What Reviewers Have Said About *Ferren And The Angel*, Book 1 in The Ferren Trilogy.

"Richard Harland's approach to entwining the perceptions, lives, and clashes between very different peoples is thoroughly engrossing … [*Ferren and the Angel's*] powerful, unpredictable brand of fantasy is highly recommended for young adult to adult readers and for libraries seeking something refreshingly new in the fantasy genre."
   –*Midwest Book Review* (Diane Donovan, Senior Reviewer)

"The worldbuilding here is addictive … This story has a great plot, some incredible conflict, and secrets just waiting to be revealed. Dystopian fans are in for a treat."
   –*Independent Book Review* (Alexandria Ducksworth)

"A richly developed fantasy that will rise quickly into a beloved classic …"
   –*Reader Views* (teenage reviewer)

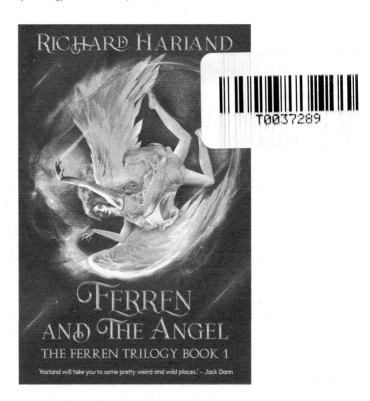

RICHARD HARLAND

FERREN AND THE ANGEL

THE FERREN TRILOGY BOOK 1

'Harland will take you to some pretty weird and wild places.' – Jack Dann

T0037289

IFWG's Masters of Fantasy line of titles

Shadows in the Stone: A Book of Transformations by Jack Dann
The Ferren Trilogy
    Ferren and the Angel (Book 1)
    Ferren and the Doomsday Mission (Book 2)
    Ferren and the Invaders of Heaven (Book 3) (forthcoming)

Ferren and the Doomsday Mission

The Ferren Trilogy
Book 2

by
Richard Harland

Ferren and the Doomsday Mission

All Rights Reserved

ISBN-13: 978-1-922856-58-6

Copyright ©2024 Richard Harland

V1 (rewritten version of *Ferren and the White Doctor*)

Printed in Garamond and Bricktown.

IFWG Publishing International
Gold Coast

www.ifwgpublishing.com

ACKNOWLEDGEMENTS

So many people to thank! A big debt to the team at IFWG who helped coax the book into its final shape: Noel Osualdini, Stephen McCracken, and of course Gerry Huntman, an infallible source of strength and support whenever things didn't go to plan.

Another thankyou to Elena Betti for another great cover—I can't even imagine the Ferren books without her visual inspiration! And belated thanks also to Liana Burrage and Andrew Enstice for the video clips they created for Book 1.

More thanks to Dmetri Kakmi as the creative editor who first saw the potential of the Morphs in Book 1 and prompted a much larger role for them in Book 2 and Book 3.

And last but not least, a special thankyou to my partner Aileen. I'm sure it's no coincidence that my period as a productive writer—actually being able to finish the books I started writing!—runs alongside our life together. For *Ferren and the Doomsday Mission*, she was my first reader (for general reader reactions) and my last reader (for backup proofing), but such help was the very least of her contributions.

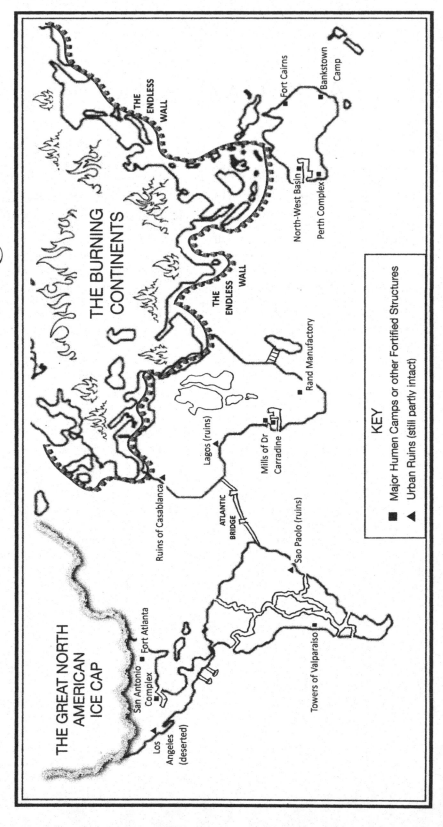

Ferren's World 3000AD

PART ONE

THE SEA-FOLK

1

Miriael looked across at Ferren: fast asleep. He lay on his side, with his head on his forearm and his back against the concrete base of one of the pylons. His features were indistinguishable in the dark, but she could hear the slow rhythm of his breath going in and out. She would take care not to disturb him while she went to investigate.

She rose silently to her feet. By now, she was well practised in moving around with the muscular power of her legs and arms, though she still missed her old spiritual power as an angel. She made her way to the side of the overbridge and looked out into the night.

It was as she'd suspected: supernatural conflict between the armies of Heaven and the armies of Earth. But what fierce fighting! She stared at the red lines of fire, the wavering spotlight beams, the eerie glows that opened up depths like caves in the sky. The fighting was further away than she'd thought, but also on a much larger scale. She hadn't seen fighting like this since the defeat and destruction of the Bankstown Doctors three months ago.

She walked away from the overbridge for a better view, twenty paces out across the bare, flat plain. The sounds, as well as the lights, came clearer in the open. Howls and whistles, sharp whip-like cracks, a thunder like a drum, the faraway singing of angelic choirs… As Miriael listened, the singing swelled louder and louder.

The rising sound told her that the forces of Heaven were harmonising together and preparing for another attack. How many attacks had they launched already? She suspected that the fighting must have been going on for a while before the noises woke her from sleep. Although she had no part in that Heavenly communion of minds, Miriael felt her nerves tingle and thrill in anticipation of combat.

Hosanna! Hosanna! Hosanna in Excelsis!

As the singing reached its climax, a horde of bright lights arced down from the sky, converging towards a spot beyond the horizon. They were warrior angels, Miriael knew, diving down in their incandescent auras. In spirit, she dived down with them. When she heard the crackle of distant explosions, she knew they were firing off burst after burst of destructive light. Instinctively, she clenched and tensed as though she still had the power to flash with light herself...

Then cold reality returned: she didn't even have an aura now. She blinked as a wetness came to her eyes at the memory of the life she'd lost.

Meanwhile, the Humen were fighting back. She heard a deep hum and banshee-like shrieks; she saw shadows moving across the sky as the red tongues of fire redoubled in intensity. She couldn't see the actual Humen forces over the horizon, but by the location of the fighting, they were probably on or close to the overbridge. Perhaps a transport convoy coming up from the south, perhaps heading north to the Banks-town Camp.

You'll never get through, she thought with grim satisfaction. *You don't have a chance now Heaven's spotted you.*

She remembered the sorties she'd flown with her own Twenty-Second Company. Many times they'd been ordered to halt a transport convoy, and not once had they failed. Swooping from a great height, incinerating the Hypers on their machines, disabling the Plasmatics inside the machines, sometimes fusing the metal of the overbridge to make it impassable. She remembered the shared exhilaration and the shared sense of triumph... The sharing was the very best part of it. She wished...

But it was no use wishing. Heaven was closed to her, even in visionary dreams. The great archangel Uriel had expressly forbidden her to make contact by means of such dreaming. She was alone on the Earth, with only Ferren to talk to.

She looked back towards the pylon of the overbridge where Ferren still lay asleep—and felt a small pang of guilt to be experiencing such regret over the past. Ferren was truly devoted to her, and she had a new purpose in the present. Together, they were building an alliance of

Residual tribes, which would surely aid Heaven's cause, even if Heaven neither knew nor cared. But she couldn't help missing the old kind of togetherness...

When she turned once more towards the conflict in the sky, the intensity of the fighting had died down. She no longer heard a crackle of explosions or saw the glow of flashes above the horizon. In the next moment, bright lights began streaming up and away from the Earth; the warrior angels were returning to Heaven. The curtains of the dark rolled open to receive them, then closed over again.

"Another successful sortie," Miriael murmured to herself, and walked back to her sleeping place under the overbridge.

2

When Miriael opened her eyes on a new day, Ferren was already up and about. He had laid out food from his pack, she saw, and was waiting for her to join him for breakfast. The sun's rays came in low under the overbridge and lit up his strong young body and matted brown hair. She had once thought of him as dirty and beast-like; now she just thought of him as a natural human being—and her only companion.

"You're awake." He grinned and gestured to the food before him. "I'm starving."

He sat cross-legged and started to eat. Miriael arranged herself sideways with her long legs tucked under her, her wings folded behind her back. Breakfast consisted of berries, mushrooms, three kinds of nuts and dried strips of meat.

Miriael couldn't come at eating the meat, but she ate everything else. Before falling to the Earth, she'd never consumed anything except manna, the spiritual sustenance for angels. Then Ferren had given her water and fed her mushrooms... Now she experienced hunger and thirst and a great many other bodily sensations. She had stopped feeling ashamed about it long ago.

"We're unbeatable!" He talked between mouthfuls as he chewed. "Seventeen tribes already in the Residual Alliance—this next will be our eighteenth! And we haven't failed with a single one! Who'd have guessed?"

Who indeed? thought Miriael. The tribes they'd encountered had been of very different kinds, but all beaten down by the Humen, their supposed allies and protectors. All had lived in fear of the Selectors, who claimed one tribesman or tribeswoman every year for military service. Yet when they'd learned the truth, their helplessness had turned to anger—and eventually determination. Although it had sometimes been hard work persuading them to take the final step and agree to a new kind of alliance…

"How many more do you think we'll join up before the assembly of representatives?" Ferren rattled on. "The Sea-folk, then two or three more? We must've covered almost the whole continent!"

Miriael smiled. Ferren was a quick and clever learner, but he still had a poor sense of geography. "No, only a tiny part of it. A hundred miles in every direction."

"Oh." Ferren digested the information as he digested a handful of nuts. "This is the furthest east we've been so far, isn't it? Have you ever seen the sea before?"

"Yes. Looking down from high up, of course."

"How big…" He broke off, frowned and stared.

Miriael was aware of it too. She spun around to face the pylon of the overbridge behind her. No doubt about it! The metal of the pylon was thrumming with tiny vibrations. In fact, the other pylons, the underframe and the deck above their heads *all* seemed to be vibrating.

Ferren sucked in breath. "Something's coming! That's what it is! Coming along the overbridge!"

He sprang instantly to his feet, and Miriael rose too.

"I'll see what it is!" he cried. "Must be big!"

He mounted the concrete base of the nearest pylon and began shinning up like a monkey. Obviously he was going to take a look out along the top of the overbridge.

Must be big. His words echoed and re-echoed in her mind. As big as a transport convoy, for example. And she could recognise the direction from which the vibrations were coming…

She shook her head at her own stupidity. She'd been so sure Heaven's warrior angels must have defeated the Humen force last night. Instead, they'd *failed!* Whatever was approaching from the south was still approaching. And it was starting to sound even bigger than a transport convoy.

Looking up, she saw that Ferren had already completed his reconnaissance. She waited impatiently as he made his way back down.

"Well?" she called out when he was still ten feet from the ground.

"I can't tell, but a lot of them. Moving fast."

"We have to get away *now.*"

He jumped down and landed heavily. "If we can get away at all."

3

The plain they had come across offered no cover. Coated with fine, grey powder, the surface was everywhere as hard and smooth as glass. They had seen many similarly unnatural effects of terra-celestial warfare during their three months' travels.

Miriael crossed to the other side of the overbridge and surveyed the route ahead. For hundreds of yards, the surface continued unchanged; then suddenly grass sprang up. There was no telling if the grass grew tall enough to hide them.

"It's our best chance," she announced.

Ferren had collected their breakfast things and came up beside her with his pack on his back.

"I don't like it," he said, and grimaced. But he made no suggestion of his own.

"Come on."

She set off running, and Ferren ran after her. With his short, powerful legs moving at twice the speed of her long, slender limbs, he soon overtook her. She focused on the grass ahead and willed herself to go faster.

Ferren, though, was looking south along the overbridge as he ran.

"They're too close!" he cried, and pulled to a stop.

Miriael looked over her shoulder where he was looking—and her heart sank. The Humen force was *very* close, and it wasn't a mere transport convoy but an army. Now visible over the sides of the deck on top, it advanced at a tremendous pace, a vast black horde glinting with shiny metal. She could see where it began, but not where it ended. No wonder the attacking angels had failed to halt it!

"Back!" Ferren reversed direction. "We'll be seen!"

He was right. The grass was still several hundred yards away, and there were surely thousands of eyes that might turn to them at any moment. She could only pray they hadn't been seen already. If they spotted her angel's wings...

Ferren waited for her to catch up, and they ran back together. The deck of the overbridge soon screened them from the army on top once again. But the army on top wasn't the only problem; further in the distance, Miriael noticed clouds of grey dust billowing by the sides of the overbridge. Clearly, more Humen forces were advancing at ground level.

"What now?" cried Ferren as they came in under the shelter of the overbridge again.

Miriael recovered her breath. "Did you see those dust clouds?"

"Yes."

"We have to stay hidden from the sides as well as the top."

"What about here?" Stepping across to where the concrete bases of two pylons didn't quite meet, he indicated the narrow channel running between them. "I used to sleep in those spaces once. Could you fit?"

She eyed the channel, which was barely two feet wide by two feet deep, and shook her head. "My wings.'

He looked from the channel to her wings and back again. "No, right. We'll use my other kind of sleeping place, then." He pointed up to the underframe that supported the deck high above their heads. "Up there."

"We hide from them by going closer?"

"Yes. Can you climb a pylon?"

Miriael wasn't too sure about the abilities of her physicalised body. "I'll have to, won't I."

The climb was a great struggle for her. The pylon had projecting bolt-heads that she could hold onto, but her fingers didn't have much strength for gripping. Nor did the necessary movements of her arms and legs come naturally; climbing like this, she had to work out how to use them in a whole new way. Ferren came up behind and guided her feet into place. Once, she slipped and trod on the top of his head.

All the time, the pylon and bolt-heads thrummed and quivered under her hands. No tiny vibrations now—it was as though the structure wanted to shake her off and jump right out of her grip. The approaching army must be very, very close!

"Hang on!" Ferren called out as she came at last to the bottom of the underframe.

She hung suspended as he clambered past her on the other side of the pylon. In the next moment, he had swung himself up into the frame and was leaning down towards her with an arm extended.

"Take my hand!" he cried.

She could hardly hear his words for the drumming in the metal all around, but she understood the gesture. She took hold of his hand, and he hauled her up into a crisscross forest of struts and braces. She found herself on all fours balancing on a horizontal girder.

"Further in!" he yelled, and she followed him as he crawled into the depths of the underframe.

Here, relatively little light entered from below. The darkness was broken only by cracks of light shining through slots in the metal plates of the deck over their heads. The deck was so close she might have touched it with her fingers if she'd dared let go of the girder.

Everything was shaking all around. The noise built up and up, the front line of the army was almost upon them—

Then the darkness deepened as a sudden blackness blanked out the cracks of light. The Humen and their machines were marching and rolling right over the top of them.

4

Ferren had travelled inside the belly of a thunderous, clanking mechanical monster, he had been in the middle of an almighty battle between Heaven and Earth—but he had never heard anything as loud as the din of the Humen war machines on the metal plates of the overbridge. Wheels, engines and caterpillar tracks passed across a mere couple of feet above his head.

He lay face up on his back, hands clamped onto the girder beneath him. Everything was going blurry around the edges. The intensity of the vibrations shook him until his teeth rattled, the girder shuddered so violently he was afraid of falling right off. Grit and dirt rained down on him until he had to screw his eyes shut.

With his eyes shut, the tremendous noise seemed to come even closer. Now it pressed directly into the bones of his skull, beating and battering, slamming and hammering. He couldn't think, he had no mind—there was only the overwhelming, annihilating tidal wave of sound.

KERLANNG! KERLANNG! KERLANNG!

WHEEE-WUMFF! WHEEE-WHUMFF!

RAKK-A-RAKK-A-RAKK-A-RAKK-A-RAKK!

BRA-LUNNK! BRA-LUNNK! BRA-LUNNK!

He felt every sound as though it ran right over him. In a stunned sort of daze, his imagination began to create different sources for the different sounds. A grinding and grating meant caterpillar tracks…a high-pitched squeal was the stressed metal of axles and drive shafts…a deep, booming rumble came from massive wheels…

On and on and on it went. His muscles ached from staying clenched so long.

It was later, much later, when the sounds changed. Emerging from his daze, he registered the tramp of marching boots. The machines had gone past, and only the foot-soldiers of the Humen army remained. There were thousands of them all pounding the deck to the same marching rhythm, but the noise they made was like a lull compared to the thunder of the machines.

He registered something else, too: no longer were bits of grit and dirt falling on his face. He opened his eyes a little, then a little more. Daylight was once more entering through the cracks between the plates of the deck. It shone through in the brief intervals between marching soldiers, flickering on and off from moment to moment. Ferren had the impression of an endless horde of shadows sweeping across over his head.

He also became aware of how hot it was. The passage of the Humen army had somehow warmed the air to a sweltering heat. Even the girder on which he lay seemed warm. But it was no longer shaking, and he no longer needed to hold on tight.

He raised himself on one elbow and looked round. Miriael was still there, stretched out on the same girder as himself. She too had propped herself on one elbow and appeared to be gazing down through the underframe to the side of the overbridge.

He crawled along the girder towards her. Head-to-head, he hoped to make himself heard above the noise.

5

She saw him and smiled. "Good hiding place here."

Ferren half-caught the words and half-read them on her lips. He brought his mouth up to her ear and raised his voice. "What are you looking at?"

She pointed by way of an answer, and he followed the line of her finger. To the side of the overbridge, a great cloud of grey dust billowed up from the ground. Of course, the Humen army had been advancing along the side of the overbridge as well as on top. When he stared into the dust, he saw dark, silhouetted shapes going past.

"They can't see us, can they?" he asked.

"No." A worried expression came over her pale face. "But I wish I could see *them*."

Ferren took a second look at the shapes in the dust. They were foot-soldiers of some kind—but what kind? Unlike ordinary Hypers, they advanced over the ground in great, springy, six-foot strides. They seemed taller than ordinary Hypers too.

"What are they?"

The angel shrugged. "No idea. They must be some new development. I saw new kinds of machine going past as well."

"New machines?"

"Like nothing I ever heard about. They must come from another part of the continent. Maybe the North-West Basin or the Perth Complex."

Ferren continued to stare into the dust cloud, vainly trying to pierce through the murk.

"I could go and take a look out," he suggested at last, and pointed to the pylon at the side of the underframe.

"Will you see better from there?"

"Don't know."

"I think they've mostly gone past."

It was true, there were fewer shapes in the dust cloud now. But suddenly a new sound came to their ears, like a thud of giant footsteps. Ordinary soldiers were still marching past on top, but the new sound rose above the tramp of ordinary boots.

Thrungg! Thrungg! Thrungg! Thrungg! Thrungg!

Miriael's expression of puzzled alarm was a mirror of Ferren's own feeling. Louder and louder the footsteps rang out on the metal plates of the overbridge.

He moved one way along the girder and Miriael the other, both seeking something to hang onto. All around, the overbridge was resonating like a gong. Ferren found a vertical strut and wrapped his arms around it. Looking towards the approaching steps, he fancied he saw the deck bulge downwards under the weight.

Thrungg! Thrungg! Thrungg! Thrungg! Thrungg!

For one brief moment, there were no shadows of ordinary soldiers marching across on top, and light shone uninterrupted through the cracks. Then came the greatest shadow of all. A giant footstep descended directly over Ferren's head, darkening the underframe far and wide. Instinctively, he ducked and crouched lower. Perhaps he was only imagining the deck buckling and bowing, but he didn't imagine the rivet that snapped and popped and went zinging past inches in front of his nose.

Then followed another *thrungg!* as the next footstep came down five yards away; then another and another. Ponderous step by step, the sounds receded.

The relative hush was balm to his ears. Whatever had just gone past must have been at the very back of the Humen army. There were no more ordinary soldiers and no more of the strange, striding soldiers by the side of the overbridge. In fact, the dust cloud there was starting to die down.

He moved back close to Miriael, whose brows were knit in a troubled frown.

"Did you feel it?" she asked at once.

Ferren didn't understand. Of course he'd felt the shaking of the overbridge—how could he not?

"I mean, like a pressure inside your head," she explained. "Like some great mind passing over. Some vast intelligence buzzing with a million calculations."

"No. I didn't feel that. What was it?"

"I don't know. I can guess where it's heading, though."

Ferren, when he thought about it, could guess too. "North to the Bankstown Camp?"

"Exactly. The Humen must be sending reinforcements to rebuild their power there. I expected it to happen eventually—just not so soon."

Ferren recalled the great battle fought over the People's Home Ground three months ago. "But their leaders were all destroyed. We *saw* them."

"Their Doctors? Yes, but leaders can be replaced. There are other Doctors."

Ferren said nothing for a while. Sounds of the army and the giant footsteps continued to diminish into the distance. Suddenly he came to a decision.

"I'll go and take a look now," he announced, and started off along the girder. He made his way past Miriael and on towards the pylon.

"Don't—" Miriael began, then changed her tone. "Just check there aren't any stragglers following behind."

He grinned and nodded. When he reached the side of the underframe, he stuck out his head and scanned all around. The dust was still rising from the ground two hundred yards ahead, but the strange soldiers were hidden inside the billowing cloud. There were no stragglers.

He hauled himself up on the outside of the underframe and came up level with the top of the overbridge. The usual cordon of coloured cables ran by the edge of the roadway. He looked along the roadway— and whistled in amazement.

Two hundred yards away, a gigantic figure lumbered along at the back of the Humen army. It was seventy or eighty feet high, like a tower against the sky, thick and heavy and lumpish—yet it had arms, legs and a head in the form of a human being.

"What is it?" Miriael had emerged from the side of the underframe and was climbing up after him.

"It's a monster." He took in the vast white medical coat that covered the figure down to its knees. So different to the puny, wheelchair-bound figures he'd seen in the past…but there was no doubt about it. "It's a new kind of Doctor!"

6

With a new sense of urgency, Ferren and Miriael continued their journey. Their route to the next tribe lay due east of the last tribe they'd visited. According to the Clanfeathers, the Sea-folk lived by the edge of the sea—which Ferren had never seen before. He could hardly imagine what it was like.

He and Miriael discussed the changed situation at the Bankstown Camp when they stopped to rest for the night.

"How long have we got?" he asked. "I mean, before they get back to the way they were."

"I don't know." She shrugged. "Not long. I expect the new Doctor will take charge now. The Bankstown Camp was always going to be the centre for their next major offensive. He'll probably send out even more Selectors."

Ferren frowned. There had been no news of Selectors in the first month after the defeat of the original ten Doctors, but they'd heard rumours and warnings from several tribes they'd visited lately.

"We have to build up our strength before the Humen do," he said. "We have to visit as many more tribes as we can."

"Yes, but it takes time to persuade them. We spent two weeks on the Longheads."

"We *have* to go faster," he insisted.

Next day, they passed through rolling hills, descended into a valley and followed a river along the bottom of the valley, as the Clanfeathers had told them. As they walked on, the valley narrowed to a gorge, and the river became a fast-flowing torrent.

"Look!" exclaimed Miriael, and pointed suddenly.

Ferren looked and saw lead and concrete pipes projecting from the walls of the gorge. The exposed ends of the pipes had broken or rusted away.

"They must have run underground originally," the angel said, nodding.

"The work of the Ancestors!" cried Ferren.

"Yes, from what you call the Good Times. Your lost human civilization from before the Millenary War."

They passed more examples as they travelled on. In one place, a latticework of plumbing spanned the gorge all the way from one side to the other. The ruins left over from the past were always impressive, always mysterious.

It was mid-afternoon by the time they finally came to the sea. Ferren heard the sound before he could see it, then smelled the smell of it too. A strangely salty, tangy sort of smell! The gorge ahead ended in a U-shaped cleft, with nothing beyond but sky and space.

He picked up his pace and ran. When he came out onto a sandy beach, he skidded to a standstill and gazed in wonder.

"The sea!" he gasped. "It's so different!"

The sheer openness took his breath away. He was dimly aware of the shoreline sweeping in a curve behind his back, but he had eyes only for the vista in front of him. He couldn't even see where the sea stopped! It went on and on forever!

Miriael came up behind him. "I've always seen it from above before. It looks bigger and better from down here."

The surface of the sea sparkled and danced in the sunlight. Close to shore, it was a green-and-turquoise colour; further out, a brilliant blue; along the horizon, it shaded to a pearly silver.

They hurried down to the water's edge and marvelled at the breakers coming in. It was hypnotic to watch the long rolls building and swelling, peaking and crashing, seething up across the pebbles, then sucking back down.

When Ferren dabbled his toes in the water, Miriael did the same. They waded out further until they were both in up to their calves. Then the splash of a wave wetted the bottom of the angel's tattered yellow robes, and she retreated laughing.

Ferren turned to look at her. She was always beautiful, with her pale oval face and bright golden hair, but right now she was happy too. Often, recently, she'd seemed distant and remote, as if weighed down by some secret sadness. But for the moment she was radiant.

For half an hour they continued moving in and out of the frothy tongues of water that hissed back and forth over the slope of the beach. Ferren tasted the clean, sharp air in his lungs and felt the breeze off the sea ruffling his hair.

Eventually, though, Miriael inspected the angle of the sun in the sky and called a halt. "We should get going again if we want to reach the Sea-folk today."

So they walked on, heading north. Successive headlands divided beach after beach of soft sand. Soon, the muscles of Ferren's legs ached from trudging over the sand. The headlands forced them to clamber over rocks and detour around slime and rock pools.

Then Ferren saw something strange ahead.

"Why all the birds?"

Another headland had just come into view: a flat promontory reaching out towards a line of islands. Above one island, a flock of a thousand seagulls wheeled and circled and dived down. Ferren shielded his eyes with his hands and tried to make out what was happening.

"It must be the Sea-folk!" cried Miriael. "They're under attack! They need help!"

"Let's help!"

They set off running.

7

As they ran closer, Ferren could see tiny figures on the islands struggling to defend themselves. There were three main islands and four smaller chunks of rock, all linked by ropes. The gulls had pinned most of the Sea-folk on the largest of the islands, where the tribespeople tried to fight back with sticks and stones.

Nonetheless, it was obvious that the birds were winning. They screamed as they circled, then swooped down and stabbed viciously with their beaks. The boldest defenders were red with blood from countless small wounds to their arms and legs.

Arriving at the headland, Ferren and Miriael sprang from the sand up onto the rock. They scrambled across seaweed, slime and shell-encrusted surfaces, and came at last to a low cliff edge at the tip of the promontory.

"What now?" cried Ferren, eyeing the twenty-foot rope that linked the headland to the first of the islands.

"Can you swim?"

"Don't think so."

"Nor me."

The rope hung down in the middle until it was barely skimming the water. The waves rose and fell, guggled and slopped in the channel they would have to cross.

"We haul ourselves along the rope, then," said Miriael. "Hand over hand."

"Dangling in the water?"

"Yes."

Ferren grimaced at the thought. "I'll go first," he said.

He shrugged the pack from his back, left it on the rocks and lowered himself over the edge. Then, seizing hold of the rope, he pushed off and swung out above the waves. Hand over hand, he worked his way across the channel. Miriael was already in position at the end of the rope and preparing to follow.

As the rope arced lower, his feet dangled down in the water, then his calves, then his thighs. Soon he was submerged up to the waist. The water seemed cold here, and floating seaweed slithered against his legs.

Cark!

A single seagull had flown down. It perched ahead of Ferren on the lowest part of the rope and fixed a beady eye upon him. It looked aggressive and malevolent, and clearly meant to block his way.

Ferren continued to advance.

Cark! Cark!

As the rope swayed with his approach, the bird gripped more fiercely with its red, webbed claws. It extended its wings and drew back its head ready to strike.

But Ferren struck first. Coming within arm's length, he heaved himself up out of the water and swung with his balled fist. The blow connected and knocked the bird sharply sidewards. It tumbled into the sea with a squawk and a splash. In the next moment, it righted itself, paddled backwards and took off with a furious beating of wings.

"Keep going!" Miriael called out. She was hauling herself along the rope a few yards behind him.

Ferren kept going. He passed the lowest point of the rope and began the upwards arc to the first island. The first island was one of the small ones, a chunk of sheer-sided rock with brown seaweed hanging down all around.

All at once, the sky went dark with wings. Ferren looked up and groaned. This wasn't a few gulls sent to block their progress; this was the entire flock. A thousand birds were now intent on their destruction.

Desperately, he lunged forward and hauled himself faster and faster towards the island. He touched the seaweed-draped wall of rock just as the first squadron hurtled down overhead. With the rope as his support, he went straight up the vertical rock and flung himself bodily onto the flat top of the island.

He expected to be pinned under a storm of beaks, claws and wings. But the birds didn't attack—and when he twisted around and looked back, he saw they had focused their attack entirely upon Miriael.

She wasn't far behind him, but the birds had struck before she could reach the island. Though she still clung to the rope, she was no longer moving forward. When the first squadron of gulls pulled away, he saw that her arms and the side of her face were bleeding.

He knelt on one knee and stretched out towards her. "Take my hand!"

It was hopeless. She tried to stretch out too, but the furthest reach of her hand was still far short of his hand.

In the next moment, a second squadron of birds dived down, and the angel disappeared under a snowstorm of wings. Ferren glimpsed pecking beaks and scrabbling claws; he saw Miriael swapping from one handhold to the other as she tried to keep her arms away from them.

He was frantic. How to reach her? Then he thought of the seaweed on which he was kneeling. Perhaps...

He jumped to his feet. The seaweed grew in long straps. He snatched up the end of the nearest strap and pulled it loose. When he drew up the other end from the water, he had a length of three yards to wield.

He lashed out with it like a whip. *Crack! Crack! Crack!*

The curling, flicking tip of the strap cut through the air all around the birds. Startled and disoriented by the sound, most drew off immediately. Ferren aimed at the few that remained and picked them off one by one.

Crack!

Crack!

Crack!

Screeching in alarm and frustration, the last of the squadron flew off too. In a moment, the attack was over. The flock circled high in the sky, still seemingly focused upon their new enemy rather than the Sea-folk.

Miriael came in hand over hand on the rope and climbed the sheer side of the island as Ferren had done. There was a look of huge relief in her eyes.

"How did you think of that?" she asked.

Ferren answered with a shake of the head. "Not finished yet." He bent to pluck up a second strap of seaweed, which he handed to Miriael. "You'll need this. I think they're massing for another attack."

8

The gulls' next onslaught was more calculated. They flew in horizontally in successive waves, first from one direction, then another. Their beaks were their weapons, and they were going for the eyes.

Ferren and Miriael stood back-to-back on the island, which was only a few yards wide at the top. The angel, still dripping with water, soon learned how to use her strap of seaweed like a whip in the same way as Ferren. They lashed out and defended one another as the attacks came in from all points of the compass. Again and again, the birds veered aside and couldn't break through.

Then one attack on Miriael's side came closer than the rest. She stumbled and fell back a step before managing to deliver a second cut with her whip. But as she stepped back, she bumped into Ferren when he wasn't expecting it. He lost his balance, slipped on seaweed underfoot and toppled right off the edge of the island.

"Yiiee!"

He hit the water with a tremendous splash. Spluttering, floundering and beating with his arms, he was barely able to keep his mouth and nostrils above the surface. There was no rope on this side of the island.

"Ferren?" He heard Miriael's cry of alarm. "Ferren! *Watch out!*"

As he beat up spray all around him, a stream of birds came arrowing in, aimed like projectiles straight at his head.

There was only one thing he could do. He took a deep breath of air, held his arms in at his sides and sank down below the surface.

Watery sounds filled his ears, and bubbles shot up in front of his face. Everything seemed strangely suspended and floating around him. If the gulls were still attacking, he couldn't hear them and they couldn't reach him. For the moment, he was invulnerable.

But the air in his lungs couldn't last. Where would the gulls be when he resurfaced? A tightness locked in around his chest, he started to gag and a gush of salt seawater invaded his mouth. He kicked with his feet and rose to the surface.

Water streamed from his hair and over his eyes. He blinked it away—and saw that the birds were waiting. They flew in a spiralling column over the spot where he'd submerged. The moment he reappeared, they exploded out from the base of the column and returned to the attack.

He gasped for air and sank down a second time. His lungs were only half full, and he knew now that the birds would stay waiting for him. Clumsily, slowly, he swam underwater towards the side of the island. But he hadn't yet touched rock when he ran out of air. As the brine found its way into his nostrils, he panicked and kicked back up to the surface.

The side of the island was no more than an arm's length away. He tried to reach it... But his muscles were like lead, and he was almost blacking out from lack of oxygen. When the birds descended once more upon him, he was helpless.

They blitzed the surface of the water with their webbed claws, stabbed and slashed with their beaks. He raised his forearm to protect his eyes, but they pecked at his hands, his shoulders and the top of his head. Soon he was bleeding from a hundred small cuts.

The sight of blood seemed to drive the gulls into an even greater frenzy. They buffeted one another in their eagerness to get a shot at him. The sea all around was a welter of spume and white water.

Dimly, through the frenzy, he heard Miriael's clear voice calling out to him. "Ferren! Grab onto this! I'll pull you up!"

She was leaning out above him from the edge of the island, and something hung down from her hand. When she was sure he was looking, she cast it further towards him, so that the end landed on the water just inches in front of his face. It was her strap of seaweed!

He gave up trying to protect himself and seized hold with both hands. At once she began hauling him in. He prayed for a few more moments before the gulls saw their chance to go for his eyes.

His feet made contact with hard rock under the surface. He pushed upwards and rose chest-high out of the water. Miriael was pulling with all her might—but she wasn't strong. Could she support his weight as he tried to tried to climb six feet of vertical wall?

He pushed up again and rose hip-high out of the water. The birds were a seething, screaming whirlwind behind him, but at least they couldn't fly straight at his eyes as long as he kept his face close to the rock.

Another upwards push, and this time he hauled himself up hand over hand. If Miriael could just maintain her position against his weight....

Then the strap snapped.

As he fell back flailing into the water, the birds retreated with a flutter of wings. But only for a moment. In another moment, they would be back to finish him off.

"*No-o-o!*" Miriael let out a great wail of frustration.

She leaned forward, looked down at him floundering in the water, spread her arms wide in despair—and a miracle happened.

As Miriael spread her arms, she also spread her wings. She had once told Ferren that her wings were only for ceremonial purposes, not for flying; nonetheless, they extended five feet on either side of her body when she spread them. Ferren, staring up from below, gaped at the sudden glorious display of brilliant white plumage.

For the birds, it was as though they'd suddenly been confronted by another bird twenty times their own size. Instead of sweeping to attack Ferren, they drew off, squawking. They seemed to have lost their bloodlust.

For a while, they circled the island, always maintaining a wary distance from the angel. Then, gradually, their circles grew wider and higher. Miriael's great wingspan had asserted superiority and intimidated them. Soon, the whole flock began wheeling away, a thousand flickers of grey and white against the blue of the sky. Their cries sounded raucous and bitter with disappointment.

Ferren worked his way around the walls of rock until he came to a rope where he could pull himself up. As he clambered onto the island's flat top to join Miriael, the Sea-folk appeared on the next island along.

9

Another twenty-foot rope linked the next island to the one on which Ferren and Miriael stood. A dozen Sea-folk waved to them; then two came across, a young man and a girl. They flitted over the rope like tightrope-walkers, stepping lightly and balancing with outspread arms.

The Sea-folk had dark, tanned skin and bleached, blond hair tied up in topknots. For adornment, they wore necklaces of coloured shells and salvaged oddments of metal, plastic and glass. When the young man and girl spoke, Ferren could hardly understand their drawn-out vowels at first. But their tone expressed their feelings: immense gratitude, wonder and a respect bordering on adulation.

Ferren told them that he came from a tribe called the People, and that he and Miriael were travelling on behalf of the Residual Alliance. At first, the two Sea-folk couldn't understand *his* accent either. But gradually they all began to make sense to each other.

"You saved us," the girl repeated over and over. "We owe everything to you."

"How did you do it?" asked the young man.

Ferren pointed to Miriael. "She spread her wings and scared the birds off. Didn't you see?"

The young man and the girl looked askance at the Celestial. Though overwhelmingly grateful, they were also a little fearful of her. It was obvious they preferred to stand close to another Residual.

"The birds nearly had us beaten this time." The young man spoke to Ferren while keeping his eyes on Miriael. "We've been fighting them for generations. They want all the fish for themselves."

"Now we'll take you to the Mothers," said the girl. "They're waiting to meet you on Fain Pellor."

She signalled, and another two tightrope-walkers crossed over from the next island. The one in front carried a pot of some kind, the one behind unspooled a coil of rope from his arm.

The new arrivals introduced themselves as Rewel and Moireen, while the young man now gave his name as Jike and the girl gave her name as Jorika. The pot turned out to contain an oily paste smelling strongly of fish. Moireen, a middle-aged woman who also smelled strongly of fish, collected paste on her fingertip and dabbed it onto the many small cuts on Ferren's arms, shoulders, neck and skull. The paste instantly staunched the flow of blood and eased the pain.

Moireen didn't dare do the same for a Celestial, but passed the pot to Ferren, who passed it on to Miriael. The angel applied the salve to her cuts with her own fingertip. Meanwhile, Rewel explained to Ferren how the extra rope he'd brought would support them as they walked on the fixed ropes.

"The worst we can do is fall in again," Ferren laughed.

It wasn't so difficult. The Sea-folk at either end pulled the support rope taut, and Ferren shuffled sideways along the fixed rope while hanging on to the support rope with both hands. As soon as he stepped off, Miriael came across in the same way.

There were four crossings before they reached Fain Pellor, which turned out to be the name of the largest island. It was partly a flat platform, partly an irregular mass of rock riddled with caves. At the centre of the flat area, three very old women sat cross-legged on the ground.

"The Mothers are the elders of our tribe," Jorika whispered to Ferren.

As Ferren and Miriael approached, the rest of the tribe crowded round. The faces of the three Mothers were lined with creases and their cheeks seamed with scars. They introduced themselves as Gweir, Lorne and Krye.

Ferren was eager to tell them about the Residual Alliance, but first had to wait while they expressed their gratitude many times over. Then their gratitude led on to something else.

"You have to stay with us," said Gweir.

"Stay and protect us," Lorne implored.

Ferren tried to explain the purpose of their journey, which meant they couldn't stay long. They shook their heads sadly.

"But you can protect yourselves," he told them. "If all Residuals band together and work together—"

"Just a few days!" said Krye.

"Just until the Selector comes!" pleaded Lorne.

Ferren jumped. "What? A Selector?"

He exchanged glances with Miriael. The Mothers looked at one another too.

Other voices spoke up from the crowd around. "They could save us from him."

"Drive him away."

"Nobody for military service."

"Not this year."

"They've taken so many already."

Ferren addressed the Mothers. "You have a Selector coming?"

Gweir answered first. "Always, this time of year."

"Three days from now," added Krye.

Lorne looked up hopefully. "If you could stay for just three days..."

Ferren consulted silently with Miriael. For the first time in a while, the angel spoke up.

"I think we could do that," she said. "We should show people here how to deal with the Humen and their Selectors."

"You can deal with them for us," Lorne suggested.

"No," said Miriael. "You'll learn what *you* can do."

"But we..." Krye began.

"We can't even fight off the birds." Gweir completed the thought.

Ferren shook his head at them. "You mustn't think like that. Our tribes have more power than we ever realised. When I tell you the truth about military service—"

Miriael raised a hand to cut him off. "Tomorrow. There'll be time for a proper meeting then. When everyone's recovered from today and ready to take in new ideas." She turned to the Mothers. "Can you arrange that?"

The Mothers shrank a little under her direct gaze.

"Of course," said Gweir. "You are our honoured guests. Everything shall be as you want."

"We are plain and humble people, but we would like to offer you our very best," said Krye.

Lorne nodded. "Our softest beds, our choicest food..."

She broke off as Gweir whispered something to her behind her hand. Then all three conferred behind their hands and came to a decision.

"We were thinking…" Gweir didn't look at Miriael, but addressed herself to Ferren. "Perhaps the Celestial would like one of our islands all to herself? There's a cave with a bed on Renna Dair."

Miriael raised an eyebrow, Ferren's brows came down in a frown.

"Why?" he demanded. "Why do you want to separate her?"

"No, no." Gweir fluttered her hands. "It's only… We thought she might prefer it."

There was a faint ironic smile on Miriael's lips as she turned to Ferren. "It doesn't matter. I don't mind." She turned back to the Mothers. "Yes, thank you. I'll have an island all to myself."

"We thought you might prefer it," Gweir repeated.

"We'll being food and drink and whatever you want," added Krye.

Ferren thought of saying he'd stay on the same separate island, but he suspected that Miriael might not agree. He was not at all happy about the arrangement.

10

The sun was setting when Ferren visited Miriael on her island. He came with Jike and Jorika, who brought a pot of soup for the angel's evening meal. They also carried a support rope to help him cross from Fain Pellor to Renna Dair.

"You ought to learn to walk on the ropes like we do," Jorika laughed.

"We could teach you, you know." said Jike, who was always the more serious of the two.

Renna Dair was smaller than Fain Pellor but larger than the rock from which Ferren and Miriael had fought off the seagulls. There was a single cave on it, shielded at the front by a wall of tightly fitted stones. Entering after Jike and Jorika, Ferren saw furniture made of driftwood and mats of woven seaweed. Miriael sat leaning forward on her bed, which was a shelf in the cave wall with dried sea sponge for a mattress. It was all comfortable enough by the standards of the tribe.

Jike placed the pot of soup before the angel, and Jorika laid a big wooden spoon beside it.

"Do you need anything else?" Jike questioned Miriael without raising his eyes to her.

"Thank you, no."

Ferren addressed the two food-bearers. "I'll stay a while and come back by myself."

"Don't stay too long or you'll miss out on dinner," Jorika told him with a grin.

In another minute, Jike and Jorika had gone, and Ferren and Miriael were left to their own conversation.

"You seem to get on well with them," Miriael commented.

"I think they've become my main helpers."

"Did you get the chance to talk about ways to deal with the Selector?"

"I have a few plans."

"What about the Sea-folk? You should involve them in the planning too. You want them to see *they* have the power to overthrow the Humen. A demonstration. The Humen aren't so invincible after all.'

"I shouldn't take charge, you mean?"

"No more than you have to. The Residual Alliance needs tribes that believe in themselves."

"All right." Ferren switched across to his own concern. "I don't like you being separated off like this."

"On my very own island?" She raised an ironic eyebrow. "You don't think it's a special privilege?"

"I think they just don't want you living close to them. Why did you agree?"

Miriael sighed. "I agreed because it'll make your task easier. You really haven't noticed, have you?"

"What?"

"Every single tribe we've visited—they're always wary about coming close to a Celestial. I'm not like them, and they know it.'

Ferren stuck out his jaw. "So they ought to get used to it. You just saved them from being overrun by seagulls."

"And they're grateful. But they're nervous around me. They can't help themselves."

"It's not right."

"You were nervous around me once. When you found me shot down and lying in the grass. You kept your distance too."

"No! I gave you food to eat and water to drink."

Miriael gestured towards the pot of soup. "And here are the Sea-folk doing the same. I think you've forgotten the way you felt."

Ferren didn't particularly want to remember. "It's not right," he repeated.

He was aware of Miriael studying him in silence for a moment.

"I'd like you to do your speech by yourself tomorrow," she said at last. "You've been taking the lead more and more, and you do it well. When I'm standing there beside you, I'm a distraction. It's you they want to hear, and you they naturally believe."

"I need you to back me up."

"I don't think so. Not anymore. When you do it by yourself, you're a Residual talking to Residuals. It'll work better with me staying in the background."

"But you know things—"

"Nothing that you haven't learned by now."

"I'll panic."

"You won't. Have confidence in yourself. The same way we want the tribes to have confidence in themselves."

Ferren was still shaking his head. But he *had* noticed how the tribes were wary around a Celestial, how they were more focused when listening to him, how they were more willing to accept what he told them...

Miriael looked him in the eyes. "Inspire them tomorrow. And keep on inspiring them. You have three days before the Selector comes."

"I don't—"

"You don't have a choice."

Her words were stern, but she was smiling too. Then she turned away and lifted the lid from her pot of soup. It was a fish soup, and rich, spicy aromas filled the air.

"And now I want to have my soup while it's hot," she told him. "What about yours?"

Ferren hung around for another minute, but the aromas made his mouth water. He couldn't persuade Miriael out of her decision anyway. He said his goodbyes, rose to his feet and headed off for his own dinner.

11

Ferren stood facing the Sea-folk. The three Mothers sat directly before him, and the rest of the tribe in a half-circle behind. Miriael sat at the very back outside the half-circle. Ferren tried not to look at her as he delivered his speech. He began by explaining the nature of the Residual Alliance.

"It's not like the kind of alliance you've had with the Humen," he told them. "Not being bullied and terrorised. This is an alliance of free and equal tribes. We band together and protect one another. You won't need the Humen protecting you. They only pretended to protect you anyway."

He looked straight at his audience and spoke in a clear, measured voice. He knew his words almost by heart, yet he still felt them and meant them.

He went on to describe the great battle fought right over his tribe's Home Ground, and how he'd seen the armies of Heaven defeat the armies of the Humen with his own eyes. "They were annihilated! All ten of their Doctors destroyed!"

He glanced at Miriael and saw her nod with approval. She'd been there through the great battle too, but this time he didn't expect her to back him up. He *could* do it on his own.

He described the Humen defeat in detail, then moved on to the most dramatic part of his speech.

"We've been afraid to break with the Humen because we thought we needed them. We don't! Heaven isn't at war with us, only with them. No tribe ever liked them or the way they treat us. But no tribe ever knew the full truth of what they do to us. *I* know, I've *seen*—and I'm going to tell you. The truth about military service!"

He paused for a moment, and there was absolute silence. His audience was with him, sharing every thought. The hatred towards the Humen he now expressed was the hatred they'd always felt but had never let themselves think. He lowered his voice, and the Sea-folk leaned forward to listen.

"You know the beginning of military service, when the Selectors come and choose someone to take away to their Camp. But the people they choose never serve in their army. They throw them in baths, packed side by side, and they dismember them. I've been inside their camp, and I've seen it. Every single one of us taken away for military service—they murdered."

He could hardly control a tremor as the image of his sister Shanna flashed before his eyes. The sister who'd brought him up like a mother, who'd been selected for 'military service' two and a half years ago, who'd marched off to her fate with her head held high… A great lump of grief welled inside him. This was the moment in his speech where he'd always relied on Miriael to step in. But he mustn't give way to tears! He must turn his grief into anger!

"What they do…what they do is steal from us. They use their machines to draw off a kind of shimmery stuff that contains all the memories and experiences in our minds. Then they cut up our bodies and scavenge muscles and tendons and nerves to make Plasmatics to power their engines. Every mechanical thing in the Humen army has bits of our bodies inside, driving the wheels or valves or pistons. And the Hypers—like the Selectors, who look human like us—the only life they have comes from the shimmery stuff injected into them. They're not really alive, they're artificial. They're parasites living on *our* memories and experiences."

He gave them time to digest the terrible information. On every face was a look of utter shock. He was in control of himself again, and the tremor in his voice was a tremor of concentrated anger.

"Yes, they're parasites," he went on. "But that means they depend on us. Do you see? We're the only real human beings, and they can't survive without us. Without what they steal from our bodies and minds, they're *nothing*. There's no actual military service, yet we're the ones who make their armies possible. I say it's time to take away the possibility.

Enough of being used! Enough of being tricked! Enough of being terrorised! We reject military service! We resist the Selectors!"

The Sea-folk were nodding their heads and murmuring approval. "They can't have our bodies." "They can't steal our minds" "We'll take away the possibility."

Ferren raised his voice. "And when you join the Residual Alliance, you join with a score of tribes all thinking the same. We'll share information and work together. If they come against us in small numbers, we'll unite and fight them off. If they come against us in big numbers, we'll warn one another and vanish where they can't find us. Together we have the power! There are a thousand people in the Alliance already!"

The Sea-folk could hardly believe it. "A thousand!" "So many!" "We'll be like the Lords of the Earth again!"

"Yes!" Ferren brandished his fist. "We're the only original human beings! We can free ourselves and live as we choose! Back to the way it should be!"

The Sea-folk cheered. All jabbering at once, they jumped to their feet in a great state of excitement. The meeting had concluded—in the best possible way. Ferren was amazed he'd been so successful on his own.

12

Miriael too was surprised by Ferren's success. She'd expected him to do well, speaking to Residuals as one of their kind, but he'd done better than well. He'd been inspirational!

She didn't get to talk to him after the meeting because he was besieged by Sea-folk all clamouring for more information. For a while, she waited on the outskirts of a mass of bleached hair and bobbing heads. Then she slipped quietly away and wandered round the edge of Fain Pellor.

In one place, there was an easy slope descending to sea level. She went down, found herself a boulder to sit on and gazed out over the waves. Water lapped and gurgled in channels between the rocks.

A fishy smell came to her nostrils—mostly from the oily salve she'd applied yesterday to her skin. The salve had proved miraculously effective in healing the small stab wounds inflicted by the birds. Today the cuts were scarcely visible, and she felt nothing more than a faint itch.

A strange mood crept over her. She *was* delighted by Ferren's success, which had more than fulfilled her predictions. The Sea-folk would certainly join the Residual Alliance, and the Alliance was all that mattered. On the other hand, she felt she'd become irrelevant.

I'm just not as necessary as I used to be, she told herself.

When they'd first started going from tribe to tribe, it had fallen to her to explain many things that Ferren couldn't explain himself. But he must have soaked up every word she'd ever uttered. Now she couldn't have done a better job of explanation even if appearances hadn't been against her. He had come so far so fast!

Somehow, she felt both pleased and sad at the same time.

She didn't understand her own mood, and after a while she stopped trying. Her mind drifted off into thoughts of Heaven, journeying in her mind from altitude to altitude. So many scenes, so beautiful and serene! And the angels with whom she'd shared that blessed state of existence! It was pleasant to remember places where she'd once truly belonged...

She had lost all track of time when two young voices broke in on her.

"There you are!"

"We've been searching everywhere!"

It was Jike and Jorika, looking down from the rock platform above.

"Would you like to go back to Renna Dair now?' asked Jike.

Miriael swivelled on her boulder. "I may as well, yes."

"I'll go and get the support rope," said Jike, and took off in a hurry.

Jorika continued to look down. She was bubbling over with excitement. "We've been hearing all about the history of the world. Ferren told us about the psychonauts going up into Heaven, and the archangels driving them out. And the Age of the Undead and the United Earth Movement. We're coming to something called the Great Collapse—I don't know what that is yet." She was obviously impatient to return and hear more.

I could give you the facts about the Great Collapse, thought Miriael with a rueful smile. Everything Ferren knew about the history of the world came from what she'd told him, which came from what Gethel and Asiel had told *her*. But it was better for the Sea-folk to hear it described by Ferren.

A moment later, Jike reappeared with the support rope coiled over his arm, and Miriael climbed the slope back up to the platform.

13

That night, Miriael dreamed of being in Heaven. It started from a memory she'd had during the day, a scene of serene beauty on the Fourth Altitude. She was walking along the Terraces of Shereth, gazing at green sweeps of lawn and long colonnades of pale blue columns. Phoenixes strutted on the upper terraces, displaying their flame-like bodies and their tails like showers of sparks.

This isn't real, it's an ordinary dream, she told herself. *It's only visionary dreams I'm forbidden to have.*

She descended to the lower terraces, where a famous rose garden encompassed the Sacred Pool. Bushes and blooms set out in concentric circles sweetened the air with intoxicating scents.

There were three angels by the central pool and a host of angels on the terraced slopes that rose on the other side. The three angels were drawing out threads of sacred water on their fingertips, weaving shapes that glistened for a moment before vanishing. The angelic host was a choir of Virtues, Powers and Principalities, singing and harmonising under the direction of maroon-robed Dominion.

Miriael felt she'd recovered spiritual peace and happiness. The clear light of Heaven…the singing of the choir…the tranquil roses and smiling faces of the three angels… There were tears in her eyes and on her cheeks, but they were tears of joy.

She stepped forward through the rosebush circles and approached the angels by the pool. One of the three was Anaitis, a high-ranking female archon who had once addressed Miriael's own Twenty-Second Company on the subject of strategy. No doubt Anaitis had been told about the new Doctor and new army marching to take over the Bankstown Camp.

But not about the Residual Alliance! The thought sprang suddenly into Miriael's dreaming mind. Someone ought to tell Heaven how the strategic situation would change when the Residuals were no longer allied with the Humen. That thought led to another. Last time in Heaven, only her hair had been visible to the angels…and even then, only a strand of it. Could she attract Anaitis' attention by waving her hair? Then she could pass on the information about the Residual Alliance…

She advanced beyond the last circle of rosebushes and stood where Anaitis could see her. She shook her head from side to side, ran her fingers through her hair and flourished it in a great cascade of gold.

The archon saw nothing. Anaitis turned and laughed in response to some comment just uttered by the angel beside her. Miriael realised she would have to step closer, right in front of the archon's face.

At that moment, the choir concluded their hymn and fell silent. In the same moment, Miriael focus suddenly shifted.

What am I trying to do?

Making contact with angels in Heaven was the very thing forbidden to her! This wasn't supposed to be a visionary dream, where the dream world was also the real world. But perhaps it was! The way she could think and choose and act—perhaps it was!

She checked the pace she'd been taking towards Anaitis and shrank back. At least the archon hadn't seen her. Step by step, she retreated in among the rosebushes, stealthy as a thief.

She was careful to avoid sudden movements, especially of her head and hair. If she could choose and act, then she could choose to fall back from Heaven and emerge from the dream in her cave on Renna Dair…

Even as she thought it, it began to happen. Soon she smelled the briny air, soon she heard the lap of the waves. The walls of her cave materialised around her, and the sea-sponge mattress materialised beneath her. The rose garden on the Terraces of Shereth blurred and faded away.

She opened her eyes and lay wide awake. She was alone in the dark. She trembled all over, and her breathing was fast and ragged.

14

Miriael couldn't go back to sleep. She lay tossing and turning restlessly for a while, then rose from her bed and went outside. Clouds half-covered the sky, and there was no moon. She chose a rocky ledge facing the open sea and sat down to reflect on her visionary dream.

She was still reflecting when she became aware of a light that had come down low over the sea. Distant at first, it moved rapidly closer. Soon she saw it as a bright oval globe skimming across the waves—and heading straight towards her. A visitation from Heaven? Her heart was in her mouth. Had she been seen after all?

A pathway of light glittered across the blackness of the water, all the way from the globe to Renna Dair. Inside the globe was the figure of an angel...a male angel wearing the white robes of the Order of Principalities. The intensity of his aura shed rays all around like a many-pointed star. He looked very solemn and very beautiful.

His progress slowed as he approached the island. Now Miriael saw a silver circlet on his brow. His sandalled feet seemed mere inches above the waves.

"I am Asmodai, also known as the Tenth Angel of Strategy," he announced. "It was you I saw on the Fourth Altitude, was it not?"

"Yes," Miriael answered in a very small voice.

He rose to hover on a level with her ledge. She lowered her gaze, awaiting punishment.

"You showed the golden flash of your hair," he continued. "Luckily for you, I was the only one to see it."

Miriael's eyes remained downcast. "I didn't see you."

"I was with all the others singing in the choir." He leaned forward, studying her. "I think I know who you are. You are that angel who crashed to the Earth. The one who survived for some reason our scholars can't explain."

"Because I ate Residual food. I mean, it was fed to me before I realised."

"Even so, it's a mystery."

"I'm Miriael the Fourteenth—" She checked herself. "I *used* to be the Fourteenth Angel of Observance."

"Yes, I know your name."

She looked up. His eyes were deep lambent pools, his hair was like finely spun glass. The curls of his hair seemed to float in the light that streamed out around his head.

"Do they still talk about me in Heaven?" she asked.

"No, you're a closed subject. But I make it my business to explore odd bits of knowledge that other angels have stopped thinking about."

Miriael wasn't sure how to understand the situation. His manner didn't appear to threaten punishment. From the way he spoke, this was an unofficial visit.

"I wasn't *trying* to make contact," she said. "I thought I was in a different kind of dream."

"Oh?" He clearly wasn't bothered about excuses. "According to the last information recorded about you, you were chained to the wall of some Residual habitation."

"Yes, those Residuals freed my chain from the wall. And another tribe broke the padlock round my ankle."

"Hmm. So Heaven's records are out of date. Not for the first time." He considered for a moment. "Are you happy staying down here on the Earth?"

Faced with the point-blank question, Miriael struggled for an answer. "I can't stop thinking about Heaven," she said at last.

"Nor dreaming about it, apparently," he said with a smile.

For Miriael, it was the most wonderful smile in the world. She was suddenly certain that everything was going to turn out all right.

"Yes," he went on. "Once you've known Heaven, it would be unbearable to find yourself excluded and shut out. I don't imagine you could ever get over it. There would always be a part of you wanting desperately to return."

He understands me so well, thought Miriael. *He can really share my experience.*

"It seems to me you've been treated very harshly," he said. "Even if you'd done something truly wicked, yet to be condemned with no prospect of forgiveness… Even the Fallen Angels weren't condemned as absolutely as that. There was a spirit of forgiveness in Heaven once."

Miriael remembered the history lesson given to her by Gethel and Asiel. "When the Supreme Trinity still ruled."

"Before the archangels of the War Council took over." He nodded. "During the Age of the Undead, while the population on Earth was wiping itself out, the Supreme Trinity allowed the Grigori and many of the Satan's followers back up into Heaven. You know about that?"

"Sort of." Gethel and Asiel *had* said something, but she wasn't clear on all the details. "The Grigori… They were the second kind of Fallen Angel, weren't they?"

"Yes, the Grigori or Watchers. They were sent to watch over the human race after Adam and Eve, but they fell in love with mortal women. That was their sin—more of a weakness than a sin. The Supreme Trinity forgave them all and called them back to their places in Heaven, along with those of the Satan's followers who'd repented of their disobedience."

"I've been weak, but I didn't deliberately sin," Miriael suggested.

"Less than the Grigori, I suspect," said Asmodai. "But even then, the great archangels of the War Council weren't happy about forgiving so many Luciferians. It was a compromise to allow about half to return. And when the Supreme Trinity wanted to allow human souls back up into Heaven… You know about that too?"

"The great archangels resisted, and the Supreme Trinity withdrew onto the Seventh Altitude. Closed off all access from lower Altitudes."

"Indeed, indeed. That was the end of the spirit of forgiveness. I'm sure the Supreme Trinity would have forgiven *you*."

He fell silent, and Miriael too held her peace. She was surprised to see a hint of wetness in his beautiful eyes. Then he shook his head, so that rays of light flew out all around.

"Here's what I'll do," he said. "I'll talk to some other angels and see how they feel about you now. I won't let your case be simply forgotten."

"You'd do that for me?"

"I believe the impulse to mercy still lingers, in some at least. As it *should*."

"It lingers in you," Miriael murmured.

He smiled, a little sadly. "I wish I could do more. You don't deserve this punishment. Or any punishment, in my opinion. At least you'll know there's a voice in Heaven speaking up for you."

Miriael stifled a sob as an immense feeling of gratitude welled in her chest. "Thank you. I never expected—"

He raised a hand to cut off her thanks. Even his hand was beautiful, with long, pale, slender fingers.

"I won't make promises, but I'll do what I can."

His departure was the reverse of his arrival. The oval of his globe moved out across the water, creating the same bright glittering pathway over the waves. Further and further he dwindled into the distance, then shot up all at once in a vertical line of light towards Heaven.

15

All through the next day, Miriael felt she was in another dream. A drizzle began to fall from the early morning, discouraging visits by Ferren or the Sea-folk, and she was happy to have it that way. No doubt Ferren was preparing the tribe with a plan to overpower the Selector in a couple of days' time. For herself, she preferred to be left alone on her own island, thinking her thoughts of Asmodai.

It was incredibly fortunate that, of all the angels whose attention she might have caught in the Fourth Altitude, she had caught the attention of one who could actually sympathise. She thought back to the angels who'd come down to her when she'd been chained to the wall of the Dwelling Place, and they'd all eyed her with revulsion. First the Junior Angels Chrymos and Neriah, then the Seraphs Nathanael, Cedrion, Bethor and Adonael, then the scholars Gethel and Asiel, and finally the great Uriel himself. Always the same reaction, the instinctive contempt of the spiritual for the physical! They couldn't have hidden it even if they'd tried. The hybrid state of her body, neither one thing nor the other, disgusted them.

But Asmodai was different. She continued to marvel over what had happened, she hugged the memory to herself. So utterly unexpected! It was a miracle come true!

She wished she'd asked him when he would next return. His mere presence brought comfort and happy associations. Truly, he represented all that was best about Heaven: the harmony, the calm, the sense of communion. Speaking to him, she'd forgotten about her exclusion; it was almost as good as being back in the Divine Realm. And he was so very, very beautiful!

Jike and Jorika came twice to Renna Dair, bringing a midday meal and a dinner meal. The first time, they deposited the food before her and hurried off at once, but the second time they stopped long enough to talk.

"Ferren didn't come with you?" Miriael asked, more in surprise than disappointment.

"He can't spare the time," Jorika told her. "We can't spare him either. He's started us making a net now."

"We're sewing lots of ordinary nets into one big net," Jike explained.

"To trap the Selector," added Jorika.

"Then tomorrow we'll practise how to do the trapping," Jike finished off.

They were full of excitement and not at all fearful. *It's always the young ones*, thought Miriael. *Always the first to take on new ideas, always the strongest supporters of the Residual Alliance.* It had been the same with every tribe she and Ferren had visited.

Jike and Jorika were soon itching to be off, and she let them go. They were too excited to explain Ferren's plans properly anyway. She supped her dinner meal, which was a different type of fish soup, both sweet and sour at the same time. But she hardly noticed the taste as she started thinking about Asmodai again.

She pictured the noble, almost sorrowing look on his face. On reflection, she was surprised he was only the *Tenth* Angel of Strategy. His relatively lowly role seemed out of proportion to the great power and spirituality she sensed in him. He was like a pure, pale flame…

16

The drizzle eased off in the evening, and Miriael resolved to wait outside for Asmodai. She used some sea-sponge from her mattress to make herself a cushion on the same rock ledge as last night. She could only hope he'd come again tonight.

But the hours went past, and sleep crept up on her. Without ever intending it, she rolled over on her side, closed her eyes and drowsed off.

His arrival began as a soft glow of light through her eyelids. Then a strange warmth penetrated her skin until she felt she was glowing all through. As the brightness intensified, she opened her eyelids the tiniest fraction.

It was him!

Her eyelids flew wide open—then snapped shut again. His aura was so dazzling she couldn't stare into it straight on. She had spots behind her eyes.

"Hello, Miriael." The brightness dimmed. "It's all right, you can look now."

She blinked a few times and managed to look. The light of his globe had become more diffuse, like a radiant haze all around She became aware of her undignified position, lying curled on her side, and sat up.

"The news is not good, I'm afraid," he said. "You remember, I was going to present your case to other angels."

"Yes."

"I spoke to Sidriel and Mendrion, who are Angels of Strategy like me. A little higher in rank, but not much. They were willing to listen, but not to form an opinion of their own. They advised me to talk to Jehoel, our First Angel of Strategy. And Jehoel…" He frowned in annoyance, and crackles of light spilled from his hands, his feet and the edges of his robe. "Jehoel told me the decision had already been made on a far higher level. He more or less said we didn't need to think about it because our superiors had done the thinking for us."

"I'm sorry," said Miriael. "I mean, sorry if you got into trouble because of me."

"Nothing I haven't experienced before. It's the injustice to you that rankles. They're all so hidebound. Blinkered minds!"

The crackles of light came faster and more furious as he spoke. Miriael was amazed to see him so fierce on her behalf.

"Thank you," she said.

"I haven't done anything."

"Thank you for caring."

"Ah, Miriael." He grew quieter. "I feel for you because I've suffered similar injustices. Not that I compare my sufferings to yours. They shut you out completely, whereas I'm only ignored. My differences aren't so obvious because they're only in my mind. But I'm too unorthodox for them. I know what it's like to be treated as an outsider."

Miriael waited to hear more. No wonder he could sympathise with her experience: he was a fellow-spirit.

"Do you know about the Weather Wars?" he asked suddenly.

"Yes, in North America. When we defeated the Doctors there by turning the weather against them. The Hundred Years Blizzard."

Asmodai nodded. "Hail, snow, storms and floods. It was my research that made it possible. I discovered techniques to make the weather into a weapon."

"But you're... I mean..."

"I'm only the Tenth Angel of Strategy?" He smiled grimly. "Indeed. I was once higher and could've been much higher again. But there were established angels who traditionally controlled the weather, and they weren't pleased with my new role. Especially Barachiel. He spread the idea that I went too far and my techniques were too destructive. As if I chose to create the Great North American Ice Cap! As if I decided how my techniques were used!"

"You should've been recognised as a hero," said Miriael.

"Unfortunately, Heaven doesn't work like that. I was moved aside and quietly demoted over the years. I had to promise to discontinue my weather research. Of course, that never stopped me doing different kinds of research."

"So unfair," murmured Miriael.

"Ah, there have been other injustices too. But you don't need to hear my story. As long as you understand why I don't have the power to help you as I'd like. In terms of influence and authority, I'm probably the very last angel for getting you back up into Heaven."

"Back up into Heaven?"

"Isn't that what you want?"

"I was thinking more of reconciliation. Being forgiven and allowed to communicate."

"Oh. Is that all?" He seemed disappointed in her.

"It's my body." Miriael lowered her eyes. "My body has weight because I'm not a pure spiritual being anymore. They told me that if I went up to Heaven, gravity would drag me down to Earth again."

"Who told you that?"

"One of the Seraphim. Bethor, I think it was."

"And Bethor knows, does he?" Asmodai pursed his lips and looked thoughtful. "The Seraphim don't know everything. You shouldn't give up."

"I don't want to ask too much."

He sighed. "All right, then. Reconciliation. That's certainly not asking too much."

"Will you keep helping me?" she asked, humbly and hopefully.

"I will." He smiled, and again his aura warmed her with its glow. "And now I think you should go back to sleep. Is this your bed?"

"No." She indicated the shelter behind her. "It's in there."

"Then you should go to it. You're very tired."

Although Miriael would have liked to stay talking to him for hours, she *was* very tired. Obediently, she rose to her feet and headed towards the cave. She glanced back just before she passed in through the entrance, and he was still watching her, still smiling.

With a feeling of great peace, she went in to her bed, lay down on her sea-sponge mattress and fell instantly asleep.

17

One day to go before the Selector turned up! Ferren had the Sea-folk practise their roles until they knew exactly what to do. By the afternoon, they were all ready for a break. The sky was blue, the air crystal-clear and the sea as smooth as glass.

"We'll show you the Kingdom under the Waves," Gweir told him, and everyone instantly took up the idea.

"What is it?"

"You'll be amazed. It was built by the Lords of the Earth."

Ferren had already heard about the Lords of the Earth, the people whom his own tribe called the Ancestors. Long ago in the past, they had created a great civilisation, since destroyed by the endless war between Heaven and Earth. Every tribe had its own name for them, and every tribe preserved relics in memory of what had once been. According to Miriael, the long-ago people were the original true human beings, and all tribesmen and tribeswomen were descended from them.

He followed as the Sea-folk led the way to the very outermost island, Mas Linn. There were two seawater channels to cross, and he crossed them walking on the ropes with outspread arms. He had learned the trick of it from Jike and Jorika: move fast and never look down. He was nowhere near as skilled as the Sea-folk, but he was skilled enough not to fall in.

Mas Linn was a particularly craggy hump of rock, with steps carved into the stone going up to the top. At the top was a wide, hollow bowl facing out towards the open sea. By the time Ferren arrived, two dozen Sea-folk were already in position, standing shoulder to shoulder.

"Make way everyone, make way!" Gweir called out as she came up behind Ferren.

The Sea-folk were so fascinated by the Kingdom under the Waves that she had to call out again and again. Even when they shifted to let Ferren pass, their eyes remained fixed on the spectacle. Ferren pushed through for a view and stared where everyone else was staring.

What he saw was a sea so calm and clear that he could look down to a great depth. There, wavering through the water, was a whole city stretching out far and wide. He goggled at drowned buildings and streets, all tinged in colours of green and blue. The buildings were roofless, often mere remnants of wall and foundation, but the lines of the layout were marked out like a diagram.

"The work of the Lords of the Earth!" cried a woman next to Ferren, and flung out her arm in a sweeping gesture.

Ferren heard the pride in her voice and shared the same exultation. "This is how we'll be again!" he shouted. "We'll bring the Good Times back!"

The Sea-folk had another name for the Good Times, but they knew what he meant.

"Such skill and craft they had," they murmured.

"Moto-cars and electrics. Flying machines and shop-shops."

"Living without war, living without fear."

The woman who had made the sweeping gesture turned to Ferren. "Do you believe it? Will it come true for us?"

"It will," he answered. "It really, truly will." He wanted it so much, the yearning was like a fire leaping up through his body. However long it took, however many lives or centuries, it *had* to come true.

For a long while they all stood in silence, lost in a dream. The Kingdom under the Waves glimmered and trembled through the water. In his mind, Ferren saw it populated with moto-cars, shop-shops and throngs of happy, smiling people. He had no doubt everyone saw it the same way.

Finally, though, it was time to return to the present. He raised his arms and clapped his hands over his head.

"Back to Fain Pellor! More practice now!"

Reluctantly, they dragged their eyes away. "But we know it all already."

"Not everything. We have to prepare for the unexpected."

Gweir chivvied them into motion. "Let's go! If it helps the Golden Days come true for us…"

They turned and made their way back to Fain Pellor. Ferren intended to keep them practising for another couple of hours; then he would pay a call on Miriael and tell her his plans for tomorrow. She would be amazed to see him tightrope-walking like one of the Sea-folk!

18

The idea of telling Ferren about her angelic visitor never entered Miriael's mind. She had heard and approved of his plans for tomorrow, but her thoughts were elsewhere.

She had something important to discuss with Asmodai tonight. It had been a mistake trying to tell Anaitis about the Residual Alliance, but she could certainly tell Asmodai. Wouldn't it work in her favour when he presented her case to other angels? Wouldn't they feel more sympathetic when they knew how she continued to aid Heaven's cause even on Earth? And if they wanted information on the development of the Alliance, they would *have* to keep communicating with her...

That night, once again, she sat on her rocky ledge while Asmodai hovered, bright and beautiful, before her. She nodded as he reported his latest conversations with other angels and their general lack of interest. By the time he finished, she had decided how to start off on her own topic.

"I know some interesting information you could tell other angels," she said. "It's about the Residuals."

He put his hands together, rested his gaze upon her and prepared to listen.

"You know that Residuals have souls?"

"Naturally. It's the spark that generates their life and consciousness."

"But the Humen don't. I've looked into the eyes of Hypers, and there's nothing there. Just a horrible, dead emptiness."

"Mmm, yes. That's long been suspected. Hypers are artificial creations, like the Plasmatics implanted in Humen machines. It's not an issue our scholars give much thought to. But *I've* thought about it."

"I can tell you how they're created. They borrow their life and consciousness from Residuals."

She described what Ferren had seen in the Bankstown Camp: the extraction process on Residual victims in the baths; the shimmering jelly stored in great glass flasks; the injection of the jelly through a plughole in the Hypers' foreheads. Asmodai nodded reflectively, and Miriael wondered if he'd guessed it all along.

"The important thing is how the Humen get their victims," she went on. "They trick the Residuals by claiming they have to make a contribution to the war. They're supposed to be allies, so they take some off for military service But what if the Residuals refuse to be taken off?"

Her dramatic question didn't have the effect she'd anticipated. Asmodai pursed his lips and shook his head.

"I can't imagine Residuals would ever do that."

"Some of them will. I've seen it."

"How many, though? One tribe, two tribes, a dozen? There are hundreds of tribes along the east coast of Australia, and the Bankstown Camp can draw on all of them."

"But if they form an alliance, and the alliance keeps expanding..."

"It would take a very long time, and they'd all need to be in it. In the meanwhile, the Humen would punish every tribe that resisted."

Miriael's hopes faded. She no longer had the heart to describe the Residual Alliance or what she and Ferren had achieved so far. "So Heaven wouldn't be interested?"

He shook his head again. "Heaven isn't interested in Residuals. I know you've lived with them, but that's not something I look to mention, talking with other angels. You know the attitude."

"Oh." Miriael fell silent. She'd once shared the attitude herself, so she understood what he meant.

For a while, he didn't speak either. She had the impression he was studying her.

"I never told you about my research, did I?" he said at last. "My latest research?"

"After the Weather Wars?"

"Even more recent. You see, I've been learning about the souls of Residuals too. There's no one I can tell in Heaven, but I can tell you. I'm investigating the souls of Residuals after death, when the soul has separated from the body."

"Morphs," said Miriael at once.

"Exactly. They've been trapped on the Earth ever since Heaven shut them out."

"The Supreme Trinity would've let them back in…"

"But the great archangels objected, and all lesser angels followed the great archangels. The end of forgiveness and the withdrawal of the Supreme Trinity."

"Do *you* think they should be allowed back in?"

"I'd like to see it happen. Of course I can't say that to anyone but you."

Miriael felt warmed by his words. He truly was a wonderful being— and she was the only one in whom he could confide!

She might have asked further questions about his research, but already he was preparing to depart. The globe of his aura bobbed and moved away from her rock ledge. Dimly she heard him promising to tell her more another time, dimly she heard him saying farewell. She only just managed to ask her crucial question.

"Will you come back tomorrow night?"

He smiled. "I will. I'll do my very best. Until then, Miriael."

In the next moment he was gone, skimming away across the surface of the sea, then shooting up like an arrow into the sky. Miriael stared at the spot where he'd vanished, and wished she could have had more time with him.

Somehow, the Residual Alliance no longer seemed as important as it had before. She'd always realised that a score of tribes couldn't change the course of the war, but she'd seen it as the small start of a movement that would become huge. Seeing it now as Asmodai saw it, she wondered if it would ever grow at all.

19

Everything was in place for the Selector's arrival. The Sea-folk were spread across the islands as if busy with their daily chores, while

Moireen was stationed among the grassy hills behind the beach, ready to give advance warning. Ferren himself was on the far side of the headland, crouching on an outcrop of rock below the level of the main platform. Looking so different to the people of the tribe, he would have to stay hidden until the last moment.

At last, the signal came. Appearing on top of the highest hill, Moireen waved her arms furiously back and forth. The Selector was approaching along the beach. Ferren ducked lower, so that only his eyes showed out. He couldn't see the rest of the tribe, but they had surely observed the signal too. He waited.

Then the black, rubber-clad figure of the Selector came into view: head, shoulders, chest and legs, as he climbed the rocks up onto the flat platform of the headland. The Sea-folk had told Ferren that this was where the selection procedure always took place. They'd also told him about the weapon to expect, long-barrelled with a cone-shaped nozzle. The Selector carried a flamethrower.

Ferren didn't expect him to pay attention to the additional loose seaweed scattered over the surface of the platform—and he didn't. He advanced across the headland and raised his flamethrower high in the air. Ferren saw the spiked metal collar round his neck and the half-human, half-animal face painted over the front of his head.

"Let's have a look at yer, then!" he roared—and a great jet of flame leaped from the nozzle of his flamethrower "Don't keep me waiting! You know what I'm here for!"

Obediently, the Sea-folk made their way to the headland, trooping across from island to island on their tightropes. They behaved as they had probably always behaved: cowed and fearful, eyes lowered, body language submissive. But this time they were playing a part. They formed up in a semicircle around the Selector, and the three Mothers stepped out in front.

"Yeah, it's volunteering time. Someone for military service." The Selector addressed himself to Gweir, Lorne and Krye. "Did yer miss me? Bet you could hardly wait to see me again, hey?"

He laughed—an ugly sound out of the corners of his mouthslit. "And guess what? A new order from our new Doctor. You're gonna like it. You can contribute *two* volunteers this year."

The Sea-folk continued to play their part. They groaned and moaned and bleated complaints. "Why two?" "It's always been one!" "We can't!" "We're not ready."

The Selector patted the butt of his flamethrower. "*This* says you're ready," he jeered.

Ferren, watching the scene from the side, frowned at the Selector's position on the headland. He was standing too far back… How could the Sea-folk draw him forward to the right spot?

Then Jorika jumped out from the semicircle and flung herself on the ground before the Selector. She burst into a storm of simulated wails and sobs.

The Selector snarled. "Shut up, you! Get back in line!"

Jorika only wailed louder at a shrieking, ear-splitting pitch. The Selector strode forward and raised a boot to stamp down on her. Jorika dodged away and stretched out her arms as if pleading and desperate. When the Selector again came forward, preparing to kick her, she clutched at his boot and pulled him even further forward.

Exactly where he needed to be! The Sea-folk moved to form a complete circle around him. Still he suspected nothing.

Ferren raised his head above the level of the rock platform. "*One!*" he yelled at the top of his voice.

Jorika sprang to her feet and darted away. The Sea-folk in their circle took a step backwards, all at the same time.

"*Two!*" The Sea-folk knelt and reached down through the scattered seaweed.

"*Three!*" When they rose again, they had hold of the edges of the special net. As they lifted it up, the seaweed fell through and revealed the full thirty-foot spread of it.

"*Four!*" The Selector was still looking about in confusion when those on the landward side ran forward and swept the net right over his head.

"*Five!*" The Sea-folk pulled hard, the Selector stumbled and fell. He let out a terrible roar of rage as they bundled him up in the mesh. Ferren climbed onto the flat top of the headland.

"*Six!*" He yelled. "Quick now!"

The Selector was fumbling for his flamethrower, fighting against the cords that entangled him. The Sea-folk ran with the net and dragged him to the edge of the headland.

The final call came not from Ferren but all of the Sea-folk in chorus together. *"Seven!"* The Selector teetered and struggled for balance on the brink. Ferren sprang forward and delivered the final kick to send him over.

It was an eight-foot fall. The black-clad figure found the trigger of his flamethrower as he fell and fired off a burst of flame. But only for a moment—until he and his weapon hit the water. There was a great splash and an explosion of steam. Then, with a stuttering hiss, the flame went out.

20

Everyone peered down over the edge and cheered. Some shook their fists, others kept a grip on their ends of the net. The Selector was only a few seconds submerged before he bobbed back up to the surface like a cork.

Ferren watched him squeeze again and again on the trigger of his flamethrower, but the weapon was waterlogged and permanently out of action. He abandoned the attempt, rolled over in the water and snarled at the audience looking down from above.

"You'll pay for this, yer dummies! Doctor Saniette will see to you! You're all gone, the lot of yer! We'll make an example! We'll make you wish…"

His voice trailed off as his eyeslits swivelled towards the other side of the channel in which he floundered. A new figure had appeared on the first island, where Ferren and Miriael had made their stand against the seagulls. Ferren gasped. It was the angel herself!

Seaweed clung to her legs, and the lower part of her robe was dripping wet. No doubt she had hauled herself from island to island hanging down from the ropes into the water. Yet she was still superb, still breathtakingly beautiful. Her hair was a golden frame around her perfect features.

The Selector had a different opinion on the beauty of angels. "You pretty-pretty," he sneered. "You airy-fairy fart!"

He refocused for a better look—and grew suddenly excited. Iridescent spittle gleamed in his mouthslit. "I know who you are! You're that freak angel, the one that survived without an aura! You're the one our Doctor wants to examine!"

He twisted in the water, struggled against the enclosing net and reached into a pocket of his black rubbery suit. The object he drew out was a small black box with a silver spike. He pressed on a button, lifted the box to his mouthslit and began to speak

"Urgent! Urgent! Message for Doctor Saniette. Sighting to report. It's what he's been waiting for. Put me through."

He paused as though expecting some reply. But the box remained silent.

"Come on, come on!" He shook the box, then shouted into it at twice the volume. "Somebody there! This is the news you want! Come on, this is urgent!"

Still the box remained silent. The Selector looked at it in disgust, then threw it away—only as far as the mesh of the net. "Blast this thing!"

"It won't work after it's been in the water," said Miriael, from her side of the channel.

The Selector looked up at her and spat—or at least made a vicious, spitting sound.

"Is that so? Won't help you, though. Soon as Doctor Saniette hears you've been sighted, he'll send out search parties and comb all around. He wants you in his surgeries so they can take you apart, see? Tiny slice by slice. They'll find out everything about you and your kind."

His malevolence was like poison streaming through the air. Miriael grimaced and turned away—and his poison grew even more vitriolic.

"Too late, you can't run off now!" he jeered. "We'll hunt you down! Doctor Saniette will get you! He put a bounty on your head, soon as he heard about *you*. Fifty extra pyscholitres for anyone reporting you, fifty more for bringing you in. Oh, he'll get you good, pretty-pretty!"

Ferren didn't know how to shut him up, but the younger members of the tribe soon distracted him. They began pelting him with stones and shells, hitting him all over his black-clad body. He snarled, swore and cursed, and turned over in the water away from Miriael. Ferren left them to it and headed for a rope by which to cross to Miriael on the first island.

21

"Don't let him get to you." Ferren tried to comfort Miriael. "You're not scared by his threats, are you?"

"Not scared, no." There was a troubled look in her sky-blue eyes. "It's nothing new. It's what the original ten Bankstown Doctors would've done to me."

"Take you apart? But why?"

"To find out how angels work. If the Humen can learn the secrets of our nature, they can devise new weapons to defeat us. It's a very real danger."

"Oh." Ferren was about to say more when he saw Miriael's gaze shift away from his face to something happening behind his back. He turned to look.

The younger Sea-folk had stopped bombarding the Selector with stones and shells, and had gone off to join the rest of the tribe at the back of the headland. Only the three Mothers remained, still holding onto the ends of the net. The Selector was speaking to them.

What's going on? Ferren wondered. This wasn't a part of the plan.

"They shouldn't be listening to him," he told Miriael. "I don't like it."

"Leave them be," Miriael advised. "You've been in charge, now let them make some decisions."

"As long as they don't decide to release him."

Ferren continued to watch, but couldn't catch what was being said. The Selector was gesturing with his arms inside the net, persuading rather than threatening. Ferren liked the situation less and less.

"He wants them to change sides," he muttered. "He'll undo all the good work we've done."

Then Gweir said something to the other Mothers, and all three of them began hauling the Selector along in the water, parallel to the side of the headland. Four yards along, there was a small bay and a small beach of pebbles and rocks.

"Don't do it," Ferren growled, addressing them in his mind. "Don't be stupid."

But the Mothers stopped hauling and allowed the Selector to scramble out onto dry land. He stood on the beach, still tangled in the net, still unable to climb to the flat top of the headland.

Ferren raised his voice and shouted across in alarm. *"Don't trust him! Keep him down there!"*

It was Krye who shouted back in reply. "He's been making us offers!"

"Telling us all the things they'll do for us," added Lorne.

"We can name our price to their new Doctor," Gweir confirmed.

The Selector nodded vigorously from inside the net. "Yeah, whatever you want! I swear! He'll do anything if you give him that pretty-pretty!"

The Selector had no expression on his painted features, but he was trying to sound sincere. Crouched at the foot of the rock-face, he couldn't see what Ferren saw. The Sea-folk who'd gone off were now returning—and they were pushing a massive, round boulder in front of them.

"What shall we do?" cried Gweir rhetorically. "Shall we accept this Humen offer? What do we all think?"

The boulder rolled closer and closer to the brink, right above the bay where the Selector crouched below. It was as high as the Sea-folk pushing it, and as wide as it was high.

"No, I think we'll turn down the offer," Gweir went on. "We'll join the Residual Alliance instead. And we'll never be threatened or bullied by Humen again!"

She stepped aside, and the Sea-folk propelled the boulder forward over the last couple of feet. "Here's our answer to you!" she yelled down as the boulder dropped.

Watching from the other side of the channel, Ferren saw the Selector's reflex reaction as the boulder hurtled towards him. He raised his arms to protect his head, but his arms were hopelessly entangled in the net—and couldn't have saved him anyway.

With an almighty splitting, crunching sound, the boulder crashed down, crushed him and cracked him apart. Zigzag cracks spread this way and that across the black, rubber-suited body.

The Sea-folk gaped at the strange inhuman sight. Even Ferren gaped, though he'd seen something similar before. Thin wisps of shimmering vapour began leaking from the cracks.

Miriael cried a warning. "Shield your eyes! Stand back!"

Everyone shielded their eyes and drew back a little—though not so far that they couldn't keep watching.

Whumfff!

With a dull detonation, the body broke open, and a million shapes and colours burst forth. An insane conflagration of images flickered in and out of existence. For a moment, the blast rocked everyone back on their heels.

When they looked again, the images had vanished into thin air. All that remained of the Selector were a few dozen scattered chunks of some inanimate material. The stuff looked dry and porous, like grey honeycomb.

Ferren recovered his breath. "Now you see what they really are!" he cried to the Sea-folk. "Like I said! Those was our memories and experiences inside him! Stolen from us and injected into him."

But the Sea-folk hardly heard. As they emerged from their surprise, they began whooping and clapping their hands. In another moment, they were all dancing wildly around and cheering, cheering, cheering.

22

The Sea-folk celebrated all through the day and into the evening. Miriael shared in the feasting and festivities, but her mind was elsewhere. She'd told Ferren that the Selector's threats hadn't frightened her, but they worried her as never before. Never had her situation on the Earth seemed more precarious.

Still, she had to put aside her worries while she sat with Ferren and the three Mothers to discuss the next steps after their tribe joined the Residual Alliance. Ferren did most of the explaining about the general assembly of representatives from all tribes to be held on the day of the autumn equinox. Miriael came in to give directions from here on the coast to the People's Home Ground, where the assembly would take place. Then the Mothers gave directions to the next Residuals they should visit, a nearby tribe called the Nesters.

Ferren was eager to start off first thing the following morning, and Miriael didn't disagree. Their journeying mattered less to her than what she would say to Asmodai tonight. If this Doctor Saniette was determined to hunt her down, then that changed everything...

It was an hour after nightfall, and the festivities were still in full swing when she slipped quietly away. She made the crossing to Renna Dair hand over hand along the rope, feet dangling in the water. Then she sat down on her ledge and composed herself to patience. Asmodai had promised to do "his very best" to visit, and she believed in his promise.

This time she observed his descent from start to finish. Appearing at first as a dot of light in the night sky, he came shooting down to sea level, then approached along the glittering path of his own reflected brightness. As always, she was struck with awe and wonder.

His globe came to rest mere inches away from her feet on the ledge. He greeted her solemnly.

"I have no news, I'm afraid." He observed the expression on her face. "But I can see you have news for me."

So she told him what the Selector had said, and explained the danger.

"This new Doctor Saniette is desperate to capture me so he can dissect me and analyse me. If he can find out how angels work, he can devise special weapons to take down *all* angels."

"Hmm. That is a very great danger."

"A danger to Heaven. It could lose us the war."

"And a danger to you. Undergoing dissection."

Miriael liked the fact that he considered her fate no less than the threat to Heaven. But it was the threat to Heaven that might work in her favour.

"Heaven can't keep ignoring me now, don't you think? They'll see they need to communicate with me when you tell them."

"More than that, I think. They can never feel safe while this Doctor is hunting for you. It's gone beyond a need to communicate. They'll *have* to let you return now."

Miriael was taken aback. "Return to Heaven?"

"Yes."

"But there's that problem…my weight. I told you what the Seraphim…"

"And I told you that the Seraphim don't know everything. I believe it can be done with a new method."

"A new method? What, something *you've* discovered?"

"Exactly." He nodded. "Yes, this makes their old excuse irrelevant."

She waited to hear him explain his new method, but the explanation wasn't forthcoming. She sensed that he wasn't ready to tell her just yet. She tried a different question. "What old excuse?"

"Oh, they claim to be cutting off all contact with you for your own good. 'To save her from hopeless frustration and yearning for the impossible,' they said."

"Is that what they said? You didn't mention it before."

"Because it's only an excuse. A nonsensical one."

"Oh."

He put his hands together as if in prayer, meditating for a moment.

"Yes, I can use this," he said at last. "They'll have to see it now. I can take it to the higher authorities. Maybe I'll even get an audience with the great archangels of the War Council. This *will* make a difference."

Miriael was a little confused. Things seemed to be moving suddenly so far, so fast…

"I'll act on it straightaway." He shone brighter in his globe and drew away from the ledge. "You've done well with this, Miriael."

A hundred questions swirled in her mind. Did she really want to go back up to Heaven right now? Would the angels accept her if she did? What was Asmodai's new method and would it even work?

But already he was retreating across the water, back to the point where he'd descended.

"Goodbye," she murmured. "And thank you."

She watched as he soared up into the sky with a coruscating trail of light.

PART TWO

ASMODAI

1

After leaving the islands, Ferren and Miriael headed north along a series of beaches. Ferren trusted Miriael to remember the Mothers' directions better than he did.

After what seemed like hours of trudging across soft sand, they came to a river and followed it inland. The walking was still hard work, over marshy ground with stagnant ponds that constantly blocked their route. The scum on the ponds was so thick it was like yellowy-brown leather, with air-bubbles bulging in blisters under the surface. When the blisters grew large enough to burst, they scattered foul-smelling matter far and wide.

Eventually, Miriael called a halt for lunch. Ferren opened his pack and brought out the food that the Sea-folk had provided. They ate honey-rolls and flatbread spread with a salty fish-roe paste.

"You never bother to remember directions yourself," the angel remarked. "Why not?"

"You're the leader."

She shook her head. "I don't want to be. Look at the way you took over with the Sea-folk."

"Only because they kept you out of the way on your own separate island."

"But you managed."

"I hated it when they did that. It had better not happen with these Nesters."

Miriael shrugged. "We'll have to adapt, whatever they do."

Ferren chewed on fish roe and flatbread, scowling.

"It's not that I can't manage," he brought out at last. "It's that I need you to inspire me. You make me a better, stronger person. I can do anything when you're with me."

"Yes, well, I'm glad to help."

"You give me hope and strength and courage. I need you more than…more than…more than…"

"You mustn't think like that."

"But I *do!*"

Miriael appeared startled by his sudden intensity. He gave up the struggle for words and thought of a better way to express his feelings. "I'll show you," he told her.

He reached for the top of his loincloth, unrolled the waistband and brought out two brilliantly white feathers. Feathers from *her* wing.

"Oh. You've still got those," she said.

He had collected the feathers three months ago, after he'd found them lying on the ground. He held them up with reverence.

"I'll never lose them. My most treasured possessions! My symbols of service! My—"

"What on earth *are* you saying? 'Symbols of service!' You make me uncomfortable when you talk like that."

"All right. I won't say it. But I feel it. What these feathers mean to me … Well, they mean it forever."

Miriael looked away. "I don't know what you think I am, but I'm *not*," she said.

Ferren rolled the feathers once more into the top of his loincloth, and they finished their lunch in silence.

They walked on through the afternoon, still following the river. The stench of bursting blisters in the scum wasn't their only problem; now hordes of gnat-like insects descended upon them. Ferren was soon bitten and itching all over. He couldn't scratch the itches because he needed both hands to beat the insects away from his face.

He was thankful when they came to a fork in the river and turned to follow a smaller tributary. Here the ground was no longer marshy, and they left the insects behind. Later again, they emerged from the valley and started across a treeless plain of hip-high grass, not unlike the Plain around the People's Home Ground.

From time to time, Ferren touched the rolled top of his loincloth, where the two feathers nestled inside. But he only did it when the angel wasn't watching.

2

Miriael was waiting for Asmodai. She and Ferren had flattened an area of grass and lain down for sleep an hour ago. But while Ferren had soon dropped off, she'd stayed wide awake. When the sky was black and the stars twinkling, she'd slipped off secretly and found another spot a hundred yards away. She'd flattened the grass here too, in preparation for her angel visitor.

She didn't like the feeling that she was deceiving Ferren. But after his strange outburst today, she was more than ever determined not to tell him about Asmodai. Ferren seemed to have formed some idea about her and himself that had nothing to do with reality. Still, she didn't want to hurt him.

She waited a long time, staring up at the stars. She was certain that Asmodai would come searching for her, but would he be able to find her? If only she'd told him the route they'd be taking... But his last visit had been so brief, had she even told him they were leaving the Sea-folk?

Then she noticed one star not behaving like the rest. It moved across the background of the constellations, and it wasn't a shooting star because it moved in circles. It had to be him! But so high and remote... How to attract his attention?

She stood in the middle of the flattened grass and spread her wings. After a moment's thought, she began flapping them slowly, open and shut, open and shut.

The star that wasn't a star circled closer. Surely he'd seen her! She wished she still had the power to loose off a flash of light. More and more frantically she flapped.

And at last she caught his attention. She breathed a huge sigh of relief. Now he was swooping down straight towards her. She blinked in the brightness of his light and felt the rush of wind as he descended.

Instinctively, she lowered herself to the ground to sit as she had always sat before. It seemed only right that she should look up at him.

"Ah, Miriael, Miriael." A deep frown creased his brow.

"What's wrong?"

"Heaven's wrong. I thought they would *have* to see sense this time. But they're so rigid and blinkered! They'd sooner fight another battle to drive off the Humen than allow you back where you belong."

"Did you talk to the great archangels?"

"No, I never got that far. They wouldn't even listen to my method for keeping you up. They all just assume the weight of your new body is too heavy for Heaven."

Miriael sighed. "Perhaps they're right."

"It's a false assumption. They don't know about Morphs."

Miriael wondered if she'd misheard. "*Morphs?*"

"Morphs. We talked about them. The souls of human beings, shut out of Heaven after death. I've been doing research into them."

"I remember. But you didn't say they could help *me*."

"They're my greatest discovery. Greater than anything I discovered during the Weather Wars. They represent a whole new form of spiritual energy. A force that's never been harnessed."

Miriael could hardly believe it. "I thought Morphs were weak and helpless."

"Which is what everyone thinks. It's what they think themselves. That's why everyone has overlooked their potential. They can be used to do many, many things. Raising you up into Heaven is just one example."

She thought back to Neath's Morph, after the old leader of the People had died. "The Morph I saw was blown about like thistledown."

"Spiritual energy isn't the same as physical strength. So you can still see them?"

"Yes, that's one angelic power that I've kept." Miriael grimaced, think-ing of so many more that she'd lost. "I saw him as a pattern of delicate lines like a snowflake. I encouraged him to float away and find a colony of Morphs like himself."

"Ah, it's the colonies I need. You don't know where he'd have gone?"

"No. I've never seen a colony of Morphs."

"If you ever do…" He paused. "I need more subjects for my research. Volunteer subjects of course. If you ever see a colony, will you tell me about it?"

"Yes. But I think they're usually in very quiet, secluded places."

"Indeed they are."

For a moment he remained absorbed, then focused intently upon her. "We need a means of communication, don't we? Now that you're travelling around, you'll need to let me know where you are."

"All right." Miriael tried not to show her delight at the idea. "Then you can keep visiting."

"I'll have to teach you how to call for me. I have a special technique."

"You have a method for everything!" Miriael laughed.

He responded with one of his breathtaking smiles. "Nothing to do with Morphs this time. This is a version of angelic communion. Like the kind of spirit-to-spirit communication you've been cut off from. Are you willing to try it? Shall we create the connection?"

"I'm ready."

"It'll be easier if you close your eyes."

Miriael closed her eyes, yet she still sensed his movement as he approached and stooped. He must be kneeling before her, his face so close to her own!

She felt a tingling vibration above her brows like the ringing of a tiny bell. A strange impression formed in her mind, as though her head was being held gently yet firmly between two hands, while her attention was being directed towards a dark space in front of her. The dark space was a kind of vacuum drawing her out… Soon it was as though her forehead had melted away.

There was a figure of light in the darkness. She couldn't be sure, but it seemed quite close and small like a doll. Then she heard words spoken.

Veni Asmodai, veni ad me.

Who was speaking? Was it the figure? Was it Asmodai referring to himself? The figure didn't have a mouth or a face, only the brightness of its light.

Veni Asmodai, veni ad me. Veni Asmodai, veni ad me. Veni Asmodai, veni ad me.

Again and again the phrase was repeated, with an insistence that created an echo in her own mind.

Veni Asmodai, veni ad me.

Suddenly, the figure seemed to jerk forward. Its light shot out—piercing and penetrating and burning right into her.

"Ow!" she cried, and opened her eyes.

Asmodai *was* there, every bit as close as she'd imagined. Surrounded by the globe of his aura, he was kneeling before her. He had closed his eyes, and his face wore an expression of intense concentration.

Then he opened his eyes, and his globe carried him a few feet further back. "I'm sorry, I should have warned you. Did it hurt?"

She considered. "Not actual pain, no. Sort of...invasive."

He hovered above the ground, still kneeling. "That was the imprinting. Now, when you need to call me, I'll receive your signal and know your location. All you need do is form a strong mental picture of me and repeat the phrase in your mind."

"What phrase? Oh, *that* phrase. *Veni Asmodai, veni—*"

He held up a hand. "Not now. Only when you want to call me. I can't promise to come at once, but I'll come as soon as I can."

"Does it have to be at night?"

"No, it can work at any time. There's a connection to me in you and you in me. Spirit to spirit, like the communion of all angels. But just between the two of us."

"The two of us," said Miriael—and out of nowhere, a sudden warmth mounted to her cheeks. She didn't understand it, but she was sure her face had gone bright red. Her newly physicalised body must be playing a trick on her...

He was still kneeling as his globe carried him further and further away. "Goodbye until our next meeting, Miriael."

She hoped he hadn't noticed the colour in her cheeks. *Just between the two of us...*

With a tremendous, roaring *whoosh*, he shot up into the sky. Miriael's head was in a whirl, and she saw spots before her eyes.

She stayed for a long while where she was, until her thoughts finally slowed down.

3

Ferren woke up in the morning still puzzled by his memories of the night. Had something really happened or had he dreamed it?

He didn't say anything to Miriael at first, but it burst out all at once over breakfast. "Did you see a weird light last night?"

"No. What sort of light?"

"Shooting up from the Earth to the sky."

"I must have been asleep, if it happened."

"Perhaps I was too. It might've been a dream."

Miriael shrugged. "Wouldn't you have woken me up if you were awake?"

"I don't know. It's all vague and muddled. You don't think it could've been some sort of Celestial?"

"Sounds more like a dream to me."

They set off straight after breakfast walking fast, aiming to reach the Nesters before nightfall. In the clear light of day, they could see distant hills painted in camouflage colours of green, grey and brown. Miriael pointed to one distinctively shaped hill.

"That's the hill the Mothers described. We head towards it."

Beyond the plain of grass, the scenery changed. They saw the change at first as a band of whiteness; then the grass gave way to bare earth; then the whiteness revealed itself as an area of dead trees. The trees were set out in rows, and their trunks and limbs were pale and dry as bone.

They passed in among the rows and walked on, until Ferren pointed to a particular tree with a silver box implanted between its forking branches.

"What's that?"

"Some Humen devilry, I expect."

He turned aside to inspect, and Miriael went with him. The box had no openings or projections or any apparent function. But several other trees had similar implanted boxes.

"It must be some old Humen experiment," Miriael commented. "Perhaps it was meant to torture trees into having different kinds of leaves or fruits or something."

They went back to following their route—then jumped when one of the boxes gave out a sudden, loud *click!* This time, though, they didn't go to inspect. When other boxes gave out random clicks at random intervals, they continued to keep their distance. Eventually they became used to the sounds and no longer paid any attention.

It wasn't until late afternoon that they emerged from the rows of white trees and came to an area like a wide, grassy field. There were low, mounded hills to the left and right; further on was a dark mass of greenery.

"That might be our destination," said Miriael. "The Nesters live in a thicket."

As they came closer, the greenery resolved into a thicket of densely growing bushes and shrubs. Closer again, and Ferren saw an arched hole like an entrance into the interior. When people emerged from the entrance and stood watching their approach, he knew they had indeed arrived.

"And those must be the Nesters," he said.

4

Ferren was always surprised at the differences between the tribes. The Nesters were nothing like the Sea-folk, nor the People either. They had sharp, pointy faces, upturned noses, and wore their hair in long braids decorated with carved wooden ornaments. Their clothes were animal pelts and hides stitched together to make wraparound garments. No doubt their customs were as different as their appearance.

The ones who came to meet them outside the entrance were all young. They eyed him with amazement, and eyed Miriael with a mixture of awe and fear. They were obviously dying with curiosity about the angel, pointing and whispering behind their hands, but none dared come too close to her.

"Don't worry, she's on our side," Ferren told them. "Don't worry, they'll get used to you," he told Miriael.

It was always the same with every tribe. He found it frustrating that people couldn't just accept and admire Miriael as he did himself. Every time, he had to prove that she wasn't a deadly threat or an enemy.

If the young Nesters were shrinking but fascinated, their elders were simply aghast. Half-a-dozen older folk followed the young ones out from the thicket. Evidently mothers and fathers, they hung back and called to their children.

"Keep away!"

"Come back here!"

Ferren spoke to the young Nesters, who were mostly his own age or younger. "I'm Ferren, from a tribe you don't know called the People. I've travelled a long way to visit you, and this Celestial with me. We have an important message about joining an alliance against the Humen."

The young Nesters were wide-eyed.

"Miles and miles!"

"A tribe we don't know!"

"Did you say, an alliance against the Humen?"

The last question came from a girl with dark red hair and very white teeth. Ferren turned to her.

"Yes, and we need to speak—"

"Have you had amazing adventures?" the young boy standing beside the girl interrupted.

"Yes, but we need to speak to the leaders of your tribe."

"That'll be the Guardians," said the girl. "I can find them for you."

"I want to hear the adventures first," the boy protested.

"No, Tadge." The girl's attractive face wore a deep frown and severe expression. "Guardians first."

"Please," said Ferren.

The girl nodded. "I'll take you. I'm Kiet of Bloodstock. Follow me."

She turned and led the way towards the thicket. Shocked expressions appeared on the faces of the older Nesters, who shook their heads and tried to stop her. "Not a Celestial." "It's not right." "Who knows what she might do?"

Kiet scowled and gestured towards Ferren. "He vouches for her. Right?"

"I do." He nodded.

"Then so do I," said Kiet. "Come on," she said to Ferren, and marched through the entrance hole into the thicket.

The arched hole became a long green tunnel. Six feet high and six feet wide, it had been hollowed out through the densely growing bushes and shrubs. Dappled sunlight filtered through the foliage overhead, dim and shady compared to the brightness outside.

Ferren walked behind Kiet, and Miriael behind him. The young Nesters trailed along after the angel, allowing a safe interval of many yards.

Soon they were passing other tunnels that opened up left and right. Evidently, the thicket spread out to a great size, and the Nesters' home went all the way through it.

Whenever Kiet encountered other members of her tribe, she stopped to question them. They answered quickly, nervously, then scurried off to the nearest intersecting tunnel to watch the procession go by from a distance. It was after the third such exchange that Kiet turned to Ferren.

"Berwin's in his nest, we'll catch him there. He's the Heartstock Guardian."

She took the first tunnel to the left, then the second to the right.

"We're in Berwin's family area now," she told Ferren over her shoulder.

They continued on through Berwin's family area, which looked exactly the same as every other part of the thicket. When Kiet pointed and announced, "And here's his nest," the bushes and shrubs looked exactly the same there too.

Only when she swung off onto a short path did the dark mouth of the nest become visible. Still Ferren had to peer and squint to distinguish the solid structure itself. It really was like a bird's nest woven into a hedge, a domed shape of twigs and branches, compacted with mud and moss.

"Wait," said Kiet.

While Ferren waited, she went up and ducked her head inside the mouth of the nest. He could hear sounds of conversation, but not what was being said.

Her head reappeared a minute later. "He's not sure he wants to speak with you. I had to tell him you're with a Celestial."

"Explain how important it is," Ferren replied. "The Nesters can join an alliance of all the tribes. Eighteen already. The Nesters won't want to be left out."

Kiet nodded and ducked inside again. This time the conversation continued for two or three minutes before she reappeared.

"He says he can't make a decision for all the Guardians, so he'd sooner not receive your message on his own."

"Perfect, then. Bring the Guardians together, and we'll have a meeting right now."

Kiet pulled a face. "I don't know about right now."

She disappeared once more inside the nest. Ferren could hear her arguing forcefully; she was certainly trying her best for him.

The next time she reappeared, she was actually smiling. "He's coming out to see you," she said.

The old man who emerged was grizzled and grey around the chin, with deeply sunken eye sockets. He stood before Ferren and Kiet with his chest puffed up, as if ready to take on the world, but he also darted anxious glances beyond and behind them. Luckily, Miriael was still back in the main tunnel, out of sight.

He spoke to Ferren, in short, gruff sentences. "Well, young stranger. You don't understand how we do things here. Whatever your request, I don't want to hear it."

"Not on your own," Ferren agreed at once. "But all the Guardians together."

"We don't come together very often."

Kiet jumped in. "You could call a meeting."

"Hush, girl." Berwin flapped a hand at her and continued to address Ferren. "In a few days' time perhaps."

"I was thinking about now."

"Out of the question." The Heartstock Guardian considered for a moment. "Perhaps tomorrow."

Ferren saw Kiet nodding at him. "Good. Tomorrow. Early tomorrow?"

"We'll see. Sometime tomorrow."

Ferren realised it was time to leave. Berwin was still casting anxious glances along the path, and Miriael might come into sight at any moment.

"Thank you," he said.

'What about their accommodation?" asked Kiet. "Where can they stay for the night."

Berwin sniffed. "Not my problem," he said, and retreated back inside his nest.

5

"It's all right, I've got an idea," Kiet told Ferren. "My family has a spare nest. You can sleep there."

"They'll accept a Celestial—?"

"I'll *make* them accept."

They returned to Miriael and the crowd of young Nesters waiting in the main tunnel. Kiet addressed the crowd.

"My family's going to put them up for the night. You should go back to your own families now. Nothing more's going to happen till tomorrow."

She swung on her heel and led the way to her family area. Most young followers drifted away, but a few continued to trail behind. Kiet strode along without looking back, zigzagging from tunnel to tunnel. Then, halfway along one tunnel, she came to an abrupt stop.

"Here's where my family area begins," she announced. "Where's Tadge?"

The boy who'd asked to hear more adventures came forward. He was about twelve years old, with buck teeth and spiky, brown hair. Apparently, he wasn't just another follower but Kiet's younger brother. She set him to keep guard and allow no one into their family area.

"All finished! No further!" she yelled, and waved away the remnants of the procession. She whispered to Ferren out of the side of her mouth. "Otherwise they'll come peeking and pestering you."

They continued on, just Kiet, Ferren and the angel. The spare nest turned out very similar to Berwin's, a dome-like shape woven into the bushes. A similar short path led to the entrance opening.

"This was my parents' nest before the Selectors took them," Kiet explained. "Me and Tadge and Rhinn used to live here. Now we live with Grandpa Niot and Auntie Nettish."

She said it in a matter-of-fact voice, not facing Ferren. Still he caught a glimpse of her features: mouth tight and jaw clenched. So her story was similar to his own...

He followed her inside, and Miriael came after him. The angel had hardly spoken since they'd arrived in the Nesters' territory. As Ferren's eyes adjusted to the semi-darkness, he saw that the smooth, rounded walls of the nest were made of clay—and smelled of clay too. The floor was of hard, packed earth.

"It's been empty over a year," Kiet told them. "I'll bring you some bedding and a table."

"We won't need a table," said Ferren. "We won't be staying long."

"Huh! You will if you want an answer from the Guardians. They won't decide at a first meeting. They'll each have to consult with their stocks, then another meeting themselves, then more consulting with their stocks."

Ferren was puzzled. "What *are* stocks? Heartstock, Bloodstock... what are they?"

"We have four stocks with a Guardian for each. Berwin makes the decisions for Heartstock, Skail for Bloodstock, Dunkery for Headstock and Clemmart for Bonestock."

Ferren chewed his lip. "I'm used to addressing all the members of a tribe together."

"Not here. The stocks don't have much to do with each other. Not adults, anyway. Everyone's born into a stock, and each stock has particular things they do best. With heart or blood or head or bone."

Ferren shook his head, not understanding.

"Like me." Kiet explained as though it was obvious. "I'm Bloodstock. So I have courage and determination in my blood. We're special at catching small animals and birds and everything that lives in the bushes. We have quickness of eye and speed of hand and foot, so we're the hunters."

Ferren grimaced. "So I have to work with the Guardians, and the Guardians work with their stocks."

"And then they'll need to consult with the Old Ones too."

"Old Ones? Who are they?"

"You'll find out if you stay for your answer.' Kiet jumped up. "Now I have to talk to my grandpa and aunt. Get them to agree to you staying here." She called back over her shoulder as she went out. "It may take a while."

Miriael looked at Ferren in the gloom. "Be patient," she said. "This is going to be hard work for you."

"For *us*," Ferren shot back at once. "We're a team, aren't we?"

6

It seemed ages before Kiet returned. The light faded to blackness outside; then a full moon rose up in the sky. It was bright enough to penetrate the foliage and shed silvery light into the nest where Ferren and Miriael sat waiting.

When Kiet reappeared, she came bearing rolled-up rugs and blankets. "Your bedding," she announced.

The rugs and blankets were made of furs and animal hides, stitched together in a random patchwork. Kiet spread them out and surveyed them with satisfaction.

"There. Table tomorrow. Have you eaten? I don't know I can get you a proper meal now. We eat all together with the stock."

"Doesn't matter, we had our own food for today," Ferren replied. "So your family agreed?"

Kiet grinned. "It was a struggle. Grandpa Niot was all right, but Auntie Nettish and Rhinn were scared. Rhinn's my older sister.'

"Scared of a Celestial?"

"Yes. That's why I put you here in the nest before I asked them."

Ferren was baffled until the girl explained. "They were scared to have a Celestial living close by, but even more scared about trying to make her leave." Kiet nodded towards Miriael. "I told them they'd have to drive you out themselves."

"If we're not welcome…" Miriael began.

"*I'll* make you welcome. So will Tadge. And everyone else will come round to it." Kiet half-turned towards the entrance. "I should be going back now."

"Wait," said Ferren. "Stay and talk to us."

Kiet needed no more persuasion. "What about?" she asked, as she dropped cross-legged to the floor.

"Well… What about these Old Ones who have to be consulted? Who are they?"

"They're the ghosts of the Old Ones. They live in the City of the Dead." She shivered and seemed reluctant to say more.

"Tell us about them," Ferren urged. "Tell us about the City of the Dead."

"It's a ruined city from the Age of Peace," she responded after a moment. "It's just on the other side of our thicket here. The opposite side to where you came in."

Ferren could guess. "The Age of Peace was a good time long ago, before the war between Heaven and Earth? And the Old Ones must have been your ancestors who built great cities with moto-cars and electrics and shop-shops?"

"Yes," Kiet agreed. "I never heard of shop-shops, though."

"It's still the same." Ferren nodded to himself. "So the Old Ones used to live in the City of the Dead, and now the Guardians go to consult with their ghosts whenever—"

"No," Miriael broke in. "It's not possible. There shouldn't be any ghosts from that time. Heaven wasn't closed off to souls until after the war began. The souls of human beings that died would have gone straight up to their eternal home."

She was very certain about it. Ferren sucked in his cheeks and turned to Kiet.

"*She* ought to know. If *she* says it's not possible…"

Kiet looked bewildered. "But I've heard them. They make ghostly, wailing sounds.'

"There must be *something* there, then." Ferren exchanged glances with Miriael.

"And whatever they are, they're going to be consulted," Miriael agreed. "So whether they say yes or no…"

"We ought to investigate. Find out what they are, and how to make them say yes…" Ferren turned from Miriael to Kiet. "Will you take us there?"

"What? Where?"

"To the City of the Dead."

"It's not allowed. Even the Guardians don't go right inside. You'd be seen if you tried to go in the daytime."

"Nighttime, then. Tonight."

"Tonight!" Kiet exclaimed with a start—then subsided again. "Don't ask," she muttered.

Ferren wasn't giving up, however. "We need your help. We need your Old Ones to say yes to the Residual Alliance."

"The what?"

"The alliance of all the tribes against the Humen."

Kiet scowled. "We *ought* to be against the Humen," she said with sudden intensity.

"Help us, then. Otherwise your Old Ones may say no."

"They answer no to most questions," Kiet conceded.

It was a first hint of yielding. Ferren continued to produce every argument he could come up with, and Kiet continued to listen—and resist. Half an hour later, he was still pleading and persuading. But eventually his persuasions won her over.

"All right, I'll take you to the City," she said. "I'm not going inside, though. Not for anything."

7

The moon was riding high when Ferren, Kiet and Miriael emerged from the thicket. For a moment they paused in the sudden openness, surveying the scene. Before them lay a wide, shallow valley, threaded by a network of a dozen rivulets. Everything was illuminated in an unearthly contrast of black and white in the moonlight.

The pale walls of the City of the Dead rose up on the other side of the valley—perhaps derelict, yet they looked solid and intact from a distance.

"Incredible," breathed Miriael. "So well preserved!"

"We watch from here while the Guardians do the Questioning," Kiet explained. "We can hear when the Old Ones answer.'

She led them along a track down the slope, then across the rivulets by a succession of stepping stones. A rubble of broken stone littered the grass as they went up again on the other side.

Eventually they arrived at an outcrop of rock surmounted by a concrete platform. From the platform, they gazed close up at the walls and buildings, pierced here and there by the dark rectangular holes of windows. Ferren couldn't begin to imagine the technology capable of constructing with such massive blocks of material. All was deserted and deathly silent.

"The Old Ones are quiet tonight," Ferren observed.

Kiet shrugged. "They only answer when the Guardians make a great noise. You have to arouse them. *No!*" she hissed, as Ferren appeared about to call out. "Don't! *Please!*"

He desisted. "We'll go right inside, then."

"You can. I'm not."

There were several gaps between sections of wall. Ferren set off towards the nearest gap, and Miriael went with him. Still he tried a last appeal to Kiet. "Just a little way?"

Kiet shook her head. She came forward as far as the gap, then stopped and shook her head again. Ferren walked on, but she stayed watching from outside. When he turned and looked back, she appeared lonely and rather frightened.

"We won't be long," he called out. "Promise."

Miriael had gone on ahead, and he hurried to catch up. They were advancing along a street with tall buildings on either side. The buildings were roofless, and there were cracks zigzagging through their facades, yet they stood as they must once have stood in the time of the Ancestors. Shopfronts and housefronts, doors and windows, pavements and gutters… He gawped in amazement.

It was like living a dream. In his imagination, he was transported back to the Good Times: crowds of people thronging the pavements, moto-cars gliding along the roadway, electrics all around lighting up the night… Occasionally he tripped and almost fell on broken slabs of concrete under his feet.

He wondered what lay behind the windows and doors. Were the buildings inside the same as they had been in the time of the Ancestors?

"Wait a minute!" he called to Miriael and crossed to a building to peer in through the nearest window. All he could see through the glass was a kind of grainy darkness.

He moved along to the nearest door and pulled on the door handle. Nothing budged. He pulled harder, then harder again. With a crack of rotted wood, the door snapped suddenly right off its hinges.

He jumped back before the door fell on him. The building inside was a mass of earth, which poured forth from the doorway in an avalanche onto the pavement. He scowled at it in disappointment.

"Nothing but dirt," he said.

Miriael had stopped to watch, but now strode on once more. Up ahead, the street opened out into a small plaza. Ferren caught up with her just as she stopped again. She was surveying a particular corner of the plaza on the left.

"Hush," she ordered. "I thought I heard something."

He listened, but heard nothing.

"What was it?" he asked in a whisper.

"Like tiny voices."

He held himself motionless and prepared to listen even harder—when a sudden clatter of footsteps broke his concentration. It was Kiet running up from behind. He whirled towards her and put a finger to his lips for silence.

But he dropped the finger when he saw the panic-stricken look on her face. She ran right up to him and grabbed onto his arm.

"What is it?"

She fought for breath. "Don't like—being left—alone!"

"Don't worry." He tried to calm her. "We're not afraid, and they're probably not ghosts. You're with us now."

Her hand fumbled for his and clutched on. He could feel how she was trembling.

"You're Bloodstock," he told her. "Doesn't that mean courage and determination?"

"Yes. That's me. That's what I'll be." Her voice steadied, and the grip of her hand felt steadier too.

Then a sound from the plaza came clearly to their ears.

"Ooo-oo-oh! Oh-ooo-oooh!"

8

Miriael was already advancing towards the corner where she'd been looking before. Ferren stepped forward into the plaza, but Kiet's hand pulled him back.

"We can watch from here," she insisted.

It was true: leaning forward, they had a clear view of the entire plaza.

"Oooh-oh-oooh!"

"Oh! Ooh! Oooooh!"

The sounds rose in pitch, increasingly excited and tremulous.

"It's the Old Ones," muttered Kiet.

Ferren didn't answer, but he was thinking furiously. He *knew* that sound. So sad and woeful... Where had he heard it before?

Miriael stopped and knelt in the corner of the plaza. She was facing a section of pavement between a broken kerb and three steps leading up to a door.

"Oooh! Oooh!"

"Oh! Ooh! Oooooh!"

He snapped his fingers. "I know!"

Miriael half-turned and flapped a hand to hush him. Kiet was looking at him, so he lowered his voice and whispered in her ear.

"Your ghosts are Morphs."

Kiet shook her head. Of course, she didn't understand about Morphs.

"They're souls of the dead who aren't allowed up into Heaven. Much more recent than the people who built this City."

She shook her head again. She didn't understand about souls—or even that she had one.

"I can't see them," she said.

"They're invisible. I met some of them in a forest once. They told me they attach themselves between the points of things."

"What does that mean?"

He aimed a finger and traced a line. "Like maybe from the edge of that broken kerb to that sharp bit of stone on the pavement—you see? Or maybe to the corner of that bottom step." He traced another line.

"You just said they were invisible."

"I'm only guessing. I can't see them."

"Oh." Kiet fell silent for a moment. "I think *she* can."

She meant Miriael—and when he took another look, he saw she was right. Miriael wasn't gazing vaguely in the direction of a sound, but focusing on a specific spot in front of her.

"Must be because she's an angel. She can see things we can't."

A sudden new sound made them both stiffen.

"What's that?"

"Shush!"

The new sound was a song with words and a tune, very clear and sweet and melodious. Miriael was singing to the Morphs.

As if soothed by the song, the "Ooohs" of the Morphs grew less ragged and chaotic. Soon their plaintive wailing quietened altogether.

"They're *listening* to her!" breathed Kiet.

Miriael repeated her song over and over, a little louder each time. Now Ferren could make out the actual words.

> Please don't be afraid,
> Please don't drift away.
> I only want to question you
> And hear what you say.

Then one particular high-pitched voice piped up in reply. It was still a kind of wail with many "ooohs", but there were words in it too—and even a musical quality, without being exactly a song. Ferren couldn't catch the words at a distance.

Miriael must have understood, though, because she responded with new singing of her own. She was obviously making up songs on the spur of the moment.

> When you had a body,
> When you were alive,
> Where was your dwelling?
> What was your tribe?

There was more piping in reply, and another high-pitched voice chimed in. Miriael finished listening to the first Morph, then swivelled to face the second. She had her back turned to Ferren and Miriael, so the words of her next song were now muffled. Ferren guessed she was asking the same questions.

Kiet had dropped Ferren's hand, but nudged him with her elbow. "They're not scary at all," she whispered.

He remembered the Morphs he'd encountered in the forest by the overbridge. "No, they're more scared of us. They're afraid we'll dislodge them from the things they've attached to."

"They sound sort of timid. And unhappy."

"They're unhappy because they're homeless. All they want is to be allowed up into Heaven. That's where they ought to be."

Miriael continued her communication with the second Morph for a while. Then she looked round and saw Ferren and Kiet waiting for her.

She signalled to them—*just a moment*—and sang a song of farewell to all the Morphs. More and more tiny, fluting voices joined in as they replied.

She bent an ear and listened, then rose and came back to the entrance of the plaza. She seemed distracted and oddly pleased with herself.

"Did he explain it?" she asked Kiet in a whisper. "Did he tell you what your Old Ones really are?"

"They're Morphs."

Ferren nodded. "I realised when I heard their sounds."

"And I suspected it when I first heard about them," said Miriael. "I was questioning one who used to belong to the Homekin. One of the tribes we visited, you remember?"

"I remember."

Miriael turned to Kiet. "And another was from the Nesters. You said you were Bloodstock, didn't you? She was called Idris, and her stock was Bloodstock."

Kiet gasped. "No!"

"You knew her when she was alive?"

"No, but my Grandpa talks about her. Idris of Bloodstock!" Kiet burst out with a strange sound that was neither laughing nor crying.

"Shush. Morphs don't like loud noises or disturbances." Miriael glanced back to the corner of the plaza. "We should leave now. Very quietly."

9

Coming back from the City of the Dead, Miriael let Ferren and Kiet walk on ahead. Their conversation drifted back to her, about Ferren's previous experience of Morphs, but she had her own thoughts to think. Now she would be able to tell Asmodai about the Morphs she'd discovered—a whole colony of them!

Kiet accompanied Ferren and Miriael all the way back to their nest. "I'll come for you tomorrow, shall I?" she offered. "As soon as I know when the Guardians are meeting. You'll need someone to take you to them."

Ferren grinned at her. "Thank you. You've been a huge help."

Miriael waited for Kiet to leave, then for Ferren to drop off to sleep. She planned to slip out, find a secluded spot and summon her angel visitor. She made a great pretence of falling asleep herself.

But her plan met an obstacle. Ferren's bedding was closer to the entrance of the nest than hers, and when he lay down, he stretched right across in front of it. She would have to step over him…

When she tried to step over him, he wasn't so fast asleep after all. Three times she made the attempt, and every time he stirred, mumbled and seemed about to wake up.

In the end, she postponed her plan. It was only a temporary postponement; now that Asmodai had created a connection between them, she could summon him at any time. Day or night didn't matter, he'd said.

By the time dawn finally arrived, she felt as though she'd hardly slept a wink. Ferren woke, yawned, stretched and went outside to look at the new morning. When he came back in, he saw she was also awake.

"I wonder when Kiet will call round," he said.

Miriael wondered too, because then Kiet would take him off to meet with the Guardians. "Soon, I hope," she replied.

He sat down on his bedding, facing her. "What a shock for the Guardians! When we tell then their Old Ones aren't really Old Ones at all."

"I don't think they should be told," said Miriael.

"Oh. Why not?"

"It's too much for them to take in all at once. You're going to have to explain about the Residual Alliance and why the Nesters should stop thinking of the Humen as allies. The truth about military service and what really happens to those who get selected. The Guardians will be struggling to digest it all anyway. Don't add another level of complication. Not at this stage."

"Hmm." Ferren looked thoughtful. "Kiet might've told people already."

"I doubt it. She'd have to start by explaining why she took us to the City of the Dead. Which she wasn't allowed to do."

"I suppose she'd be in trouble." Ferren looked even more thoughtful.

"You need to tell her to keep last night to herself. She shouldn't say anything to anyone until the time's right."

"When will that be?"

"I don't know." Miriael didn't want to consider that prospect right now. "When the Guardians decide to consult with the Old Ones."

"And we decide what to do about it."

"Yes. Then."

Ferren bowed to her advice and asked no more questions.

Not long afterwards, Kiet herself turned up. She stood silhouetted in the entrance of their nest, bright daylight all around her.

"The Guardians are ready for you," she announced. "You have to come now."

"Coming," cried Ferren, jumping to his feet. "We'll be out in a minute."

Miriael took a deep breath. This wasn't going to be easy. "Not me. I'm too tired, I hardly slept last night. I wouldn't be much use this morning."

The face Ferren turned to her showed all the emotions she'd anticipated: bafflement, hurt, opposition, protest.

"But you *have* to come!" he cried. "We work together!"

"No, you do better on your own. If I'm there, you have to persuade them to accept me as well as persuade them to accept the Residual Alliance. It's simpler to leave me out of it."

"But...but..."

"She could be right," Kiet put in.

Ferren argued, but Miriael was adamant. He might have kept on arguing forever if Kiet hadn't forced his hand.

"Come *on*. The Guardians won't wait. If you don't come now, you may as well not bother."

He left in the end, shaking his head. His parting words sounded almost like a threat. "I'll come back to report. You'll have to be awake for *that*."

Then he was gone, and Miriael breathed a sigh of guilty relief. She counted slowly to a hundred before setting out for her own meeting. At last!

10

Miriael retraced last night's route towards the side of the thicket overlooking the City of the Dead. Assuming all Nesters shared Kiet's fears about the supposed ghosts of the Old Ones, this would be the part of the thicket with fewest nests and fewest people. Certainly, none of the Nesters would be likely to wander out beyond the sheltering vegetation, or even gaze out towards the City.

She was ready to hide if anyone approached, but saw only one woman and two men crossing the tunnel ahead of her. Soon she emerged from the bushes and stood in the spot where they'd paused last night. The grassy slopes looked very green, dotted with chunks of rubble and stone.

On the far side of the valley, the City's walls drew an irregular outline at the bottom of a bright blue sky. But Miriael didn't intend to go there.

Instead, she headed up the valley, following the edge of the thicket. The bushes came forward or retreated in a succession of small bays. She chose one bay and sat on the grass with her back to a particularly dense mass of vegetation.

Veni Asmodai, veni ad me.

She formed a picture of him in her mind and focused on it hard. She remembered every tiniest detail of his appearance: his beautiful, pale features … his flowing, curling hair … the silver circlet on his brow. Again and again, she murmured the phrase he'd taught her.

Veni Asmodai, veni ad me. Veni Asmodai, veni ad me.

How long would it take? Would she know when the connection went through?

Veni Asmodai, veni ad me. Veni Asmodai, veni ad me.

There was no signal to tell her she'd made contact—but suddenly she became aware of a movement in the sky. A small, white cloud was scudding towards her. She watched with one eye while still murmuring Asmodai's phrase, still holding his image in her mind. The cloud came to a stop directly above her.

For a long minute, nothing happened. Then a sudden stream of light burst forth from the underside of the cloud, shooting earthwards. She let out an involuntary cry and closed her eyes against the dazzle.

When she opened them again, he was there before her, exactly as she'd pictured him. The cloud itself remained hovering overhead.

"I have the impression this is urgent." He smiled his serene and perfect smile.

"It is. I've found some Morphs for you!"

She told him about last night's visit to the City of the Dead, and the ghosts of the Old Ones that had turned out to be Morphs.

"The City of the Dead? Is that…?" He swung to look out at the ruins across the valley.

"Yes, over there. We went in through that gap"—she pointed—"and along a street to a plaza at the end."

"How many of them?"

"I don't know. A lot, from different tribes. I only sang to two."

"Sang?"

Miriael laughed at his puzzled expression. "I borrow the tunes of hymns and make up rhyming songs for them. They like that. It's the best way to communicate."

Now he looked thoughtful. "I can communicate with them, but it's always been a struggle. They're never eager to answer questions."

"Because they're so jittery. My way soothes and relaxes them first. Shall I show you?"

"Please."

Miriael sang some of the songs she'd sung last night, as well as she could remember them. She sensed a new kind of respect in his eyes as he listened.

"And you make up words and rhymes as you go along?"

"It's not difficult. You could do it too."

"Perhaps I could." He smiled and turned to gaze at the ruins again. "Perhaps I should go and try now."

"I could come with you. Shall I?"

"Hmm. You'd have to move physically, wouldn't you? Feet on the ground, walking with your legs?"

"Yes."

"Then, no. I only want to see for myself and make contact at this stage. Maybe with a song to introduce myself. I'll be finished before you could walk across."

"Oh."

"Then I'll come back and tell you what's happened. This is all thanks to you. And it matters to you too, of course."

"Me?"

"It's the Morphs that can lift you back into Heaven. You haven't forgotten?"

"No, no. But…"

She didn't have time to complete her sentence; his aura lit up, and he flew off across the valley in a direct straight line. A moment later, he had disappeared through the gap in the ruined walls.

A confused welter of emotions ran through her as she sat waiting for him to return.

11

Ten minutes passed, then twenty, then thirty. Miriael stared across at the silent City and wondered why Asmodai was taking so long. Still, she trusted him to return...and eventually he did.

"I'm sorry, I was longer than expected." He bobbed before her in the globe of his aura, a few inches off the ground. "It's because you did so much better than you realised."

"I did?"

"Those Morphs in the plaza were just the beginning. There are more all over the City. They've settled in corners of streets and buildings everywhere. There must be hundreds upon hundreds upon hundreds of them."

"Did you sing to them?"

"Yes, and they responded. Many different groups. I did it exactly as you showed me." He laughed. "All of my painstaking. investigative research, yet I never discovered what you did. A simple method of communication! Crucial!"

His regard was like a warm glow that enveloped her all over. "Will they help you with your research?" she asked.

"Help me? Yes, I believe they will. They'll cooperate. But there are so many of them, and they're cautious about making decisions on their own. It'll take time to bring them to a consensus."

"They're very timid. You have to treat them carefully."

"Indeed I will. But they won't be so timid when they know their own strength. I shall have to teach them their potential."

His wings stirred, and he clasped his hands before his chest. When he spoke again, there was a thrilling intensity in his voice. "It's not mere research anymore, you know. I'm ready to put it into practice. That's why I need so many Morphs."

"I *did* wonder about that," Miriael murmured.

"I'm ready to put it into practice for *you*. As soon as these new Morphs cooperate, we'll have the power we need to lift you back into Heaven."

She gulped; it was all so sudden. "But I thought... I mean... Heaven hasn't agreed to have me back up."

A dark scowl came over his face. "No, nor likely to. Their minds are so closed, they won't open them even to what's in their own best interest."

He fell silent for a while, and Miriael respected his silence. She had the impression he was struggling in himself.

At last, the struggle produced a question. "What would you say to going up into Heaven without their approval? Unsanctioned, as it were."

She gaped. "They'd only send me back down," she answered, when she recovered her breath.

"I doubt it. They won't agree now because they don't believe it can be done. They dismiss the possibility out of hand. But when we've actually done it—you and me and the Morphs—they'll see what a good thing it is. With you out of reach of the Humen, you're safer, Heaven's safer, everyone's safer. I guarantee they won't send you back once you're up there and able to stay up. They'll accept the fact after it's presented to them."

"But that's...that's..." She couldn't say what it was. Disobedience to Heaven went against all her instincts and training as a junior warrior angel.

"Unthinkable?" He raised an eyebrow. "But I'm thinking it. And now you are too. We'll be helping the hosts of Heaven in spite of themselves." He focused a penetrating look on her. "Don't *you* believe I can do it?"

"Yes, I do. If you say so." She faltered. "But I don't know..."

"You need time to adjust. I understand. Do you think you'll have an answer by tonight?"

"I suppose. Will you come again tonight?"

"Of course I will." He smiled. "It matters a great deal to have you believe. I'm not used to other angels believing in me."

His aura intensified to a blinding brightness. In the next moment, he lifted off the ground and soared into the air.

Miriael raised her eyes and saw the cloud still hovering overhead. It lit up briefly with an interior light, then became a perfectly ordinary cloud moving across the sky. The only extraordinary thing was that it moved without a breath of wind.

As you controlled the clouds in the Weather Wars, thought Miriael. *Yes, I believe in you. You can do it.*

12

When Miriael returned to the nest she shared with Ferren, she found Kiet waiting outside on the path.

"I want to be here when he comes back," said the girl.

Miriael, who had been lost in memories of Asmodai, collected her thoughts. "You mean Ferren. Did you leave him with the Guardians?"

"Yes, I wasn't allowed to stay myself. But I want to hear what happened." Kiet gave Miriael a quizzical look. "Didn't you say you needed to sleep?"

Miriael shrugged. "I couldn't. I was too wide awake."

"So where…?"

"I found a quiet spot to sit and relax."

She invited Kiet inside, but the girl preferred to wait in the sunshine. It was a while later when Ferren finally returned. Miriael heard their voices and went outside to join them.

Ferren turned to her and repeated what he'd been saying. "It's so slow! They have to consult with their stocks, then hold meetings between themselves, then I don't know what. It's like Kiet predicted. They don't *want* to make up their minds!"

"Who was for and who was against?" Kiet put in.

"Berwin and the one called Clemmart just wanted to sit on the fence. Dunkery was a bit more in favour." He addressed an explanation to Miriael. "She's the only female Guardian."

"Guardian of Headstock." Kiet added to the explanation. "And Clemmart's the Guardian of Bonestock."

"The one most against was Skail," Ferren went on. "He was negative about everything."

"I could've told you that. He's my stock, Bloodstock."

"Why is he so much younger than the rest?" Ferren asked.

Kiet sniffed. "Don't know. He's sharp as a tack, but he hides it. Nobody I know likes him. He's not old in age, but he thinks and acts like he's a hundred."

Ferren nodded. "He had his guard up from the start. He kept asking about other tribes in the alliance, and which tribe's the biggest. How many in your tribe?" he asked Kiet.

"About two hundred."

"So you *are* the biggest."

Miriael brought him back to the point. "Did you tell them the truth about the Humen and military service?"

"Of course. They were shocked and horrified. Even Skail."

"What truth about military service?" Kiet asked at once.

"Tell you later," Ferren answered in an aside and continued speaking to Miriael. "You should've come with me. You could've told them what you told me about the Humen not having souls."

"I'd have been a distraction." Miriael shook her head.

"They all know you're here in their territory. They're all getting used to the idea."

"But at least they don't have to look at me."

Kiet raised her voice. "What do you mean, the truth about military service? *What truth?*"

Miriael was grateful for the interruption. "You'd better explain," she told Ferren.

He switched his attention back to Kiet. "Won't you hear it all from your Guardian anyway?"

Kiet snorted. "Skail? He only consults with the adults of Bloodstock. And not always all of them."

Ferren drew a deep breath and prepared to explain. But Miriael stopped him before he began.

"Wait. Why don't you do it outside in the sunshine? I've heard it so many times, I don't need to hear it again."

Ferren looked a little hurt. But Kiet snapped her fingers and jumped at the idea.

"You can tell my friends too! Can you? They'll want to hear. Shall I get them together? All right?"

The hurt expression faded from Ferren's face. "All right."

Kiet grinned and headed outside with Ferren following.

13

K iet collected two members of her family and three other friends.
She introduced them to Ferren one by one. He'd already met her
spiky-haired younger brother, Tadge, and he'd heard about Rhinn, her
older sister. Then there was Flens, thin and gangling with a bugle of
a nose, a cheery, roly-poly girl called Ethany, and Gibby, who had fair,
curling hair and pretty, dainty features. Flens was from Headstock,
Ethany and Gibby were from Heartstock.

They gathered under a flowering rhododendron bush that came
down all around them like a tent. Rhinn, Flens and Ethany sat on a log,
Tadge and Gibby sat on the grass, and Ferren and Kiet sat facing them.

"This is special, just for us," Kiet said, and pointed to Ferren. "He's
going to tell us about the Humen and military service."

Ferren began by explaining about the Residual Alliance, which
would look after the interests of the tribes, whereas the alliance with
the Humen only exploited them. He had begun in the same way to the
four Guardians. But suddenly he decided on a different approach. He
had plenty of time, and his audience would respond better if he told it
as a story.

So he told them the story of his own life. Growing up with the People
in the Home Ground...discovering the angel shot down and disabled...
feeding her and talking to her...then exile and the overbridge...going in
search of his sister who'd been taken for military service...journeying all
the way to the Humen Camp...

When he told them about breaking into the Camp, they leaned
forward, mouths open, holding their breath. They were living every
moment with him in imagination. They shuddered as he described what
he'd seen the Hypers doing to Residuals in the bath—and he shuddered,

describing it. He continued with the story of his return journey in the belly of the mechanical monster...seeing the Plasmatics that drove the engine...watching as the Hypers were injected with doses of jelly...

The revelations of Humen evil drew mutters of rage from his audience. Kiet and her friends weren't cowed, they were seething for revenge.

Ferren raised his voice as he arrived at the most inspiring part of his story. "But the Humen can be beaten! I saw them smashed in a great battle. My tribe was right in the middle of it—and we didn't need anyone else to protect us. We protected ourselves!"

He told of the bunker that the People had built under the angel's guidance, and how it had shielded them from all the terrible forces and energies flying around. "We protected ourselves," he repeated. "We have the power!"

The young Nesters cheered and began bombarding him with questions from all sides.

"Weren't you scared?"

"Is it the same angel with you now?"

"What was it like in the belly of the monster?"

"Did you never find your sister?"

The oddest question came from Tadge, who was spluttering with excitement. "Will you...if you go back...that Camp again...will you take us with you?"

Ferren goggled and laughed at the same time, and it was Kiet who answered for him. "Why would he go back there, Tadge?"

"To wreck their things! Sabotage their machines!"

"No, he's here to build the Residual Alliance."

Ferren nodded agreement, though he couldn't help thinking, *This is the reaction I want!* If only the Guardians had half as much fight in them...

Then Kiet jumped to her feet and held out her arms to her friends and family. "The Nesters ought to join the Residual Alliance, right?" she cried. "All those in favour of the Residual Alliance! Raise your hand!"

Every hand went up in favour.

"And we'll help make it happen! Any way we can!"

Again every hand was raised. Tadge raised two hands in a double show of support.

14

Veni Asmodai, veni ad me.

Miriael had slipped out in the quiet of the night, having rearranged Ferren's bedding so that he no longer lay across the entrance of their nest. Now she sat in her secluded spot overlooking the valley with the thicket behind her. She had her eyes closed as she concentrated on her image of Asmodai and repeated the phrase to summon him.

Veni Asmodai, veni Asmodai, veni Asmodai, veni ad me.

She still hadn't decided whether to agree to an unsanctioned return to Heaven, she only knew she needed to see him again before she could make a decision. It was as if she had a hundred questions to ask, although she wasn't sure what they were. She needed his serene presence before her, his quiet voice explaining, the calm wisdom in his beautiful eyes...

It was easy to concentrate on a mental image of him, much harder to *stop* thinking about him. And when he finally arrived, the reality was even better than the image. She opened her eyes as he came to rest in front of her, a lambent glow in the dark. He was solemn yet smiling.

It occurred to her that this time his light hadn't descended from above. "Did you come across the valley?" she asked.

"Indeed I did. I have been singing to the Morphs in the City of the Dead, trying to win their confidence. As you said, they are very, very timid."

"But *you'll* win their confidence."

"Yes, I will in the end. What about you? Have I won your confidence?"

"For going back up into Heaven? You don't have to win my confidence. Of course I trust you."

"But you don't like to act without Heaven's approval?"

She considered. It was true she would have *liked* Heaven's approval, but she'd gone against it once already. "I did that when I decided to eat mortal food," she told him.

"So...?"

"It's not only that. It's the Residuals too. They helped me, and I've been helping them. I'd be sorry to abandon them."

"You feel they depend on you?"

"Well, not as much as they did. But there's one in particular... I've been travelling round with him for three months now."

"Ah, a Residual assistant?"

"Not exactly. It's more as if I'm *his* assistant."

No sooner had the words left her mouth than she wished she hadn't uttered them. Asmodai stared at her, but said nothing. She didn't know how to explain it to him. Did he look down on her now?

But when he spoke again, there was no hint of condescension. He didn't despise her, and he didn't despise Residuals.

"Miriael, your feelings do you great credit. Truly they do. You see the Residuals as being exploited by the Humen, treated like mere raw material. And you want to protect them and save them. Your compassion is admirable, and I would never wish to reason you out of it. I would never wish to reason you out of it, except that there are higher stakes involved."

He lowered his eyes and collected his thoughts. His face wore the gentle, sorrowing expression that made him even more beautiful. His appearance put her in mind of the deep, resonant notes of the *Amen* that came at the end of every Heavenly hymn...

"How can I appeal to you?" he murmured. Then he raised his eyes and looked at her. "Ah, Miriael, I know I can't ask you to do this for your own sake. You wouldn't defy disapproval merely because you long to return to the joys of Heaven. Nor because you fear the suffering that awaits in this new Doctor's surgeries. You'd never value your own happiness above all other obligations." He shook his head. "And I can't ask it for my sake."

"Your sake?" Miriael didn't understand.

"I mean, because lifting you up into Heaven would be a proof of my methods. Using the spiritual energy of the Morphs in a way my superiors dismiss as impossible. No one would be able to ignore my research after such a demonstration. But that's not a reason for asking you either.'

"I suppose not." Miriael agreed.

"No, I'm asking you for Heaven's sake. It has to be done because it's the ethical thing to do. Even though Heaven doesn't see it and doesn't approve. The survival of all angels depends on you. If this new Doctor gets hold of you, dissects you and analyses you, he'll work out ways to destroy us all."

"You think he *will* get hold of me?"

"Sooner or later. It's inevitable. And when he does…" He raised his eyes to the night sky. "They're rigid and stubborn and hidebound up there. But Heaven is still Heaven. You have to save them from themselves."

When he put it like that… As he stood with his eyes looking up, she studied his hands, his robes, his wings and sandalled feet. Everything about him reminded her of the goodness of Heaven. Yes, she had to do it for *their* sake. And in some obscure way, she wanted to do it for him as well.

"All right," she said.

He lowered his gaze. "You'll do it?"

"I will."

His sorrowing expression had gone, replaced by a look of relief. "Unsanctioned?"

"Yes." She smiled at him. "It matters a great deal to you, doesn't it?"

He smiled back. "More than you can imagine."

Yes, she thought, *I've made the right decision.* He hadn't answered all her questions—she hadn't even asked them—but she trusted him to make everything turn out for the best. She had the feeling of giving herself into his hands…

Lost in her reflections, she didn't immediately register that he was still speaking.

"Sorry," she apologised. "What were you saying?"

"I was saying, everything's in place except the cooperation of the Morphs." He gestured towards the City of the Dead. "I think I had them almost won over when I answered your summons. Shall I go and sing some more to them now?"

Miriael didn't want him to go, but couldn't think of a reason for him to stay. Not a *serious* reason…

"I'll go then, shall I?" The globe of his aura bobbed a few inches further away. "You've inspired me with new purpose."

Yes, go," she said. "Go and win them over."

15

Ferren was frustrated, having nothing to do while the Guardians wasted time over meetings and consultations.

"No, Skail hasn't called all Bloodstock adults together yet," Kiet told him. "I'll hear from Grandpa and Auntie Nettish when he does."

They were walking along one of the green tunnels not far from Kiet's family nest. Ferren was by now familiar with the general layout of the tunnels and the four clearings and firepits where the stocks did their cooking and eating.

"I wanted to ask you something," said Kiet.

"Yes?" he prompted.

She didn't respond directly. "Let's go somewhere quiet," she suggested. "I know a place we can talk."

She led him from a main tunnel into a side tunnel, then along a narrow, overgrown path. Finally, she left the path and plunged through a tangle of bushes, creepers and vines. They came out into a bowl-shaped area of sandstone with a pool in the middle. Rays of sunlight descended through the overhanging foliage and danced on the tranquil surface of the water.

Kiet sat and wrapped her arms round her knees. Ferren sat alongside. The stone was surprisingly warm to the touch.

"Tell me about your sister," she said.

"My sister? Shanna?"

"The one you went searching for. You said you broke into the Humen Camp because of her."

"I thought she might be a worker or a slave in there. I'd have worked or slaved along with her. Then I found out what really happens." His jaw clenched and his eyes narrowed.

"You must've really loved her."

A hot, painful lump rose in his throat. "She was like my mother. The Selectors took my parents before I was two years old. Shanna taught me and protected me and *everything*."

Kiet blinked. "Selectors took my parents too. One and a half years ago."

Ferren remembered that Kiet's family had lived in the nest where he and Miriael were staying. "Both at the same time?"

She looked at him, not understanding. Her eyes were wet with tears. Brown eyes, he noticed, so dark they were almost black.

"Don't they normally select just one a year?" he asked.

"No. Always two."

"Oh, right. Must be because you're a bigger tribe."

For a while Kiet said nothing, then she exploded in sudden anger. "I would've killed them!"

"The Selectors?" Ferren was surprised.

"I grabbed a heavy bit of wood and ran at them from behind. I was going to bash in their skulls."

He couldn't even picture it. "I don't think you could kill Selectors as easy as that."

"No, they'd have killed me. But they never saw me. The rest of my family pulled me back." She screwed up her face. "Everyone's been worried about me ever since. Especially Auntie Nettish. I've had to be extra well-behaved. But when you arrived and spoke about an alliance of tribes against the Humen…" She turned on him, eyes flashing. "Why do you think I've been helping you?"

"I don't know. I never thought about it."

"That's why. I *hate* the Humen."

Ferren could believe it; she had an inner ferocity he'd never noticed before. There was a long silence between them.

"Tell me more about your sister," she said at last.

Ferren didn't think he wanted to talk about Shanna, but once he'd started he couldn't stop. He told Kiet how brave and clever she was, and how she'd trained *him* to disguise all signs of cleverness. He described her plan for building a roof over the Dwelling Place to keep the rain off, and how her plan had got her into trouble with Neath, the People's leader.

"So then she knew Neath was going to hand her over to the Selectors. She thought up a plan for that too. She stored a supply of food in the Rushfield and made a hollow to hide in, covered with rushes. Nobody knew except me. But when the Selectors came, Neath kept the whole tribe searching for her for days. They found her in the end, and the Selectors took her off."

For a moment, he couldn't continue. Kiet was listening intently, nodding sympathetically.

"When she went off…you should've seen her! She walked so tall and so proud! She'd probably have fought them, but she didn't want them taking me too."

"I wish I could've met your sister," said Kiet. "She sounds like a wonderful person."

Ferren brought out his favourite dream. "Perhaps she survived somehow inside the Humen Camp. Perhaps she escaped the baths."

"She would if anyone could," Kiet agreed.

He shook his head and shook away the dream. "No, nobody could," he said.

The silence that followed was by far the longest yet. Sparkles of light bounced off the surface of the pool; dragonflies darted into view, hung glittering in the air, then darted off again.

"Let's think happier thoughts," Kiet suggested. "You tell me good things you remember about your sister when you were growing up. And I'll tell you good things I remember about my parents."

"Turn and turn about?"

"Yes. I'll start. I've got plenty to tell."

So they shared memories: first Kiet, then Ferren, then Kiet, then Ferren again. As the day wore on, the sadness passed, replaced by a strange sense of peace. Their memories were in many ways similar…

Eventually, the talk lapsed. Kiet lay full length on the sandstone, and Ferren followed suit. He felt the warmth seeping through his limbs and the play of golden sunlight on his face. Time stood still. His frustration with the Guardians faded away, and he forgot about Miriael's strange mood of distance and detachment. Although his consciousness seemed to float on, he slipped into a kind of drowse.

He was startled out of his drowse by the realisation that Kiet was standing over him.

"I have to go now," she announced. "Duties at home. You stay if you think you can find your way back."

"I think so." He stretched lazily.

She grinned. "I brought you these." She bent down and balanced two small, yellow pears on his chest. "To keep you going until dinnertime."

"Thank you," he said—but already she was gone.

In the next moment, the two pears rolled off his chest and onto the sandstone. He reached for one and bit into it. It tasted sweet and delicious.

16

Miriael had spent the whole day wondering if Asmodai had won over the Morphs. Since he hadn't come back to report, she suspected he hadn't. But she was impatient to hear from him.

Many times she had returned to her special spot looking across to the City of the Dead. Several times she had tried to call him by picturing his face and reciting the phrase of summoning. Perhaps he was too busy talking to the Morphs or preparing other angels for her reappearance among them. He'd warned from the start he might not always be able to come at once. Yet surely he should have found time for her by now?

She made her final attempt after nightfall, but the connection still didn't work. When a light rain began to fall, she gave up and returned, dispirited, to the nest.

She lay for a long while listening to Ferren's breath going in and out to the slow, regular rhythm of sleep. The rain outside grew heavier and heavier, pattering on the dome of the nest.

Then an idea came to her. It was a wild fancy when it first surfaced, but the more she considered it, the more reasonable it appeared. When she'd gone up to Heaven in her last visionary dream, many angels might have caught sight of her, but only Asmodai actually did. Would the same thing happen if she deliberately dreamed a visionary dream now? No one in Heaven would know except *him*.

She visualised the rose garden on the Fourth Altitude, then waited for sleep. If she could drop off remembering the scene from her last visionary dream, hopefully it would carry over into a new visionary dream. She felt herself drifting off…

But when she dreamed, the rose garden wasn't there. She was fully aware she was dreaming, so it wasn't an ordinary dream…and by the clear light and sweetness of the air, she had surely dreamed herself up into Heaven. But this part of Heaven wasn't familiar to her.

She stood on a mosaic path of marble stones and coloured glass laid out in pictures. As she glided forward, the pictures unfolded in sequence, depicting all of Heaven's greatest victories in the Millenary War. To her left and right, rainbows played in the spray of fountains that shot high in the air. The path led to the grand portico of a building she didn't recognise.

Only when she stared past the spray of the fountains did she discover a definite landmark: a line of trees with symmetrical curving branches like sixfold candelabras. Even at a distance, the golden orbs of their fruits were visible. When she counted the trees, she had no doubt that these were the twelve Trees of Wisdom.

So she wasn't on the Fourth Altitude at all, but the Fifth!

No sooner had she had that thought than she found herself passing between the red and bronze columns of the portico. As though someone had spoken in her ear, it came to her that this must be the College of Strategy, which she knew was on the Fifth Altitude…

Behind the columns the entrance door stood wide open, and behind the door was the high, vaulted space of a great chamber. Arches crisscrossed in the vault, beams of light slanted down through the arches. The scale of the chamber dwarfed its furnishings, which were massive enough in themselves: a heavy, circular table surrounded by chairs like thrones. Equally massive was the blue-and-green globe mounted nearby, representing the Earth with its oceans and continents.

At present, the chairs were empty. Miriael scanned all around for Asmodai, but the only two angels in the chamber were unknown to her. They were collecting papers from the table as though from a meeting that had recently concluded.

She moved closer, confident she wouldn't be visible to them. They talked as they worked…perhaps they would say something about Asmodai? She wished she still shared in that Heavenly state of communion where spirit touched spirit and thought touched thought; then the question in her mind would immediately link to a thought in theirs. But their thoughts were closed to her.

In fact, their talk was typical of angel speaking to angel: more a weaving of togetherness than an actual exchange of information. They both knew and thought the same already. Their words were a mere accompaniment, like a duet where both knew their parts and contributed to the same music.

They were talking about the meeting just concluded and the strategic decision on which all participants were agreed. "The Forty-Third Company will handle it…" "Watch and wait…" "No need to act…" "See what they intend…" Miriael heard the phrases without really following. Naturally, everyone was in harmony over the decision—a harmony that would eventually include the Forty-Third Company too. She remembered the sense of perfect fellowship among the warrior angels of her own Twenty-Second Company.

The movements of the two angels were as harmonious as their conversation. Each angel was collecting papers of a particular kind, and they helped one another by passing across papers that belonged to the other's collection. Movement fitted together with movement as they circled the table… Like many activities in Heaven, it was almost a dance.

She listened more closely when their talk progressed to participants at the meeting who'd taken on the task of sending instructions to the Forty-Third Company. They chimed in on one another like a chorus. "Sabaoth the Fifth Angel of Strategy." "Mendrion the Twelfth Angel of Strategy." "Zophiel the Tenth Angel of Strategy." Miriael waited to hear the name of Asmodai, but he wasn't mentioned. It seemed that the dream had nothing to tell her.

She wondered if Asmodai had sounded out either of these two angels on the subject of her case. He'd approached some Angels of Strategy, she recalled, who'd listened but refused to form an opinion. Watching these two, though, she felt sure it wasn't *them*. They were so much in tune with one another and with all other angels, they would have never listened to a question about an angel discarded by Heaven. They'd have reported the questioner to a higher authority.

In fact, it was difficult to imagine any angel giving Asmodai a hearing on such a subject…

A thought struck her then—so simple and obvious, she was amazed she'd never thought it before. How was it possible for Asmodai to work on his own research without giving himself away? And his plans for her and the Morphs, his unauthorised visits to the Earth… How could he do all of that when spirit touched spirit in a state of communion? How could he conceal such tremendous secrets without other angels becoming aware?

Was this another special technique he'd developed? How strange it all was!

Immersed in her own thoughts, she was starting to lose contact with the dream. The two angels were still visible, but their brightness was diminishing into darkness. She heard a sound that might have come from the roof of the great chamber, but she knew it to be the patter of rain on the dome of the nest. And that other sound was the slow, regular rhythm of Ferren's breathing as he slept…

But the dream still had something more to reveal. As the names of the angels who weren't Asmodai still echoed in her mind, one name suddenly leaped out at her. "Zophiel the Tenth Angel of Strategy."

Yet Asmodai had called *himself* the Tenth Angel of Strategy! She couldn't be mistaken! That was *his* role!

The angel in the great chamber said one thing, and Asmodai said another. They couldn't both be right! What did it mean?

17

It was mid-morning when Kiet stuck her head in at the entrance of the nest. "News!" she cried. Her gaze focused first on Ferren, then on Miriael's bedding rolled up against the wall. "Angel not here this morning?"

Ferren shrugged as though Miriael's disappearance wasn't important to him. "No. I think she went out as soon as the rain stopped."

"Yes, it's sunny now. Come with me, and I'll tell you the news."

Ferren didn't see why she couldn't give her news inside the nest, but he followed anyway. She led him to the same rhododendron bush where he'd addressed the young Nesters. Although the grass and undergrowth were wet everywhere else, the leaf litter where they sat under the bush was dry.

"So." Kiet cleared her throat. "There was a meeting for all the Bloodstock adults yesterday evening. I heard it from Grandpa and Auntie this morning. Skail told them everything you said to the Guardians."

"And?"

She pulled a face. "He wasn't pushing for the Residual Alliance. He buried it under reasons for and against, like he always does."

"So Bloodstock doesn't support the idea?"

"They haven't decided. It'll come down to what the Old Ones think, same as I said."

"Huh!" Ferren grumped. "Not much news, then."

Kiet tossed her head. "There's other news too. We've been going round all the stocks and persuading everyone to support the Alliance."

"Who's *we?*"

"Me and Flens and Gibby and Ethany. Everyone's totally in favour."

"Who's *everyone?* You don't mean the adults?"

"No, young Nesters like us. We've got thirty-five supporters."

"That's good." Ferren cheered a little.

"Of course it's good. Listen." Her voice took on an urgent tone. "I've been your greatest helper here, haven't I?"

"You have," he agreed. *More than Miriael,* he thought to himself.

"Well, then, can I tell my friends the truth about the Old Ones?"

Ferren was taken aback. "About the Old Ones being Morphs, not ghosts?"

"Yes. They'll keep it secret. *I've* never breathed a word to anyone, and I didn't even do a proper swear to you. But they'll have to do a proper swear to me. They can't break a proper swear."

He considered. He'd agreed to Miriael's suggestion not to reveal the true nature of the Old Ones—"too much to take in all at once," she'd said—but they'd have to reveal it sometime. Although he ought to talk to her about it first, of course...

"Go on," Kiet urged. "Say yes."

"Hmm." He ought to talk to Miriael about it first, but he could hardly talk to her about anything anymore. She was always going off, and he never knew where…

"Say it! Yes, yes, yes!" cried Kiet, jumping up suddenly. She seized a branch of the bush above Ferren's head and shook it until a great spatter of rainwater came down over him.

He laughed. "Stop!"

"Say yes!" She continued to shake the foliage.

"Yes! I've said it! Yes, as long as they swear to keep it a secret."

Kiet was flushed and grinning. She was about to sit down again when a voice called her name.

"Kiet! Kiet? Where are you? I can hear you!"

A moment later, Rhinn peered in under the rhododendron bush. As usual, Kiet's older sister wore a worried expression on her long, thin face.

"I guessed I'd find you here. They're all waiting, and Skail's not pleased. You haven't forgotten what happens today?"

Kiet grimaced. "First Intimacies. I know." She turned to Ferren. "Sorry, gotta go."

18

Kiet expected a lecture from her older sister about taking First Intimacies more seriously. But Rhinn only studied her curiously as they walked along.

"You seem very pleased with yourself these days," she said.

"Do I?"

"You've hardly smiled the last year and a half. Not since—"

"Don't say it!"

"I won't. But now you seem happy all the time."

Kiet strode faster. "So that's all right, isn't it?"

"Yes. So long as you remember your First Intimacies with Bross."

Skail was waiting outside the family nest, along with Grandpa Niot and Auntie Nettish. They started off as she came up.

"You're late," said, Skail, and clamped a hand on her elbow.

Skail was in his late twenties, thin and wiry, with tightly drawn features dominated by a smooth, wide curve of forehead. All his movements were fast and flickering, like a bird.

Kiet eased her elbow out of his grip. "I'm not going to run away."

"Remember your duties," he told her. "It's time you grew up and began behaving like a proper woman. You need settling down."

He didn't have to spell it out. She understood that he was thinking of the time when she'd wanted to bash the Selectors with a length of wood.

"You should know your place and accept it," he went on. "Bross is an excellent partner for you. I had to work very hard to arrange it. You had nothing in your favour but your looks."

They arrived at a small clearing, and the special nest reserved for the ritual. The nest was decorated all over with dried flowers and lucky charms. Dunkery, the Guardian of Headstock, stood there with folded arms, and Bross's parents beside her.

"Last minute nerves?" she asked.

"Something like that," Skail agreed.

"He's already inside and waiting," said Bross's mother, Mevan.

Then Bross's father, Trebb, came up to Kiet with a bowl of oil.

"You know what to do?" asked Skail, as she took it.

Auntie Nettish answered on Kiet's behalf. "She's been well taught."

"There you go," said Grandpa Niot, propelling Kiet forward with a gentle pat on the back.

She ducked in through the entrance. Bross was at the back of the nest, sitting cross-legged in the semi-darkness. She couldn't see clearly, but she knew his body was hard and muscular, while his face was mild and pleasant and sprinkled with freckles. She also knew he would be wearing only the ritual moleskin loincloth round his waist.

"Bross?"

"Here. Are you going to do it?"

For First Intimacies, she was supposed to rub his body all over with oil. She placed the bowl on the ground between them.

"Do you want me to do it?" she asked.

"No, but it's what they expect."

"You don't want me to do it?"

"Seems silly. Why would I want to be covered in oil?"

"I think it's supposed to be the touch of my fingertips."

"What's so special about your fingertips?"

Kiet laughed. "Nothing I ever knew. I think they're meant to make you feel all relaxed and melting."

"I don't want to feel relaxed and melting. I'll be wrestling Stogget in a month."

Stogget was the tribe's champion wrestler; Bross, though only a year older than Kiet, could match him in everything except experience.

"It's a distraction for me right now," he added.

"Same for me." Kiet clicked her tongue. "Do you want to rub the oil on yourself? Then we'll pretend I did it."

Bross considered for a moment. "All right. Better than going all relaxed and melting."

He picked up the bowl and began applying the oil.

"Don't go too fast," Kiet advised. "We have to stay here a while, or they'll think I didn't do it properly."

Even going slowly, Bross was finished in a matter of minutes. In the meanwhile, Kiet had come up with another idea. Bross was as trustworthy as anyone she knew, and she, Flens, Ethany and Gibby had already gained his support for the Residual Alliance when they'd talked to the young Nesters of Headstock. Now seemed like a good time to try out the next step.

"Do you want to know the truth about the Old Ones?" she asked.

She began by swearing him to secrecy. They interlocked little fingers, and he repeated the phrases as she recited them. "I solemnly swear. Never to reveal. What I am about to hear. Unless by permission. Of Kiet in person." When they parted little fingers, the swear was made.

Then she told him everything she knew about the Morphs in the City of the Dead, what they were and where they came from. She had to explain over and over before he absorbed it all, and then some more before he believed it. By the time she'd finished, almost half an hour had passed.

Peeking out through the entrance, she saw that the Guardians and family members still stood around, looking bored.

"They'll think we did the best First Intimacies ever," laughed Kiet. "Wait!"

She caught him by the shoulder as he joined her at the entrance, then rubbed her hands over his back.

"What was that for?" he asked.

"To get oil on my hands, of course."

She laughed again, and Bross looked at her curiously, much as Rhinn had done.

"You seem very happy about things," he commented.

"Do I?"

"Happiest in a long time."

19

Miriael had made up a hundred excuses for Asmodai, then dismissed them again. Why would that angel in the great chamber have lied about the Tenth Angel of Strategy? But if not... She felt sick at heart.

At first, she didn't want to meet Asmodai again. She couldn't think how to question him and dreaded his response. But she was angry too—and her anger included the fact that he no longer seemed to care about meeting with *her*. So many times she'd tried to summon him yesterday... It was as though he didn't need to talk with her once he'd secured her agreement.

All day she wavered, but couldn't make up her mind. She lay awake half the night as well. Yet her resolution was growing, and finally she came to a decision. She *had* to meet him again.

She stepped past Ferren, walked out through the thicket and arrived at her usual spot overlooking the City of the Dead. She closed her eyes and murmured the call-phrase under her breath.

Veni Asmodai, veni ad me.

Her mental image of him kept sliding off into memories of the two angels in the College of Strategy. She struggled to maintain concentration, *willing* his image to stay fixed in her mind. For minute after minute after minute, she clenched her muscles and screwed her eyes tight shut. She *would* summon him! She *would* demand an explanation!

Finally, she became aware of a light percolating through her eyelids. She opened her eyes, and there he stood before her.

"Asmodai," she said.

She didn't know whether he'd descended from the sky or crossed the valley from the City of the Dead. But he had come, and he was speaking to her. Perhaps he was apologising for his failure to come yesterday? She didn't listen.

"*Asmodai*." She pronounced his name more forcefully.

That silenced him. He looked at her, eyebrows raised.

"I went up to Heaven in a dream last night," she told him.

"Another visionary dream?"

"Yes."

"Ah, I wasn't there to see you last night."

"This was the Fifth Altitude. The College of Strategy. *Your* College of Strategy."

She studied him as she said it, searching for a guilty conscience. He showed no sign, merely waited to hear more.

"I overheard two angels talking about the Tenth Angel of Strategy."

He said nothing, but she saw him react.

"The Tenth Angel of Strategy wasn't you. Some other name. Not Asmodai."

Now he lowered his gaze, and the light of his aura dimmed.

"I used to be the Tenth Angel of Strategy," he said at last. "You remember, I told you how I helped control the weather during the Weather Wars? I was Tenth Angel then, and deserved to go higher. But they dragged me down."

"So you're not anymore?"

"No. I still think of myself as Tenth Angel, but it's only in my mind."

His face wore the sorrowing look that pulled on her heartstrings— but this time she didn't believe it.

"What else isn't true? How I can trust you about anything?" She brought out her biggest challenge. "How is it you can do unorthodox research and think unorthodox thoughts, and no one in Heaven is ever aware of it?"

"You mean, because of the communion of angels?" He hung his head, and his voice was very humble. "Touching thought to thought and spirit to spirit?"

"Yes."

"I'm not allowed into the full communion."

"Not—? But that's impossible!"

"No, there are some angels… You didn't know?"

"What?"

His grandeur had gone; now he looked utterly vulnerable.

"I'm one of the Fallen Angels," he said.

Miriael opened her mouth, then closed it again. She couldn't find words.

"It's almost a relief that you've found out," he went on. "It's been such an effort, covering up."

She continued to stare at him. "Were you…a Luciferian?"

He took a deep breath. "I want to tell you everything. I was one of the Grigori sent down to watch over the human race on Earth. The other kind of Fallen Angel. We fell through weakness, not pride. We were supposed to guide human evolution, one small step at a time. Instead, we formed too high an opinion of them, and instructed them in many kinds of knowledge before they were due to learn it."

"You also fell in love with mortal women."

"We did. Two hundred of us. I was one of the two hundred. I experienced the wrong kind of love and a desire no angel is ever meant to experience."

Miriael felt a strange tightness in her chest. "This was how long ago?"

"Six thousand years."

"And you were allowed back up into Heaven…?"

"A little under a thousand years ago. We thought our fault had been forgiven, and it was, in a way. But never forgotten. And after the Supreme Trinity withdrew and the great archangels took control, our fault seems to be remembered more and more all the time."

"Hmm. So *that's* why you miss the spirit of forgiveness. Heaven has lost it, you said."

"Yes, and why I feel like an outsider among other angels. I'm in the same situation as you, except you're exiled on Earth and I'm exiled in Heaven."

"You should've told me. Why didn't you tell me?"

"I was ashamed. I *am* ashamed. You've fallen in an unusual way, but I'm a Fallen Angel. I can never live that down."

Miriael thought about it. "Did you ever ask other angels about me coming back up into Heaven? You didn't, did you?"

He shook his head, almost despairingly, and his fine-spun hair flew out all around. "I *couldn't!* I don't have that sort of influence with anyone. They'd never have listened to me."

"So everything you told me—that was all lies."

"Yes." He let out a sound that was almost a sob. "I lied. It felt so glorious talking to you and not being judged. I could imagine myself as a normal, righteous angel. You weren't looking sideways at me or thinking things about me in the back of your mind. I had your respect. I can't explain how wonderful that felt."

"But you *lied*."

"You believed in me and needed help. I wanted so much to be able to do something for you. I wanted to feel I could do a good act and not have it seen as just an attempt to make up for past sin."

Miriael struggled for perspective. On the one hand she sympathised... yet the sheer size of his lies!

"I've fallen a second time, haven't I?" His head had dropped, his voice had sunk to a whisper. "I was tempted to see myself through your eyes, and I've shown my weakness again. Now you can never forgive me or trust me."

"Look at me," she said.

His head remained bowed. "I can't. Just tell me."

He was cast down and mortified, waiting to hear his final sentence.

"Look at me, Asmodai. Raise your head and look at me."

Very slowly, his head lifted. She refused to speak until he met her gaze.

"Your lies to me are unforgivable," she said. "But I'm not so perfect either. We're both weak. I forgive you."

The relief in his eyes was a tentative light flickering into life.

"But how can you? After everything..."

"I forgive you. That's all there is to it. Just tell me the truth from now on."

His aura increased in radiance until it was back to its normal intensity. "It wasn't *all* lies. I lied about myself and my position in Heaven, but I told the truth about my research and the power of the Morphs. I really do have a special way to lift you back into Heaven."

"You still want to do that?"

"More than ever." He spread his hands. "It's the only kind of help I can give. I don't know if you can trust me enough now?"

His look was a silent appeal. Shorn of his grandeur, he was somehow even more beautiful. Miriael hardly needed to think about her reply.

"I already said yes. I haven't changed my mind."

"It's the same as before? Back as we were?"

"So long as you've told me everything now."

"I have."

"Then yes, I accept your help." She smiled. "Don't you feel better to have it all out in the open?"

"Much, much better." The joy and thankfulness in his eyes told her more than any words. He clasped his hands as if in prayer. "I'll *make* Heaven value you as you deserve," he vowed. "They have to treat you the same as any other angel. When you're redeemed, then I am too!"

His fervour lifted him off the ground, higher and higher in his globe of light.

"It will come true!" he cried. "For me! For you!"

He shot off in a rush, neither up into the sky nor across to the City of the Dead, but further along the valley. He skimmed parallel to the dark mass of the thicket; when the valley curved, he continued straight up and over the low, mounded hills at the side. Miriael followed his glow until it vanished from view.

20

No, I don't want you to be perfect, Miriael thought. *You don't need to be on a higher level than me.*

She sat on in the dark for hours, looking at nothing in particular, seeing only the scene that had passed. She felt emotionally exhausted, with an inner sort of trembling and an inner sort of happiness. At last, the pieces of the puzzle all fitted together. Even before her visionary visit to the College of Strategy, there had been things that didn't quite made sense—but now they did. Although it wasn't the answer for which she would have wished, somehow it was even better.

So strange, so very strange! She'd admired Asmodai to the point of adoration, yet now she realised it had never been simple admiration. It was a much more complicated feeling.

She remembered the joy and thankfulness in his eyes when he'd understood that she forgave him. The memory redoubled her inner trembling—and her happiness. He *was* brilliant and remarkable, beyond any angel she'd ever known, yet he was also vulnerable. She'd never expected it, but she was so glad he'd admitted it. In one great leap, she'd suddenly moved much closer to him.

One thing he'd admitted kept reverberating in her mind: as a Watcher, he'd fallen in love with a mortal woman. "A desire no angel is ever meant to experience," he'd said. He was capable of *that* kind of love, one individual for another, quite different to the communal love that all angels experienced. And when she looked into her own feelings…

It was the same thing she felt for him. She couldn't deny it. One individual for another! No one else! Only him!

"Asmodai, Asmodai, Asmodai," she murmured aloud.

And if he'd fallen in love once, he could surely fall in love again. A mortal woman then, why not a hybrid angel now? She'd lost her aura, she ate mortal food, she lived and moved in her body like a physical human being. Oh, it was very, very possible!

Her thoughts turned into a hazy kind of musing, and her musing turned into a pleasant kind of daydream. She was in no hurry to move.

She was still in her spot when the first streaks of dawn appeared in the sky. She remained sitting until the sun rose clear above the horizon. Then she stretched and rose to her feet.

Time to get back to the nest she shared with Ferren. No doubt he'd discovered her absence by now. She hoped he'd go off somewhere else today; she needed peace and quiet for a chance to catch up on her sleep.

Heading back through the green tunnels, she almost collided with a young Nester running the other way. It was Ferren's friend Kiet, of all people. They both pulled to a halt.

"Where are you off to?" Miriael asked.

"Family errand." Kiet's eyes narrowed. "What are *you* doing out here?"

"Just talking a walk."

"So far from your nest? You'll get lost. I didn't know you went roaming this far out."

"I only walk the route you showed us. The route we took to the City of the Dead."

"You haven't been *there!*" It sounded like an accusation.

"No, I sit looking out from this side of the valley. I have a favourite spot to sit and think."

"Oh, well." Kiet still seemed suspicious. "If that's all it is…"

Afterwards, Miriael wondered if she'd revealed more than she needed to tell.

21

Returning from a meeting with the Guardians, Ferren was buzzing with excitement. He was relieved to find Miriael back in their nest, asleep.

"Wake up!" he cried. "We have to talk!"

She rolled over and opened her eyes. "What about?"

"The Questioning's tomorrow."

"Questioning?"

"When the Guardians consult the Old Ones about joining the Residual Alliance."

"Ah. Right. The Questioning. That's good."

"They've decided at last. So we have to make it work in our favour."

Miriael merely yawned. Ferren frowned at her.

"We know the Old Ones are Morphs," he went on. "And you can

communicate with them. So how do we do it?"

"What?"

"Get the Morphs to tell the Guardians to join the Residual Alliance."

"I don't know."

Ferren stared. "I thought you had an idea. You were developing a plan."

"No, I haven't had much time to develop anything."

"Not much time! What else have you been doing?"

"You wouldn't understand."

A faint, secretive smile had appeared on the angel's face. Ferren hated the sight of it.

"You have to work out what to do," he insisted.

"You could communicate with the Morphs yourself, you know. You saw how I did it."

A prickly tension was rising inside him. Why was she backing away?

"I could never make up songs. You'll be there anyway."

"I expect so," she said, and yawned again.

The tension exploded. "Expect? What do you mean? Why wouldn't you be there?"

"I said I expect to be. I'm sure it'll turn out well, whatever happens."

"Doesn't it matter to you now?"

"Of course it does. But the fate of the Residual Alliance doesn't depend on one tribe more or less."

"Why are you like this? You used to believe in our cause! You've changed!"

"I don't think so. But you have."

"No!"

"Yes. You've become perfectly capable of building the Alliance on your own."

"Don't want to! I want you helping me!"

"Now you sound just childish. If you could hear yourself—"

"I want you helping me! I *saved* you! I fed you and kept you alive on the Earth!"

"Yes, you did that. You saved me, and then I couldn't go back up to Heaven." Her tone had grown suddenly cold and remote. "You really have no idea, have you?"

"Idea about what?"

"You don't understand, and I'm afraid you never will." She pushed aside her patchwork blanket and rose to her feet. The top of her head brushed the roof of the nest.

"I'm really not in the mood for tantrums," she went on. "Since I'm clearly not going to be left in peace here, I'll find somewhere else. You can nurse your grievances by yourself."

"But tomorrow—"

She swept out of the nest without answering. Ferren gazed after her in a state of complete confusion. What had just happened?

22

Ferren worried about Miriael all day. Surely they'd be reconciled when her anger wore off? Surely she'd come back to discuss the Questioning with him? He waited all day for her in the nest. But he waited in vain.

In the end, he went out searching for her. He called first on Kiet, to ask her to help, but Kiet wasn't in her family nest.

"She's been gone for hours," Auntie Nettish told him. "Rhinn and Tadge too. Wouldn't tell me where they were going. They'd better be back for chores before dinner."

So he searched on his own. Presumably she wouldn't have gone far... He walked up and down every green tunnel in the Bloodstock area, he peered into the bushes on all sides. Then he tried calling on the nests in the area, asking if anyone had seen the Celestial today. The Bloodstock adults weren't used to meeting him without Kiet and looked at him askance. They looked even more askance when he mentioned "the Celestial"—they very definitely didn't want to see *her*. And nobody had anyway.

His spirits sank lower with every negative reply. He didn't know what to think. The sun was already setting, and the day was coming to an end. Then, quite by chance, he ran into Kiet after all.

She was in a small clearing close by her family nest, a tub of water before her and piles of wooden bowls and spoons all around.

"Where have you been?" he cried.

She paused with a drying cloth in one hand and a fistful of spoons in the other. "You said it was all right to tell my friends if they did a proper swear. I've been going round explaining that the Old Ones are Morphs." She scrutinised him with narrowed eyes. "What's the problem?"

"Problem! It's a disaster! Miriael!"

"What about her?"

"She walked out this morning, and she hasn't come back."

Kiet shrugged. "She often goes off on her own, doesn't she?"

"Not like this. We had a quarrel this morning. A really bad quarrel."

"So?" Still Kiet seemed unperturbed.

"You know there's a Questioning tomorrow?" he demanded.

"Of course. Everyone knows. That's why I was in a hurry explaining about the Old Ones."

"She might not turn up for it! She might not come at all!"

Now Kiet was perturbed. "And she's the only one who can talk to them..."

"The only one who can *see* them, even!" Ferren waved his arms about. "We can't do it without her!"

"What were you planning to do?"

"I don't know. She never said. She doesn't care about the Alliance anymore. She's lost interest!"

"All right, all right. Calm down. I should've guessed. She doesn't even know what happens in a Questioning. She couldn't have a plan unless she talked to me first."

"We have to find her. Then we can work out a plan with her."

"*If* we can find her. Have you searched?"

"Everywhere! This whole area!"

"What area?"

"The Bloodstock area."

"Hmm." Kiet looked suddenly thoughtful. "She might've gone further than that."

"What? What do you know?"

"Nothing. I'm just remembering something she said. Perhaps she's right outside the—

She broke off as a voice rang out. "Dinnertime! Ready to serve!"

Kiet jumped to her feet and began stacking up bowls. "I have to go. I'll be in trouble if I don't take these."

More and more voices chimed in. "Dinnertime! Dinnertime! *Dinnertime!*" The hullabaloo came from the direction of the Bloodstock firepit nearby.

"Come and have dinner with us all," Kiet suggested.

Ferren shook his head. "I want to keep searching."

"Up to you. I'll search after dinner."

"Where—"

"It's only a possibility. Don't get your hopes up." Kiet rose with the stacked bowls in her arms and the spoons in the topmost bowl. "You picked a really smart time to have a quarrel, didn't you?"

23

Miriael saw Asmodai in a different light now. When he approached along the valley to stand before her, he was as beautiful as ever, but with a more personal kind of beauty. Not the perfection of all angels, but distinctive features imprinted with his own individual story—noble yet fallen, pure yet with a weakness. For the first time, she wondered about the silver circlet on his brow. Was it a personal adornment he'd chosen or a mark of his status as a Fallen Angel who'd been forgiven?

"I was hoping I'd find you here," he began.

"I was hoping you'd come," she said.

"But you didn't summon me."

Miriael shook her head. She'd wanted him to come *without* being summoned. He smiled as though he understood what was in her mind.

"I came because I wanted to see you," he said.

His aura grew more radiant in the darkness of the night, yet Miriael found she could look into it—and into *him*—without being dazzled. For a long moment, their eyes rested on one another.

"I do have some news too," he added. "Good news."

She guessed at once. "You're ready to lift me up?"

"Ah, you've stolen my thunder." Again he smiled his wonderful, beatific smile. "Yes, everything's in place for your ascent into Heaven."

"The Morphs?"

"Everything. Are *you* ready?"

"As I'll ever be. When?"

"Tomorrow at dawn. I was thinking to lift you up to the Second Altitude, by the Pavilions of the Rose."

"My old battle squadron! The Twenty-Second Company!"

"Exactly. You like the idea?"

"I love it!"

"I don't know how all angels will react, but I'm sure your old companions will welcome you back. I've already called by and dropped a hint."

"About me coming back up?"

"No. Just about preparing for a surprise."

Miriael's pulse was racing. Her return to Heaven had suddenly become very real and very immediate. Then a thought struck her.

"You're taking a huge risk for yourself," she said.

"I am?"

"If nobody welcomes me back, I'm no worse off than before. I've got nothing to lose. But *you*..."

"I'd lose my position and what little status I have. I'll take the risk."

"But you could be expelled all over again. If they don't see the potential of your discovery, they'll condemn you for disobedience. You'd face the ultimate judgement."

"So be it."

"Why? Why are you doing this?"

He broke eye contact and made no reply. Miriael persisted.

"Is it all to save Heaven from these new weapons Doctor Saniette could develop?"

He shook his head, mutely, unwillingly.

"Is it for *me*?"

He looked up. "I believe you've been treated unjustly. You deserve to be happy in Heaven."

"So you're doing it out of a general sense of justice?"

He looked down again. "No," he muttered.

"There's something more, isn't there?"

The answer emerged as if wrung out of him. "I want to be happy too."

"You're doing it for yourself?"

"I'm ashamed to tell you."

"Go on. It's too late for shame with me."

He raised his eyes, which glowed with a new kind of light. "I want you up in Heaven with me, I want to be close to you all the time. It's utterly selfish, but I don't care. You matter more to me than the whole community of all the angels in Heaven. There, I've said it. That's the truth."

"Oh!" Miriael was taken aback, but she was more pleased than shocked. "Is that such a wrong thing?"

"It's weakness. I thought I'd left such weakness behind long, long ago."

"I'm glad you haven't."

"Glad?"

"I don't think it's so wrong anyway."

He shook his head. "I persuaded myself that the communal kind of love was enough for me. But this... I can't help myself. This is a hundred times more intense."

"Don't feel bad about it. I don't."

"You...?"

She nodded. She couldn't say any more...and nor could he, apparently. They searched in one another's eyes; then, as though by mutual agreement, they looked away.

"Tomorrow at dawn, then," she said in a whisper.

"Your return to Heaven." His voice was equally soft and low. "I'll meet you here at first light."

"In this very spot?"

"Yes. Look for me as a cloud. Then follow where I lead."

"I will, Asmodai."

"Until first light, Miriael."

24

The dawn was clear and fresh and quiet. Not a breath of air stirred as the sun showed its head above the horizon. A faint, pink pearliness appeared on the undersides of a few dove-grey clouds dotted around the sky.

Miriael was still in her special spot, stretched out on the grass next to the thicket. She hadn't wanted to spend her last few hours on the Earth enclosed in a nest, smelling the smell of clay. This period of time was no ordinary time—and Asmodai had made it even more extraordinary when he'd declared his feelings.

She sat up now and scanned the sky for one particular cloud unlike the others. She expected it to resemble the cloud from which he'd appeared once before—and it did. Seemingly out of nowhere, it came bobbing towards her, the one thing that moved in a motionless scene.

She rose to her feet as it approached. "Asmodai?"

She wasn't sure if she should raise her voice to call out. She would have liked to see him in person, this morning of all mornings, but presumably he used a cloud for disguise when he visited the Earth during the day.

The cloud floated to a stop before her, and his disembodied voice addressed her out of the vapour. "It's a mile's walk, Miriael. I'll try not to go too fast."

She followed as the cloud moved off. They were heading upstream, parallel to the edge of the thicket. It was hard going at first. The grass grew thick and tussocky in some places, and there were half-buried lumps of stone everywhere. She kept an eye on the cloud ahead while watching for obstacles under her feet.

By and by, they passed beyond the thicket on this side of the valley and the City of the Dead on the other. Now came a succession of low, rounded hills like grassy mounds. Miriael continued along a more level route at the bottom of the valley.

The sun rose higher. Splashes of light appeared on the green crowns of the hills, and the pale sky changed to a serene shade of blue. Sounds of birdsong started up like falling drops of water in the clear, fresh air. Somehow, the birdsong only accentuated the silence.

When the valley curved away to the right, the cloud continued straight on. Asmodai was leading her in among the hills. She shielded her eyes and hurried to keep up. They hadn't gone much farther when the cloud came to a sudden stop.

In the next moment, the cloud opened up, a line of light burst from it—and Asmodai himself descended to the ground. Her heart leaped to see him there in person. He raised an arm and beckoned to her…and she had the impression that he was smiling.

She strode forward with renewed vigour. Never had he looked more beautiful…and he *was* smiling.

"Is it here?" she asked as she approached.

"Not far," he answered. "Now we can go side by side."

He turned and moved on as she came up beside him. The sun, entering in gaps between the hills, shone brightly on the grass all around. She noticed several crimson flowers showing out against the green.

"Let me tell you about it," he said. "What I've built is a structure for flying up to Heaven using the power of the Morphs. A great triangular shape"—he sketched it with his hands—"a bit like a wing. I think of it as the wing of a bird or an angel.'

He laughed. Miriael could see he was excited to a degree she'd never seen before. Her own heart pounded with nervous anticipation: the moment of her ascent was very close at hand!

A sweet floral perfume filled the air. He was moving along faster and faster, and she struggled to stay walking side by side.

"I can't keep up!" she cried.

He slowed at once. "Sorry, I can't help myself."

"Tell me more about your flying wing. Where do the Morphs fit in?"

"They're incorporated into the structure. They'll fly up to Heaven too, you see."

"Ah. That's what they've always wanted, isn't it?"

"Exactly."

He veered to pass through the gap between two hills. Beyond the gap were more hills and a smooth-sided trough running between them. A shaft of sunlight fell upon a great patch of crimson flowers that seemed almost glowing in their intensity of colour.

So bright, thought Miriael. *But not as bright as the flowers of Heaven will be.*

"How did you construct your flying wing?" she asked. "I mean, is it metal? Surely you couldn't do that yourself!"

"No, I needed help. I can do many things, but I can't work with metal." He laughed. "Come on, you're so slow. You'll see in a minute. Just over that hill there!" He pointed. "I promise you'll be amazed."

The hill was exactly the same size and shape as every other low mounded hill, covered in the same green grass, dotted with the same red flowers.

"Do we have to climb over the top?" Miriael asked.

"No." He turned to face her. "Stop."

"What?"

He whirled away and raised one hand high in the air—than brought it slicing down.

"*Now!*" he cried in a great ringing voice.

Over the hill came a horde of black-suited Hypers. An evil gleam shone in their eyeslits, pointed metal teeth showed in their mouthslits. They surged down the slope and raced towards her.

25

M iriael was overpowered without a fight. She couldn't think, couldn't act, couldn't believe. The Hypers kicked her legs out from under her and knocked her to the ground. All she knew was a sick, hollow feeling in the pit of her stomach.

Spiked boots pinned her down, rubber-covered hands clamped round her wrists and ankles. Asmodai had moved ten paces away.

"Help!" she called to him. "Help me!"

He heard her cry and raised his eyebrows. Then he turned to begin a discussion with one particular Hyper who came up to him. Miriael struggled against the hands that held her, keeping her eyes on him. With one part of her mind, she understood—yet she didn't *want* to understand.

The Hypers surrounding her brought out spools of silvery plastic tape for binding her. They taped her wings to her arms and her arms behind her back. Soon she was completely immobilised.

Still she focused on Asmodai. The Hyper he was talking to had six sets of wings painted on his rubber-clad chest, signifying six angel 'kills'. No doubt he was the commanding officer. She caught fragments of their conversation.

"My side of the bargain…"

"Yes, a high-speed transport machine…"

"The rest of your men…"

"Stay and do the other job for you…"

When the Hypers finished binding her and stepped back, Asmodai turned from the commanding officer and came across. He smiled down at her, helpless on the ground.

"Well, well. Didn't I promise you'd be amazed?"

"Everything you said was a lie!" she spat at him. Yet even now she didn't entirely believe it, still hoped for some impossible reprieve. "You never meant to lift me back into Heaven! You never had a flying wing!"

"Oh, the flying wing is true enough. Fully assembled, almost ready to fly. It's just a few hills further away." He swung an arm in the direction. "I really do possess a new source of power that no one's ever discovered before. Much too important to waste on you, of course."

"You sold me off! It was all a petty little bargain with the Humen!"

"I wouldn't say 'petty'. You're a precious commodity in Doctor Saniette's eyes. I believe I extracted top value for you."

He broke off as a mechanical sound came louder to their ears: *guzz-a-dack-dack-dack! guzz-a-dack-dack-dack! guzz-a-dack-dack-dack!*

Miriael twisted her head and saw a transport machine approaching through a dip between the hills. It had the usual trolley top, but more wheels and cylinders than she'd ever seen on a transport machine before.

The Hyper commanding officer barked a mathematical formula. "4a plus 3b times 7.892!"

Obediently, the machine swung to the left, came up alongside Miriael and slowed to a halt.

"Load her up!" the officer ordered.

His men advanced once again, took hold of Miriael's immobilised body, lifted and dumped her on the flat trolley top. From the back of the machine, they produced a camouflage sheet of mottled green and brown, which they prepared to pull over her.

"One last word!" Asmodai checked them with a raised hand. The Hypers waited as he bent down to Miriael with a smile.

"Not quite the journey you imagined, I suppose. Your journey now is to Doctor Saniette in the Bankstown Camp. I may see you there if you last that long."

"You're a monster!"

"Not at all. I'm a Fallen Angel."

"Phah! *You* never fell in love with a mortal woman! You only love yourself!"

"Well, yes, I'm not *that* kind of Fallen Angel. Much more fallen—not the pathetic weakness of a Watcher." He laughed. "I was a Luciferian, of course."

He drew back with a wave of his hand. In the next moment, the Hypers pulled the sheet over Miriael's face, and she was enveloped in darkness. She heard another sharp mathematical command and the sound of an engine speeding up: *guzz-a-dack-dack-dack! guzz-a-dack-dack-dack!*

Then the transport machine rolled forward, carrying her away.

PART THREE

MIRIAEL GONE

1

Kiet had some information for Ferren, but she'd decided to put off telling him until later. Although she didn't understand the implications of what she'd observed, she guessed he would react badly when he heard about a *second* angel.

It was lucky she hadn't told him last night. When she'd come back from spying on Miriael outside the thicket, she was bursting with the need to tell someone. But then she'd looked in at the entrance of Ferren's nest and had seen him stretched out with his head on his arm, fast asleep. She would have to wake him...

Immediately she'd thought of a dozen reasons why it was better *not* to wake him. So she'd backed off from telling him then—and now that morning had come round, she didn't intend to tell him now either. If she started describing what she'd observed, she would also have to say what she thought was going on between the two angels. And the consequences of that could be highly unpredictable.

The one thing she knew about Ferren's relationship to the angel was that he was somehow odd about her. He would probably hate hearing she'd been meeting with a male angel behind his back. Either he would explode with anger or he would plunge into senseless despair—and both reactions would make him useless when they needed to manipulate the Questioning in favour of the Residual Alliance.

Yes, he could have his tantrums afterwards, but he needed a cool head today. They both did, because they'd most likely have to do the manipulating themselves. Having seen Miriael with the second angel,

Kiet no longer expected her to turn up. She had other priorities…

But how to manipulate the Questioning? When the Guardians interpreted the Old Ones' responses, they usually heard the answer as no. Kiet racked her brains, and could see only one possible way.

She left her family nest very early in the morning. She had a great deal to do, and not much time to do it. She would need to visit and prepare all the young Nesters who already understood that the Old Ones were Morphs.

As for Ferren, she decided to keep away from him. If she met him now, he would only want to quiz her about last night, and whether she'd found Miriael in the place she'd gone searching.

2

When Ferren awoke and saw that Miriael wasn't there in the nest, a leaden weight settled upon him. He couldn't concentrate on today's Questioning; his mind was lost in a thousand aimless thoughts.

It was Rhinn who brought him his breakfast instead of Kiet.

"Today's the day," she said. "We'll be ready to help when you ask."

He ate his meal in gloomy solitude. He had not long finished when he became aware of a murmur outside. A stir of noise and movement seemed to rise from all parts of the thicket at once.

He ducked out through the entrance and along the path to the main tunnel. Nesters were going past, all in the one direction.

"Is it the Questioning?" he asked one young mother who carried a baby.

"Yes, we're going to watch."

He was surprised that Kiet hadn't come calling for him. He joined in with the Nesters, heading through the thicket towards the City of the Dead. As tunnels converged, more and more people packed in and jostled together. So far as he could see, they were all adults—no sign of Kiet or her friends or any young Nesters.

He heard them talking in low, excited voices as they walked. One bald and bearded man addressed him directly.

"This is a Questioning about your alliance of all the tribes, isn't it?"

"And breaking away from the Humen," added another voice. "That's what I heard."

Ferren nodded. "The Nesters have to decide," he said.

"The Old Ones will tell us," a third voice put in.

Ferren had the impression that they weren't opposed to the Residual Alliance and quite liked the idea of breaking away from the Humen. But he could also see they would never act to bring it about by their own initiative.

When he came out of the thicket onto the side of the valley, most of Nesters were already there. They stood grouped along the slope in their four stocks, thirty or forty in a group. But there was a separate, less organised crowd lower down the slope, a crowd of all the young Nesters. Ferren spotted Kiet with her dark red hair, surrounded by several others he knew by name.

Every face was turned towards the City of the Dead, everyone was watching the Guardians as they crossed the rivulets and made their way up the other side of the valley. Four young Nesters accompanied them, bearing huge gongs and drums. Ferren recognised spiky-haired Tadge as one of the four.

What had Kiet once said about the Old Ones answering when the Guardians made a great noise? He realised he still didn't know how a Questioning actually worked.

The Guardians climbed over the outcrop of rock and onto the concrete platform on top. By their hurried actions and anxious glances, they only wanted to get the business over as quickly as possible. The young bearers followed them onto the platform and began setting up drums and gongs right under the walls of the City of the Dead.

Ferren decided to push forward and join Kiet lower down the slope. But a great many adult Nesters stood in his way, all pressed in shoulder to shoulder. Although they didn't deliberately block him off, they were too absorbed in events on the other side of the valley to think of letting him pass.

He had finally managed to reach the crowd of young Nesters when a great blare of sound stopped him dead. The Guardians had begun beating their drums and banging their gongs. It was nothing like music, just a discordant cacophony, which rose to a thunderous crescendo, then hushed.

"Old Ones, Old Ones!" the Guardians yelled at the tops of their voices. "Should we join a new alliance, should we break with the Humen, should we ally with other tribes? Old Ones, Old Ones, what do you say?"

Immediately, they began beating and banging again; then paused to yell out their question again. After repeating the ritual three times, they stepped aside from their drums and gongs, and stood listening. Everyone across the valley stood listening too.

In the sudden silence, a new kind of sound could be heard from inside the City.

"Ooo-ooo-ooh! Ooo-ooo-ooh!"

Faint and plaintive, it was the wailing of the Morphs. The Guardians made a great show of cupping their hands to their ears. Then they turned to one another and began a very earnest discussion.

Ferren pushed forward through the young Nesters and came up to Kiet.

"They've disturbed the Morphs from their peace and quiet," he said, as she turned to him. "That's all the sound is. The Morphs are upset."

"I know," Kiet agreed. "Wait for the Guardians to interpret it."

"Then what?"

"Keep watching. Follow my lead."

The wails of the Morphs were dying away by the time the Guardians finally swung towards the rest of the tribe on the other side of the valley. One by one, they crossed their arms in front of their faces.

Kiet snorted. "That means a no," she said.

Mutters rose from the young Nesters. "Never!" "It wasn't!" "Don't believe it!"

But the adult Nesters higher up the slope believed it. The sigh that came from them was a sigh of acceptance.

"Right!" Kiet held up a hand and looked around. The young Nesters looked back at her. "This is it! We're going to find out! Right?"

"*Right!*" answered a chorus of fierce young voices.

In the next moment, she had started off down the slope. Ferren and all her other followers ran after her.

3

On the concrete platform, the four young bearers were already arguing with the Guardians. Skail visibly smouldered with rage, while Berwin, Clemmart and Dunkery appeared bemused by the unexpected challenge. Coming up over the outcrop of rock, Ferren saw Tadge raise his fists in frustration.

"An ooo-oooh isn't a no!" he shouted at Skail. "You interpreted wrong!"

Then Kiet's followers clustered round and joined the argument. Skail glared at them.

"You little fools! You don't know a thing about the Old Ones."

"Nor do you, then," retorted bugle-nosed Flens.

"Enough!" cried Kiet, stepping forward in front of Flens. "Easy settled. Let's all go inside the City. We can hear them better there."

The Guardians' jaws dropped. They looked nervously towards the walls of City of the Dead, then back at Kiet.

"Not possible," muttered Skail.

"Nobody does that," agreed Berwin.

"*We* can." Kiet appealed to the young Nesters. "Who's with me? Who'll come in and listen *properly?*"

Although Ferren nodded along with the rest, he didn't understand. How could Kiet even see the Morphs, let alone question them?

The Guardians appeared unsure what to do. As heads of their stocks, their role was to show leadership. It wouldn't look good if they hung back while mere youngsters took the lead.

"We're going in anyway," Kiet told them.

"We're not afraid of *ghosts*," added Flens, with a wink.

Dunkery, the only female Guardian, was the bravest of the four. "I suppose we *could*," she said.

"I don't know," Clemmart scratched his chin.

"I will if you will," Dunkery told him.

Flens laughed. "Don't worry! We'll be with you all the way."

"How dare you!" snapped Skail, and white spots of anger burned on his cheeks.

Kiet was already striding towards the gap in the walls through which she and Ferren had entered before. Since they were the ones with past experience, they had to prove there was nothing to fear, he realised.

"Come on," he said to both Guardians and young Nesters, and strode after her.

The young Nesters, following behind, collected the Guardians and swept them along too. Dunkery, Berwin, Clemmart and Skail came forward in a small, tight knot, very close together—but they came.

The street beyond the gap looked different by daylight. As they passed the blank facades, Ferren could see the full extent of the deterioration: cracks in almost every stone, grass sprouting in the cracks, fallen fragments of stone scattered everywhere across the roadway. The City seemed as if asleep and dreaming in the sunshine.

The young Nesters whistled and cried out in wonder. "Look at that!" "And that!" "See over there!" "What about the size of those blocks!" "Whew!"

Ferren caught up with Kiet and walked alongside. "What are you going to do? Have you got a plan?"

"Half a plan. I'm going to try singing to the Morphs like your angel did."

"What, in the plaza?" He pointed ahead to the end of the street.

"Yes."

"But you won't see them."

"Fingers crossed they're in the same place." She clicked her tongue. "I can't sing like an angel, but I'm a pretty good singer. I can remember the tunes she sang."

"How about words?"

"I'm working on them. Shush up and let me think."

They continued on past shopfronts and housefronts, past the door he'd pulled off its hinges, past the avalanche of earth that had spilled out onto the pavement. Behind them, the young Nesters were still uttering cries of amazement. Ferren swung round and put a finger to his lips.

"Walk quietly now!" he warned. "You'll unsettle the Morphs if you make sudden noises."

The exclamations ceased, the sound of footsteps fell away. Kiet leaned across to him and whispered.

"You said 'Morphs'. You shouldn't have said that."

Ferren hadn't noticed and didn't much care. They arrived at the entrance to the plaza, and both looked towards the corner where the Morphs had been before. There was the same broken kerb and the three steps leading up to the door.

"Wish me luck," said Kiet. "Make sure the Guardians are paying attention."

She set off across the plaza to the spot where Miriael had knelt and sung to the Morphs. The young Nesters spread out to watch all across the entrance to the plaza. Ferren noted with approval that they pushed the Guardians forward for a particularly good view.

Kneeling as the angel had done, Kiet pretended to focus on what she couldn't see. Then she raised her voice and sang.

> Please don't be afraid,
> Please do, please do stay.
> I want to ask some questions
> And listen to what you say.

She'd been telling the truth about being a good singer. Her tune was a perfect match for Miriael's tune, and the words were at least very similar. Ferren held his breath along with everyone else. He remembered that, with Miriael, the Morphs had been making sounds long before she even knelt down. The silence drew out and out…

Then came a tiny "Ooo-ooh!" A moment later, another voice joined in; then half a dozen all piping together. The sounds weren't wails of panic, like the Morphs' response to the banging of drums and gongs. Kiet's singing had soothed them and calmed them.

Ferren clenched his fists in triumph. He couldn't see Kiet's face with her back turned, but he was sure she felt the same. She raised her voice again.

> Do you like the Humen
> And what they make us do?
> Should we stay allied with them
> Or look for someone new?

The Morphs chittered and cheeped quietly among themselves for a moment. Then they responded with a chorus of "Ooo-oohs!" Yet it wasn't quite the same wordless sound as before.

"They're saying 'new'," murmured someone next to Ferren.

Young Nesters whispered in excitement and looked at one another with shining eyes.

"I can hear it!"

"They're talking to us!"

"They want us to look for someone new!"

Ferren could hear it too. He scanned along the line of onlookers and saw the Guardians nodding. They seemed more fearful than excited, but they were nodding.

Kiet signalled over her shoulder for attention, then sang again.

> If we look for someone new
> Do we look for other tribes?
> Should we join people just like us
> And be their true allies?

This time the response was immediate and more confused, with half-a-dozen voices piping up all at once. The onlookers leaned forward and strained their ears.

"I think they said 'tribes'!"

"And 'people'!"

"I heard 'true'!"

"True allies with other tribes—has to be!"

There were so many tiny, high-pitched voices, any and all of the interpretations could have been correct. Ferren grinned to himself. Whatever the Morphs did or didn't say, they *ought* to favour a Residual Alliance, since their own colony was composed of many tribes.

He moved along to the nearest Guardian: Berwin of Heartstock.

"You heard the advice?" he asked in a whisper.

"I heard some words in it."

"They want the Nesters to join the Residual Alliance."

"Maybe, yes."

"We'll have to have a meeting of the Guardians," said Skail, who had been listening in on the conversation. "We'll decide how to interpret it then."

Ferren didn't like the postponement. "Perhaps you need to hear it more clearly." He turned and spoke to the young Nesters. "Let's go up close! Let's hear it so there's no mistake!"

The young Nesters were willing enough. They began to bustle forward into the plaza, carrying the Guardians along with them.

"Wait!" gasped Berwin, pushing back. "No need! I already heard it!"

"What?"

"They want us to join the Residual Alliance."

"No mistake about it," agreed Dunkery, from further along the line, and Clemmart chimed in, "No mistake."

Ferren turned to Skail. "What do you think? Shall we go in closer while Kiet sings the questions again?"

"No." Skail's face was a picture of frustration, but he was no braver than Berwin. "The Old Ones want us to join the Residual Alliance. Enough. Now let's go."

The forward push into the plaza had already come to a halt. Ferren raised his arms and waited until everyone was looking at him.

"They've given their advice, let's leave them in peace!" he said. "Time to go back and announce the answer!"

4

Buoyed by euphoria, Ferren led the way back along the street to the platform. For the moment, he seemed to have taken charge. They looked out across the valley to where the rest of the tribe still waited.

"You can change your signal to them now," he told to Dunkery.

Dunkery stepped forward and waved a single arm from side to side. The other Guardians came up beside her and followed suit.

"That's the signal for yes," a young Nester explained to Ferren, in case he hadn't worked it out for himself.

There were many nodding heads and even a few cheers from the other side of the valley. As Ferren had suspected, the adult Nesters quite liked the idea of the Residual Alliance.

"All thanks to those mysterious 'ghosts'," Flens commented ironically.

Skail must have heard, because he swung round to stare at Flens. Then he swung again to confront Ferren.

"You called them something else," he said. "'Morphs,' you called them. What did you mean by that?"

"Not now." Ferren swept an arm to encompass the young Nesters. "They understand. They'll give you the whole story."

Still Skail persisted. "You don't think the Old Ones are ghosts at all, do you? What do you think they are?"

But Ferren wasn't listening. He had suddenly realised that Kiet hadn't followed the group back to the platform. "Has anyone seen Kiet?" he demanded.

Everyone looked round, everyone shook their heads.

"Must be still singing and chatting back there." Flens hooked a thumb in the direction of the plaza.

"I'll go and get her," said Ferren, and turned to address the Guardians. "You should lead everyone home now. Nothing more to do here."

He wasn't worried about Kiet, he just wanted to share the success of the Residual Alliance with her. Thanks to her idea, they'd triumphed against all odds.

He hurried along the street and back to the plaza. She was still there in the same corner, still on her knees. She heard his footsteps as he approached, and looked round.

"I've been talking to them!" Her voice was an excited whisper. "Talking without singing! They don't need a tune now they're comfortable with me." She grinned from ear to ear. "Easier than making up rhymes."

"But you did that too," he whispered back. "You were incredible."

He halted a couple of paces away, wary of stepping on invisible Morphs. She guessed the reason for his caution.

"There's one between those two bits of stone, that blade of grass sticking up and the bottom step." She pointed. "And another all across the top step and door frame and doorsill. I can almost see their patterns."

"But not *actually* see?"

"Of course not. They told me where they were. They're so interesting to talk to. I just wish I knew how to cheer them up. They're very, very unhappy."

"Because they're not allowed into Heaven." Ferren changed the subject. "Did you realise the Guardians accepted the Residual Alliance?"

"Yes." Kiet remained focused on the Morphs. "They told me one thing very interesting. An angel has been visiting them."

"An angel? You mean Miriael?"

"No, a different angel. He could be the one I saw last—"

She clammed up too late. Ferren had heard, and now he saw the tell-tale look on her face.

"*What!*"

"Shush! You'll upset the Morphs." She tried to turn away as though nothing had happened.

But it had—and Ferren's euphoria vanished as though it had never existed.

"You were going to say 'last night'!" he fired at her.

"No."

"Yes! Don't deny it! Is this when you went searching for Miriael?"

"All right, I *will* tell you." Still she didn't look at him. "I was going to, anyway. But wait till we get back home."

Ferren would have liked to drag it out of her—but he took a deep breath instead.

"Everyone else has gone back already."

"I'm coming."

Kiet said goodbye to the Morphs and rose to her feet. Their fluting replies floated in the air as she followed Ferren out of the plaza.

"Goodbye-eee! Goodbye-eee! Goodbye-eee-eee!"

5

"Tell me!" Ferren demanded. "Everything!"

Kiet had accompanied him back to his nest—he wouldn't allow a minute's more delay. They sat facing one another in the semi-darkness.

"Well, yes, last night," she began.

"You *did* find her. She was in the place you expected, right?"

"She mentioned it earlier, and I worked it out, more or less. It was—"

"Why didn't you tell me?" He jumped in again; he couldn't wait.

"Because she—"

"You should've done something! You should've made her come back!"

Kiet let out a huff of exasperation. "Do you want to hear or not?"

"Yes. Yes."

"Then stop interrupting. If I tell it, I'll tell it in my own time."

With an effort, Ferren held himself in and nodded for her to go on.

"So. Her special place was just outside the thicket, not far from where we all stood today. A bit further upstream, in a kind sheltered spot back against the bushes. I went there in the dark after dinner. I didn't see her at first, I had to wander round for a while. Then I noticed this strange glow."

Ferren's heart was pounding. Still he nodded and said nothing.

"It wasn't Miriael, of course. It was the glow of this other angel with her. I crept up closer in the shadow of the thicket. They couldn't see me because the bushes stuck out, and they were on the other side. The way they were talking, they weren't thinking of anything but themselves, anyway. I could watch peering out around the twigs and leaves. She was sitting and he was standing—"

"Did you say *he?*"

"Yes."

"Not a female angel?"

"No, male. But very, very beautiful. If you think Miriael's beautiful… And he had this light that came out of every part of his body and made a sort of oval around him. You should've seen him. The most amazing sight I ever saw."

Ferren ground his teeth. "Go on."

Kiet looked at him with sudden concern. "You probably won't like this."

"Go on."

"All right." She shrugged. "I suppose Miriael thought he was beautiful too. I couldn't hear what they were saying, but they sounded like they knew each other really, really well. The way she was looking up at him, hanging on every word, bathing in his radiance. Like there was no one else in the world for her. Nor him neither."

Ferren felt a great mass of emotion boiling inside him. He didn't know what it was or where it came from, but it was rising…it was irresistible…

"I expect that's why Miriael has stopped caring about the Residual Alliance," Kiet went on. "You said she'd lost interest."

"So that's it!" The words burst from him as if squeezed out under pressure. He was hardly aware of uttering them.

"She's had this angel coming to see her. Maybe the same one who's been visiting the Morphs—"

"*Betrayed me!*" Ferren exploded. "*Betrayed me!*"

He jumped to his feet and kicked at his bedding. If there had been anything to break and smash, he'd have broken and smashed it.

"She's been lying to me all along! Secret meetings! Sneaking off to him!"

He began striding blindly back and forth in the confines of the nest. Kiet drew her legs up out of the way, and he whirled and shouted at her too.

"Don't you see? She's gone off to be with him for good! Left me, and never said a word!"

"Don't shout at me." Kiet scowled. "So she likes to be with her own kind. What do you expect?"

"Loyalty! I expected loyalty! I thought I mattered to her! And the Residual Alliance! All tossed aside—for *him!*"

"If you can't talk sensibly…" said Kiet, and made a move towards the entrance of the nest.

"I'm nothing to her—well, she's nothing to me! I never want to hear her name, I never want to *think* of her again!"

He reached for the rolled-up band of the loincloth round his waist and drew out the two white feathers from Miriael's wing. He glared at them, then threw them away from him. Gently, they sailed down through the air.

"My symbol that I followed! I'd have been always true! I'd have died for her!"

He let out an inarticulate roar. As the feathers touched ground, he raised his foot and stamped on them.

"This is what they're worth to me now!" He trampled them with one foot, then the other, grinding them into the earth. "Out of my life! Out of my life! Out of my life! You see!"

But when he looked round, Kiet had already gone.

6

Next day, the Guardians called an unusual meeting attended by all of the stocks together. Ferren attended too; as envoy for the Residual Alliance, his presence was indispensable. From the start, it was an accepted fact the Nesters would join the Alliance. The discussion was all about the details.

The big surprise was the turnaround in Skail's attitude. The Bloodstock Guardian, who had always been the most negative of the four, suddenly became the Alliance's strongest supporter. He must have been questioning the young Nesters in his stock about the true nature of the Old Ones, because he now knew as much about Morphs as anyone. Seeing how cleverly he came up with reasons for pursuing a completely different policy, Ferren understood why Kiet had once called him "sharp as a tack." No doubt he had seen which way the wind was blowing.

Skail's cleverness was on display again when Ferren came forward to explain about the forthcoming assembly, to which all tribes in the Alliance would send a representative. Skail immediately proposed that the Nesters, being the largest tribe, should have double representation. He even claimed they deserved two representatives because the Selectors had always taken away two tribe members a year for 'military service'. Ferren argued against him, but his heart wasn't in it, and eventually he gave way.

It's harder on my own, he thought. *I'd have made more of a stand with Miriael to back me up.*

After the meeting came the celebration feast, then the dance. Ferren wasn't in the mood for either, but since he was still at the centre of events, he had to stay and smile and talk. Nesters kept coming up to him with all kinds of questions, especially about his own tribe, the People, and other tribes he'd met on his journey. The one subject no one asked him about was Miriael and her unexplained absence. So far as they were concerned, it was as though the Celestial had never really existed.

The feast took place outside the thicket on the flat grassy field that Ferren and Miriael had crossed on their first approach to the Nesters' territory. When the feast had been cleared away, the musicians positioned themselves on the same ground. There were six of them, led by the familiar figure of Kiet's Grandpa Niot. They blew, plucked, sawed and pounded on their instruments, and the dancing was fast and furious.

Ferren had noticed Kiet at the meeting and the feast, but they had hardly exchanged glances. He felt a little ashamed of his outburst yesterday, and didn't know how to explain or excuse it. He was surprised when she came up to him after the music and dancing began.

"Want to dance?"

He shook his head automatically; he had been hoping to slip off quietly for so long he couldn't adjust to the idea of becoming more involved. Kiet didn't ask a second time, but found herself another partner and was soon whirling and twirling among the other dancers. She was a mad ball of energy, more wildly unrestrained than any of them. He watched her in moments when he wasn't having to respond to questions.

The sun went down, but the festivities continued. Ferren still couldn't manage to get away. Since joining the Alliance, the Nesters seemed to feel a new friendliness towards him. On his side, he struggled to smile and keep up a conversation. Overhead, the sky smouldered in colours of orange, red and purple.

It could have been the normal sunset flight of birds when a great flock went streaming across the sky. Perhaps a little after the normal time... They came from the direction of the thicket, cawing and fluttering. Ferren looked up and noticed, but the Nesters were too absorbed in dancing and talking to pay attention.

Everyone noticed ten minutes later, though. Ferren was engaged in yet another conversation when someone standing near him announced, "I smell smoke."

Others began sniffing the air.

"Me too."

"Peculiar kind of smoke."

"It's coming from the thicket."

As more and more voices sounded the alarm, the dancing slowed and stopped. Ferren inhaled, and it *was* a peculiar kind of smoke. It reminded him of something...

"Fire in the thicket!" yelled Dunkery of Headstock. "Get back and put it out! Everyone, save your nests!"

In the next moment, they were all racing back into the green tunnels, seeking the source of the smoke. But there was no fire anywhere among the bushes. Pursuing the burning smell, they ran all the way through the thicket and came out on the other side.

Then they saw it. From one side of the valley, they looked across to the other side, aghast. Thick, black, oily smoke was billowing above the walls and buildings of the City of the Dead.

7

With a dozen adult Nesters and almost all of the young Nesters, Ferren crossed the valley and came up towards the concrete platform on the other side. Bushes and clumps of grass were burning outside the City, but he couldn't imagine what there was burning inside.

He was first to scramble onto the platform. As others scrambled up behind him, he heard a cry: "The Morphs! What's happened to the Morphs?" It was Kiet's voice, and her cry was filled with desperation and despair.

He studied the strange sooty film on the City's walls. The peculiar smell was stronger here, quite unlike the smell of burning vegetation. But at least the clouds of oily smoke were drifting up into the air, further and further away from the ground. With luck, the worst of the fire was over.

He made for the gap in the walls and would have led the way in, except that Kiet was already sprinting ahead of him.

Beyond the gap, the facades in the street were streaked with black smuts, doors and window frames were scorched and charred, newly fallen blocks of stone lay scattered everywhere. It was a scene of desolation.

However, the doors and window frames weren't the source of the fire. Most of the flames still burning came from slick, black blobs and tar-like patches on the roadway. As Ferren approached, a biting smell caught in his throat and made his eyes water.

"I know what this is!" he announced. "This is the smell of flamethrowers. *Humen* flamethrowers."

There was a moment of reflection, then several voices murmured agreement. "We've seen flamethrowers!" "Like the Selectors carry!" "It's the smell of the fuel they use!" "This wasn't ordinary fire!"

"Here's the proof!" cried Grandpa Niot, another of the adults. "Come and look at this!"

They gathered round him on the pavement, and the proof was plain. One of the Hypers must have trodden on a patch of unburnt fuel, and the black shape of his boot had printed itself on the stone surface. The Nesters glanced nervously over their shoulders.

"Don't worry, they're not here now," said Ferren. "They must've finished and—"

A grieving cry cut across his reassurances—a cry from the plaza at the end of the street.

"That's Kiet!"

"What has she found?"

Or not found, thought Ferren, with sudden foreboding. He set off running towards the plaza, and the others ran after him.

Kiet was in the plaza, in the same corner as before, facing the same three steps and door where the Morphs had been. She turned wide, wet eyes to them as they came up.

"They're not here anymore! Not answering! All lost and gone!"

Lines of yellow flame flickered on the wooden door, which had cracked half open, exposing the earth packed in behind.

"They've been burned alive!" Kiet howled. "Burned alive!"

Ferren didn't know if Morphs were exactly alive, but he doubted they could catch fire.

"No," he said firmly. "They must have floated off. Gone somewhere else."

"Why would the Humen do it?" asked Flens. "Don't they like Morphs?"

Ferren shrugged. "We have to have a proper search. Search if there's any left in the City."

"Except we can't see them," someone pointed out.

"We can listen for them."

Grandpa Niot flourished the musical instrument he'd been playing at the dance. He'd brought it with him: a shaped wooden board with pegs and strings, called a zither. "I could make a lot of noise, like at a Questioning."

Ferren shook his head. "If there's any left, they're already scared. We want to soothe them, not scare them."

He turned to Kiet, who understood at once. "I'll sing," she said. "They'll more likely answer if I sing to them."

She took up position in the middle of the plaza, thought for a minute, then tilted her head and sang at the top of her voice.

> Are you there, are you there, are you there?
> Please answer, anyone!
> We want to help and keep you safe,
> Make a sound if you hear my song!

They strained their ears in the silence that followed, but there was no sound in response.

"We'll have to try all over the City," said Ferren.

Over the next half hour, Kiet tried her song many times. The group tiptoed along deserted streets and across empty squares, past countless blank-faced buildings. In some places, roads fell away in yawning craters and entire housefronts had collapsed. In other places, only skeletons of stonework remained: windowed walls with nothing behind them, staircases ascending with no rooms to go up to. Everywhere, they saw scorch marks, coatings of soot and black blobs of flamethrower fuel.

The Hypers must've burned the whole place, thought Ferren hopelessly. *There must've been hundreds of them.*

Still, he wouldn't give up searching as long as Kiet wanted to go on. Other Nesters began casting quizzical looks at him, having clearly decided that the search was useless. By now, there was desperation in

Kiet's singing, and her voice sometimes cracked or choked on the final notes. Tears made tracks down her cheeks, where she'd rubbed at her face with dirty, sooty hands. She cared more about the Morphs than anyone.

It was on the ninth or tenth attempt of singing her song that a very faint "ooo-ooh!" replied.

8

"Where was that?" The Nesters gazed in all directions.

"Maybe over there," suggested young Gibby, pointing.

Others thought the same, and the group converged towards the side of the street, where a gap ran back between two buildings. The gap might once have been a paved alley, but was now blocked with a pile of fallen masonry. The two buildings had both lost most of their upper storeys.

"Sing again," Ferren prompted Kiet.

Kiet lifted her voice and sang with a will. "Make a sound if you hear my song!" she concluded.

Once more they heard it, very small and tremulous. "Ooo-ooo-ooh!"

Kiet came up in front of the pile of masonry. "Where are you, little one?" She spoke rather than sang, but in a gentle, crooning voice. "Are you in here? Are you buried very deep?"

Ferren, standing right behind her, could make out some words in the answering wail.

"No-o-o, not dee-eep! Close to you-ou-ou! Under the big sto-one! It fell on me-e-e-e-e-e!"

Big stone? He saw one chunk of fallen masonry that was far bigger than the rest. It wasn't a single block of stone, but many blocks cemented together.

"I think he means that one." He pointed over Kiet's shoulder while whispering in her ear. "It must weigh tons."

"Get Bross," Kiet replied without looking round.

Ferren turned back to the group on the pavement. "Bross?"

The lad who stepped forward was solidly built and muscular. Ferren remembered him as one of Kiet's friends.

"Can you shift that?"

Bross frowned thoughtfully at the big chunk of masonry, then nodded. "With help."

"I'll help," said Ferren.

"No, I'll help," growled one of the adult Nesters, coming forward. He was even more muscular than Bross, with massive forearms.

"Go, Stogget!" cried Flens, and the others laughed.

"If those two can't do it, nobody can," said Grandpa Niot.

Ferren and Kiet drew back as Bross and Stogget climbed up on the rubble. They took hold of the huge, fallen chunk on either side.

"Be careful!" Kiet warned as they heaved and strained. "No jerking movements!"

It was almost more than they could do to move it at all—but finally they did it. They staggered back down to the pavement with the huge chunk between them, then let it drop with a crash.

"Ooo-oooh!"

Kiet was back to the pile of fallen masonry in a flash. "It's all right, little one," she crooned. "Everything's going to be all right for you."

Where the huge chunk had been lifted away, a dark hole now gaped. Kiet stretched towards it, half leaning and half lying over the rubble. Ferren leaned forward to watch from behind.

The tiny voice, recovering from its fear, now fluted in lamentation. "All alo-one! Others all gone! Me alo-o-o-o-o-ne!"

It was a heartbreaking sound. Ferren could see nothing inside the hole, but he could tell exactly where the Morph was. So could Kiet.

"Come out and be safe with us," she crooned. "Do you want to come out with us?"

"I do, I do-o-o-o! What do I hold on to-o-o?"

"They have to attach themselves…" Ferren whispered in Kiet's ear. But already she was reaching with her arm into the hole.

"Take hold of me," she crooned.

Inch by inch, further and further… Then, all at once, she let out a gasp and laughed with surprise.

"He feels so cool and ticklish!" she exclaimed.

Ferren guessed that the Morph had attached itself to her fingertips. She withdrew her arm from the hole as slowly and carefully as she'd slid it forward. But the Morph didn't come with her.

"No-o-o-o-o-o!"

It was a wail of sheer terror. Kiet froze.

"I think you're stretching him," said Ferren. "He's still attached to points of stone inside the hole. He needs more than just your fingertips."

"My arm?" Kiet leaned forward again, advancing her whole arm inside the hole for the Morph to attach to. But after a minute she shook her head. "I'm not feeling anything."

"Your arm must be too smooth and rounded for him," said Ferren. "They need something with sharp bits sticking out."

"Like what?"

"I don't know."

"We don't have anything like that."

"Perhaps we do," said a familiar voice. Ferren spun around—and it was Grandpa Niot, holding out his zither. "How about this?"

Ferren noted the many pegs that fixed the strings to the board of the instrument. "Plenty of bits sticking out there," he agreed with a grin.

He accepted the zither from the old Nester and passed it on to Kiet.

"Try holding it over the hole," he advised. "Let the Morph attach himself when he's ready. No hurry."

"I'll wait a hundred years," promised Kiet.

In fact, they only had to wait a few minutes. They couldn't see the Morph attach himself to the pegs, but they heard a peaceful peep-peeping sound when he'd succeeded.

Kiet lifted the zither away from the hole. Then, holding the instrument in both hands, she stepped carefully away from the rubble. Ferren saw her look of concentration as she thought up the words for a song to the Morph. When she sang, it was to a bouncy new tune.

> We're going home, we're going home,
> So safe and snug we'll be!
> We'll talk and laugh and play at games,
> So happy you and me!

9

They made their way back to the platform and across the valley. Most of the adult Nesters still waited on the slope outside the thicket. They clustered around in excitement, and plenty of those returning were willing to tell the story. But Kiet pushed forward with her arms round the zither, and the Morph was of course invisible.

Ferren helped shield her from questioning, though he was dying with curiosity himself. Why had Hypers come to the City of the Dead? Where had all the other Morphs gone? But he could see that Kiet was determined to let *her* Morph recover in peace.

"Go away!" she snapped at anyone who came too close.

To Ferren, she said, "Whatever happened is over now. He'll tell us when he's ready."

They were near the front of the crowd as the Nesters streamed back along the tunnels, returning to their nests. From the chatter going on behind him, Ferren guessed that people had now learned about the Morph on the zither.

He accompanied Kiet to her family nest and saw her settled inside. But she didn't stay settled for long. A moment later Auntie Nettish came bustling up. She looked in at the entrance, saw Kiet with the zither and shook her head.

"I won't have that thing in my home!"

"He's a Morph, not a ghost," Kiet retorted.

"He's still invisible! I couldn't bear it! Can't trust what you can't see!"

Grandpa Niot stepped up and tried to reason with her. "He's fixed himself to my zither. He won't be roaming around."

"No! He's not a proper living creature! Not natural! I'll go mad if he's there in the nest with me! He goes or I go!"

Rhinn and Tadge added their voices in support of Grandpa Niot, but it was no use. Auntie Nettish was growing more and more hysterical. Inside the nest, Kiet had fallen silent—until suddenly she marched out with the zither.

"If you put him out, you put me out too!" she declared.

Grandpa Niot looked uncomfortable. "Perhaps it's best if you find somewhere else," he said. "Just for tonight."

"I won't stay where I'm not wanted!" Kiet snorted, and marched back to the main tunnels.

Ferren went after her. He hadn't said a word during the quarrel—partly because Auntie Nettish wouldn't listen to him, and partly because he hoped to offer his own solution.

"You could stay in the spare nest with me," he suggested.

"With him too?" She held up the zither.

"Of course."

"Hmm. I suppose there's room now, isn't there?"

"She won't be coming back," said Ferren, meaning Miriael.

She looked at him thoughtfully. "All right," she said at last.

Was she thinking I might fall into a rage again? he wondered. He still felt guilty about that. He knew that his real feelings for Miriael were on an altogether higher and nobler level.

When they arrived at the spare nest, he made a point of offering her Miriael's bedding to sleep on. She nodded as though she'd expected nothing else. Then she propped the zither against the wall and crooned to the Morph.

"Here's a good place for you, here you'll be safe. We'll look after you. Sleep and forget, little one."

The Morph let out a soft peep-peep. Kiet watched over him for a minute, then turned to whisper to Ferren.

"I think he'll sleep now."

"Or whatever Morphs do," Ferren whispered back.

Another peep-peep came from the zither, a quietly contented sound.

"I love it when he does that," Kiet murmured. "Don't you love that sound?"

Ferren yawned. He was ready for sleep himself.

"I'm going to call him Peeper," she went on. "Peeper the Morph."

"He'd have had a very different name once," said Ferren.

"Yes, but he left it behind. Now he's Peeper."

10

Ferren awoke to Kiet shaking him by the shoulder.

"I think he's ready to talk. You have to come and hear."

Ferren rubbed his eyes and sat up. Bright daylight was pouring in through the entrance of the nest. Kiet went back to the zither, sat cross-legged and rested the instrument on her lap.

She was already communicating with Peeper by the time he came across.

"Go on, go on," she murmured, leaning forward to listen.

All Ferren could hear were faint, fluting sounds. He willed himself to patience. After a while, the sounds grew more and more agitated.

'Slow down, slow down," Kiet crooned to the Morph in a soothing tone. "Don't over-excite yourself, little one."

She turned to Ferren. "It *was* the Humen with flamethrowers. He says an army of them swept across the whole City like a line of fire. The Morphs had to let go of their attachments, and the hot wind from the flames drove them and carried them all into one last corner. Then the angel came to rescue them."

"What angel?" Ferren demanded. "*What angel?*"

"Not so loud!" Kiet tried to hush him, but it was already too late. Peeper burst out in a frenzy of chirruping.

"It's all right, little one. Tell us about this angel, then."

She lifted the zither from her lap and held it so that Ferren could bring his ear closer too.

"Beautiful, beautiful angel!" piped Peeper. "So-o-o beau-ootiful!"

The Morph's voice had grown louder and clearer. Ferren, leaning forward, could now make out every word.

"He came to see us. Sing to us. Many ti-i-imes. He promised to lift us up into Heaven. He said it was our true home. True-oo! Ho-o-o-o-me!"

"Did he wear a silver circlet round his brow?" Kiet drew a finger across her own forehead in illustration.

"Oooh, silver, he did, oooh. And we wanted to go up into our true ho-o-ome. But we didn't know if we should trust him. We didn't kno-o-ow! Then we had to trust him because of the Humen. They came through with their fire, and he flew in to save us. Rescue-oo-oo."

Ferren had a question to ask, but Kiet signalled him to silence.

"He came in a flying wing," Peeper went on. "So hu-u-u-u-ge! With Morphs already on it. He stopped right above us. We were in the last corner of the City. Ooo-ooh!"

"Go on," Kiet prompted.

"He said to let ourselves float up to him. Then he would rescue us. Lift us up into our true ho-o-ome. And we were all floating up to settle on his wing. But a wall fell on top of me-e-e, I couldn't get free-e-e! And nobody knew-oo! They flew away, and nobody knew-oo-oo-oooo!"

The story ended on a long, woeful wail. Ferren took the opportunity to ask Kiet his question.

"This angel was the same one you saw with Miriael, right?"

"Yes, with a silver circlet."

"Ask Peeper about Miriael. Was there another angel there too?"

"He'd have said." Kiet shook her head. "Anyway, I'm not going to ask him now. He's too upset, you can see."

"Just ask."

"No."

Kiet lowered the zither flat on her lap and hummed a gentle tune without words. Peeper's wail diminished to a small, mournful sound.

Ferren wasn't looking for an argument. He rose to his feet.

"I'll go and tell the Guardians what Peeper told us," he said. "Everybody ought to know."

Kiet wasn't looking for an argument either. "Yes, do that. Even though they won't understand."

Ferren headed for the entrance.

"Tell my friends too," she added. "*They* will."

11

Ferren had worked it all out. This other angel who could lift Morphs up into Heaven could surely lift Miriael up into Heaven too. That must be where she'd gone, back to her own kind. And now the two of them were both up there together...

He didn't mention his new explanation to Kiet. In fact, he didn't intend to talk with her about Miriael at all. However, the subject came up in a different way.

"When are you going on to the next tribe?" she asked him.

"Next tribe?"

"For joining up to the Residual Alliance."

"I haven't thought about it. The assembly of representatives is only a few weeks away."

"But still. There's time for a few more tribes first."

"Maybe."

She scowled. She was stretched out on her bedding with the zither beside her; Ferren sat gazing vacantly out through the entrance of the nest.

"Is this because of *her?*"

"Who?" he asked, although he already knew.

"Your angel. Miriael. Doesn't the Residual Alliance matter anymore if she's not helping you with it?"

"It's not that." He shook his head defensively.

"Then why?"

"You wouldn't understand."

"Understand what?"

"What she means to me."

"Ah, I was right!" She stared at him until he looked away. "You *can't* be in love with an angel."

"How do you know what I can be?"

"She's a different sort of being. Far above and beyond beings like us. You can admire her or adore her, but you can't be in love with her."

"We've been going round together for three months. We've been sharing everything."

"That's friendship, not love."

Pursuing his own thoughts, Ferren hardly heard. "I think I've been in love with her right from the start."

Kiet was silent for a while. When she spoke again, her voice was sharp and hard and scoffing. "You're not still hoping she'll come back? Are you serious?"

"I don't hope anything."

"She doesn't love you, you know."

"She doesn't have to."

"No?"

"No. I can devote my life to her and love her regardless. I don't ask anything in return."

"Seems to me you do."

"I wanted to serve her, and have her accept my service. I vowed to be loyal and true to her, so I thought she'd be the same to me. I was disappointed before, when you saw me angry with her."

"'Angry'? More like a jealous rage."

"I was wrong." His relationship to Miriael was coming clearer even as he spoke. "It makes no difference, what she does to me. I can't reject her. I'll always be loyal and true, no matter what. That's my love for her."

Kiet sniffed. "Weird sort of love."

"It's the only kind I want."

"But if you can't have her?"

"There'll never be anyone else for me, after her. She's my ideal. She'll always be my ideal. Forever and ever."

"So you'll never get over it?"

"I don't *want* to get over it."

"Hrrph!" Kiet uttered a strange sound that might have been contempt.

"I said you wouldn't understand," Ferren told her loftily.

"You're right about that." Kiet rolled over on her bedding and picked up the zither. "Me and Peeper are going out for some fresh air.

We'll leave you with your forever love. I'm sure you…"

Instead of completing the sentence, she ducked out through the entrance.

Yes, thought Ferren. *It must be hard for an ordinary Residual to understand.*

12

"Why are boys so stupid?" Kiet addressed the question to Peeper, though she didn't expect an answer. "Stupid, stupid, *stupid!*"

She had come to her special pool with the overhanging foliage. It was late in the afternoon, the weather was changing, and there was no sun to warm the sandstone. She propped Peeper's zither against a root and sat facing it. She had to have *someone* to listen to her bitterness. A welter of feelings still churned inside her.

"Did you hear him, Peeper? Going on about his great love! It's all in his head! She doesn't love him back, she can't, she's an angel. But he'll keep loving *her* all on his own. Forever and ever! Can you believe it?"

Peeper uttered a chirrup that might have meant anything.

"An *angel*, Peeper! As if! Aiming so high above himself! He'd sooner have an impossible love that can never happen rather than anything real that could. His ideal, he calls her! And he wants to preserve the ideal in his head when even *she* doesn't live up to it. He knows she doesn't, yet still… *Stupid!*"

She banged the flat of her hand on the sandstone, then rubbed her palm where it hurt. A moment later, she went on in a quieter voice.

"Such a weird idea of love. All worship at a distance. So pure and bloodless." She shook her head. "And I thought First Intimacies was silly!"

She remembered the ritual with the oil that she and Bross had been supposed to enact. She didn't know what her own idea of love would look like, but she knew it was very different to Ferren's worship at a distance *and* First Intimacies. Perhaps something that grew between two people without either of them willing it to exist…

She gazed at the zither without really seeing it. Peeper's soft peeping sounds ran on like a background to her thoughts.

"I'd have gone with him, Peeper. I was going to offer, when he went on to the next tribe. I could've shown him where the Fieldsfolk live, or the Skinfellows. For the sake of the Residual Alliance, I'd have left my home and family and—"

Peeper came suddenly to life with a wail of protest. Kiet interpreted the sound and soothed the Morph with a more gentle, crooning tone.

"No, no, not you, of course not. I'd have taken you with me. Anyway, it won't happen now. He's lost his commitment to the Alliance since his angel left him. You'll see. He'll just keep delaying and putting it off."

Peeper subsided once more into soft peeping sounds. Kiet went on with her own reflections.

"Yes, he'll stay moping around, and call it love. He's fixed on his idea, Peeper, he won't give it up. Just like a boy!" She curled her lip. "It has to be the end of the world when things go against them. But it's *never* the end of the world. Life goes on, whether they like it or not."

She realised suddenly that the light was sinking and the air was damp: not cold, but humid. She shivered.

Yes, life goes on, she thought, *and I have to look after you, little one.* Ferren's stupid idea of love wasn't worth worrying about. She couldn't do anything about his unhappiness anyway. Whereas Peeper's unhappiness...

She wondered. Was the Morph a little less unhappy than when she'd first found him? Of course, he still missed all the other Morphs who'd gone off up into Heaven, but he did seem a little more cheerful now. He knew he wasn't completely alone, at least.

In fact, she wasn't sure that his fellow-Morphs *had* gone off up into Heaven. It seemed such an odd coincidence that the other angel and his flying wing had turned up at just the right moment to rescue them. And why had the Humen chosen to burn them out of their City? A doubt had nagged at the back of her mind ever since she'd heard Peeper's story.

But she couldn't do anything about that either. She picked up the zither and rose to her feet.

"Time to go home, little one," she said.

'Home' meant the spare nest and Ferren still nursing his great love.

She hoped he'd said all he had to say on the subject. Even so, she felt depressed at the mere thought of it.

13

The weather had changed. For days, a mist enshrouded the Nesters' territory, and the sun was no more than a lighter patch in the sky. Inside the thicket, the bushes and shrubs looked grey and ghostly; outside, the visibility was down to thirty paces. It was like being in a cloud.

Ferren was glad of the mist, which gave him an excuse for postponing his journey. He could hardly find his way to the next tribe if he couldn't see the landmarks by which to direct himself.

He had collected the two feathers from Miriael's wing that he'd trodden into the ground. With loving care, he restored them to their original whiteness, then rolled them into the top of his loincloth, as before. He touched them frequently through the cloth, and every time it was as though he renewed the vow he'd made three months ago.

Forever and ever, he told himself. He would be loyal and true to the angel even if she wasn't loyal and true to him. He'd never expected his love to be returned, but now it was all sacrifice, all self-denial. He felt a kind of moral elevation in his thoughts as he touched the feathers through the cloth.

He had had no more meetings with the Guardians. The Nesters he met in the tunnels often looked at him with curiosity, seemingly surprised that he was still in their territory. But they didn't ask questions, and he didn't explain.

Kiet kept casting looks his way too, and he sensed her unvoiced disapproval. *She* thought he should be adding more tribes to the Residual Alliance, and was disappointed by his inactivity. Sometimes he wondered if she wanted him gone, so that she and the Morph could have the spare nest to themselves...

On the other hand, she relied on him to take care of Peeper when she had to go out. She couldn't take the zither to mealtimes with her stock, when Auntie Nettish and others would be present. Ferren was pleased to be trusted with the role, though not so pleased when she said, "You'll be good company for each other. Both left behind and down in the dumps."

One time, she went off for lunch, then came back just a few minutes later.

"Do you want to hear something interesting?" she said. "I know you're not interested in much these days."

"What is it?"

"There are lights moving around over the City of the Dead. They think it could be angels."

Ferren *was* interested. "How many?"

"Three, I heard."

So, not Miriael and that other angel, thought Ferren. *And Miriael has lost her light anyway.* Still, something was happening.

"Go and see for yourself," Kiet suggested.

"What about you?"

"I'll come. Soon as I find someone to look after Peeper."

Some minutes later, Ferren emerged from the thicket and joined a crowd of Nesters peering out through the mist across the valley. The walls and buildings of the City of the Dead were obscured, but three blurred glows of light showed through the obscurity. They moved and hovered over various parts of the City.

"What are they doing?"

"Inspecting."

"Searching for something."

"Because of the fire."

"Because the Humen came there."

The guesses flew thick and fast, but they were only guesses. Some of the Nesters looked to Ferren for answers, but he could only shrug.

A little later, Kiet turned up. She made her way through the crowd to stand beside Ferren. She observed for a while in silence, then said, "We should go and find out what they're doing."

There were shocked gasps from the Nesters around, and even Ferren was taken aback.

"What, walk up and question them?"

"No, spy on them."

"I'll do it," said a voice nearby, and Ferren recognised Kiet's friend, Flens.

"Me too!" This time it was Kiet's brother, Tadge.

"Wait!" cried someone else. "They're coming out!"

It was true: the three lights were no longer hovering over the City of the Dead. Now flying close together, they passed over the City's walls, which were momentarily illuminated through the mist. They came swooping across the valley, and for a moment it looked as though they were heading straight towards the thicket.

"They've seen us!" "They're coming for us!" The Nesters shrank back and made ready to run.

But the lights turned aside midway across the valley. Now they were heading upstream. There was a general sigh of relief.

"I'm going to follow them," said Kiet, and strode off at once.

Flens set off after her, then Tadge, then several other young Nesters. After a moment, Ferren went too.

14

The lights sailed further and further upstream. It was easy to follow them through the mist; Ferren hoped that the followers weren't so visible themselves.

He hurried to catch up with Kiet at the head of the group.

"Where are they going?" he asked, and pointed ahead. "What's *there?*"

"Nothing. Just hills." Kiet appeared puzzled. "A whole lot of small, grassy hills."

Everyone was puffing and panting by the time they left the valley. The lights passed over the tops of the hills, and the group followed in the troughs between the hills. Although they had fallen a long way behind, a distant glow still led them on.

Then, all at once, even the glow disappeared.

"They must've come down behind the hills," said Ferren. "They'll be on the ground now."

"They'll have reached the place, then," Kiet agreed. "Whatever it is."

They fixed the direction in their minds and headed towards it. It took another ten minutes' walking before they arrived.

The place turned out to be a level area of grassy ground like an arena encircled by hills. Mysterious, flat-roofed structures occupied most of the space, dim shapes in the mist. The three lights had separated out and were moving about among the structures.

"I never knew *this* was here," muttered Kiet.

"I bet the Humen built it," said Ferren.

The regular rows in which the structures were arranged reminded him of huts in the Humen Camp. However, these structures were much simpler, mere canvas awnings erected on metal poles.

Ferren and Kiet advanced towards the nearest awning, with the other young Nesters following. Then Kiet made a sudden hop. Ferren wondered why—until something sharp stabbed the sole of his foot. He stifled a cry of pain, looked down and saw a small shard of shiny metal.

In fact, many bits of leftover metal lay scattered in the grass, along with screws, nuts, bolts and rivets. Kiet was already turning to the rest of the group, putting a finger to her lips and pointing out the hidden hazards. More cautiously, the group continued forward to stand under the awning.

Meanwhile, the three lights had finished inspecting the structures; now they converged to a central spot. They seemed to hover a foot in the air without ever actually touching ground.

"What're they doing now?" Ferren muttered.

"Maybe going to talk," Kiet whispered behind her hand.

Her guess proved correct. Even muffled by mist, their angel voices sounded melodic and beautiful.

"Discussing what they've discovered," said Kiet.

"You can hear what they're saying?"

"No. Just what it looks like."

"We need to go closer."

Ferren scanned the possibilities. The awnings were all open, and there were no screening walls. But two rows ahead, under one particular awning, stood a solid-looking workbench.

"Behind that," he whispered, pointing.

Kiet nodded, and they set off in a crouching run. The rest of the group followed close at their heels. If anyone stood on sharp metal, they kept their mouths clamped shut.

The workbench wasn't perfect cover, but it was good enough in the mist. Everyone crowded behind with their heads ducked low. On top of the bench were massive, lumpish shapes of Humen machinery.

When Ferren peered out around the machinery, the three blurred lights appeared to be bowing to one another as they talked. They were now only twenty or thirty yards away, and he could hear fragments of their discussion.

"What were they..." "Assembling something big..." "A dozen transport machines..." "Strange place to..."

All at once, the talk broke off, and there was a moment of silence. Then one of the lights shone out suddenly brighter.

"Show yourselves!" came the command. "Who's there?"

Ferren and Kiet looked at one another. Nobody in the group had made even the tiniest sound.

"On the count of three, we shall blast you out of existence," said another voice, equally authoritative.

The mist seemed to dissolve under the intensifying radiance of the light in the middle. Ferren found he could now see the angel at the heart of the light: a tall, majestic figure with sixfold wings. He held a raised sword in his right hand.

"*One!*"

"What will they do to us?" whispered Kiet.

"Fry us to a crisp," Ferren whispered back.

"What do we do?"

"*Two!*"

The radiance of the angels on either side was also intensifying. They weren't as tall as the figure in the middle, but hardly less awe-inspiring. They wore purple robes, and their swords were sheathed in scabbards.

"They probably think we're Humen," whispered Kiet.

"We're not."

"No."

"I'll show them."

Ferren rose to his full height and walked out from behind the workbench.

"Me too," said Kiet, and walked out after him.

15

It was the hardest walk Ferren had ever walked. He kept putting one foot in front of the other, but his legs trembled, and he expected to collapse at any minute. Although he tried to look straight at the angels, their dazzle grew overwhelming. He narrowed his eyes to the thinnest of slits, almost blinded. Their radiance seemed to beat on his skin like a midsummer sun at noon—except that the rays felt cool, not hot.

At least he had support: Kiet came with him every step of the way. Even without turning, he could sense her constant presence always half a pace behind.

When the angel in the middle made a movement, he was sure his last moment had come. But it was only a lowering of the arm, a lowering of the sword.

"These are Residuals," said a deep and resonant voice.

Immediately, the light from all three globes diminished to a more bearable glow. Ferren heard Kiet's gasp of relief. As the spots cleared from before his eyes, he saw that he'd advanced much further than he'd realised. The angels were now a mere half-dozen yards away.

"Stay where you are!' ordered the angel in the middle, as Ferren went to take a backwards step. Ferren froze.

"Residuals!' the other two murmured in surprise. "What are they doing here?"

All three angels had long, flowing hair and sharply etched features, with wide, pale foreheads and intensely blue eyes. They appeared very stern and severe.

"We were…" Ferren began; then his throat closed over.

"We saw your lights and followed," Kiet brought out.

"Just curious," Ferren concluded.

"Where are you from?" asked the angel on the right. "Do you live near here?"

"Yes, in our thicket." Kiet pointed the approximate direction, and Ferren let her answer for both of them. "The tribe of the Nesters."

The angels looked at one another. Then the one in the middle took charge again. "Do you know anything about *this?*"

He swept out an arm to encompass the rows of awnings all around. Crackles of energy accompanied the sudden gesture.

"No." Ferren shook his head.

"None of us knew in the Nesters," added Kiet. "These things couldn't have been here long."

"They haven't," said the angel on the left.

Ferren was still in awe of the angels, but no longer so fearful. Apparently, he and Kiet weren't about to be incinerated in a flash of light. Kiet must have felt the same, because she ventured to speak unprompted.

"We followed you from the City of the Dead," she said.

"The ruined city?" The angel in the middle frowned. "Yes, we were there. What do you know about the fire?"

"It was the Humen," said Kiet.

"With flamethrowers," added Ferren.

"And they drove out the Morphs," Kiet finished off.

"Ah, there were Morphs?" The angel in the middle raised his white, craggy eyebrows in surprise. "What does that mean, I wonder."

"Perhaps we should tell them all we know," the angel on the right suggested. "They may be able to contribute some information."

The angel in the middle was clearly the highest in power and authority. He thought for a moment, then came to a decision. "Very well. Let them be told."

The other two took a step forward.

"I am the Seraph Cedrion," said the one on the right. "A high archon and a commander in the South."

"I am the Seraph Bethor," said the one on the left. "I share in the rule of the provinces of Heaven."

"And here"—both turned towards the angel in the middle—"you

stand before Uriel, Angel of the Presence and Angel of Destruction. One of our four greatest archangels."

Ferren bowed his head, with a sense that humility was expected. Uriel said nothing, and it was Cedrion who began the telling.

"Several days ago, one of our angel observers over the Bankstown Camp reported a large force of two hundred Hypers and fifteen transport machines leaving the Camp and travelling south. We sent the Forty-Third Company to keep watch on them."

"They travelled as far as this spot in the hills." Bethor indicated the mist-shrouded scene around them. "They set up these camouflage awnings so that our observers couldn't see what they were doing from above. Then, later, they abandoned the place, marched to the ruined city and set fire to it. They're now on their way back to the Bankstown Camp."

Cedrion took over again. "But in the meanwhile, one special transport machine had already left to return to the Camp. Naturally, the Forty-Third Company had their orders and stayed watching here. But our observers above the Camp saw it approach and were puzzled by the speed it was travelling."

Cedrion paused and handed the narrative back to Bethor. "They decided on an impromptu discovery operation. One angel swooped down to distract the Hypers, the other swooped down and plucked away the camouflage sheet over the trolley top. Underneath was an angel captured and bound. Of course, they couldn't rescue her, they didn't have the numbers to fight. They had to watch as the machine carried her on into the Camp."

"No doubt to the surgeries," added Cedrion.

Ferren could hardly breathe for sudden hope—and dread. "What angel?" he whispered.

The archangel Uriel uttered an angry sound and chose to answer himself. "We call her an angel, but she was an abnormal case. She had lost her aura, yet still survived in this terrestrial atmosphere. She had taken to consuming mortal food."

Ferren gasped "*Miriael!*"

He might have fallen if Kiet hadn't steadied him with a hand on his shoulder.

"Yes, Miriael. Previously a junior warrior angel and the Fourteenth Angel of Observance. How did you know the name?"

But Ferren was beyond words, and it was Kiet who answered. "I knew her too. She was travelling with *him*, and they were visiting my tribe. He thought she'd gone back up into Heaven."

"Of course not." Uriel's expression was grim. "We don't know what happened to her. Only her end in the Bankstown Camp."

The world spun round and round in Ferren's head. Everything he'd believed had been wrong! Miriael hadn't gone back up into Heaven! Doctor Saniette had captured her! He struggled in vain to take it all in. It was a mere background noise in his ears when Kiet addressed Uriel.

"You haven't heard about the other angel, have you?"

16

Kiet had been thinking it through. The facts she already knew and the information from Bethor and Cedrion…a force of two hundred Hypers engaged in some mysterious activity close by the Nesters' territory…Miriael captured and transported to the Humen Camp. She fitted the pieces of the puzzle together in her mind.

When Uriel said, "What other angel?" she was almost ready with her answer.

"One question first." She held up a hand. "Have you had a lot of Morphs arrive recently in Heaven?"

"Morphs? Of course not."

"About four days ago?"

"No."

"We don't allow Morphs into Heaven," Bethor confirmed. "None have been admitted for a thousand years."

"All lies, then!" Kiet snapped her fingers. "Thought so."

The three angels were growing impatient, especially Uriel.

"Explain yourself!" he commanded.

So Kiet told them about the beautiful male angel she'd seen having a very private conversation with Miriael. "Like they were a couple in love or something." Then she repeated what Peeper had said, about the same angel visiting the Morphs in the City of the Dead and promising to take them up to Heaven. "But when they couldn't decide, the Humen came with flamethrowers and *made* them go with him." She also described the flying wing as Peeper had described it. "They had to float up and attach themselves to it."

The angels looked incredulous. "A flying wing? What sort of a thing is that?"

Kiet swept a hand towards the awnings all around. "Maybe the sort of thing those two hundred Hypers were assembling here?"

Uriel's brow was black as thunder. "Let me understand this. Are you claiming that one of our angels actually *collaborated* with the Humen?"

"Yes."

The shock showed on their faces.

"Impossible," murmured Cedrion.

"Inconceivable," agreed Bethor.

Uriel's voice rose threateningly. "No angel would ever do that!"

"Nor lie neither?" Kiet stood her ground. "So what happened to those Morphs that were supposed to be coming up to Heaven?"

Bethor shook his head. "Describe this angel, if you saw him."

"Very beautiful, like I said. Very pale. He had a silver circlet round his forehead."

The angels looked at one another, startled. "A silver circlet?"

Then Cedrion pursed his lips and grew thoughtful. "I never imagined this could be relevant," he said slowly. "Last night I received a report that the angel Asmodai has been missing for several days."

"Asmodai?" Uriel grew thoughtful too. "One of the Fallen Angels?"

"A Luciferian. Supposedly repentant. But there have been questions about him ever since the Weather Wars."

"Overreach, as I remember." Uriel nodded. "He went off on his own research."

"Does anyone know what he'd been researching lately?" asked Bethor.

"You believe me now?" Kiet tried to break in, but the angels weren't listening.

"This will need investigating," said Cedrion.

"It will need reporting to the War Council," said Uriel. "Evil beyond all evil, if it's true."

"Nothing like it since the Satan himself," Bethor agreed.

Their globes pulsed with a stronger radiance, and all three lifted their eyes up to the sky. They were obviously about to leave.

"*Wait!*"

The sudden cry made Kiet jump. It came from Ferren, emerging from his stupor. The angels paused their ascent as he flung out his arms.

"What about Miriael?" he demanded.

"She's with the new Doctor now," answered Uriel. "There's nothing we can do."

Ferren was aghast, and Kiet spoke up for him. "But *she* never collaborated with the Humen. Don't you see? All she did was fall in love with an evil angel."

Uriel looked stern but also sorry. "Yes, I see. He may have used her as the price of Humen assistance. But there's still nothing we can do."

"We would rescue her in our own interest, if we could," said Cedrion. "The last thing we want is for an angel to fall into Humen hands. But the Bankstown Camp is too well shielded."

"We've tried to break in before," added Bethor.

"*I* broke in!" cried Ferren. "If I can do it, why can't—"

"Then *you* should rescue her," said Uriel. "Believe me, I hope you can. But we can't."

In the next moment, all three angels soared upwards into the sky. Kiet felt her hair lift from her head in the rushing wind of their departure. Ferren still stood with his arms outstretched and pleading.

17

No sooner had the angels vanished upwards into the mist than the other young Nesters came rushing out from behind the workbench. Kiet swung to face them.

"We heard!"

"We saw it all!"

"You were so brave!"

They were all yammering at once. She flapped her arms to quieten them down.

"What did you hear?" she asked.

"You were talking about the Humen!"

"And the Morphs."

"The fire in the City of the Dead."

"And some other evil angel."

Kiet had the impression that half of what they'd heard had gone over their heads.

"Then they wouldn't rescue *his* angel!" cried young Tadge, pointing to Ferren. "She's being held prisoner in a Humen Camp. But they won't even try!"

"Worse than 'held prisoner'," muttered Ferren, who had stopped staring up at the sky.

"It's the same Camp *you* broke into, isn't it?" Flens addressed Ferren directly. "You told us about it, when you went searching for your sister. You broke in, but they say they can't."

"I crept in low down through a pipe," said Ferren. "I suppose they couldn't do that."

Kiet snorted. "Or *wouldn't!* Wouldn't want to dirty themselves!"

"I bet we could do it," said Tadge.

A sudden silence descended on the group. For a moment, nobody looked at anyone else.

"I'd do it," said Tadge. "If *he* leads the way."

Rhinn spoke dismissively, as older sister to younger brother. "It's not an adventure, Tadge. You're far too young."

"But I'm not," said Kiet.

"Nor am I," said Flens.

"Nor me," said Bross.

Rhinn shook her head. "You must be mad."

"Maybe we are." Flens grinned.

"We're in the Residual Alliance now," Gibby piped up. "So we *ought* to fight the Humen."

"In our own way," said Ethany. "Secretly."

In the next moment, they were all shouting and clamouring over the top of one another.

"A rescue mission!"

"A secret expedition!"

"Into the enemy Camp!"

"Save the angel!"

Not every voice spoke up, but the general mood was all in favour.

"And *he* has to lead us," cried Tadge, pointing. He'd already included himself in the adventure again.

"No," said Ferren.

Kiet spun towards him with a frown. "What do you mean, *no?*"

"No, I won't lead anyone on an expedition into the Bankstown Camp. It's a doomsday mission. You don't understand the danger."

"We understand what Selectors are like," Ethany protested.

"We followed you into the City of the Dead," said Flens.

"No," Ferren repeated. "This isn't your business."

"Don't you want to rescue your angel?" Kiet demanded.

"I'll do it on my own."

Kiet was dumbfounded. The other young Nesters bombarded Ferren with objections.

"Why would you do that?"

"We *want* to help!"

"Give us a chance!"

"If it's so dangerous—"

"You need all the help you can get!"

But Kiet had been studying Ferren's face. "You've been crying," she said.

"I have not."

"Yes, I can see wet on your cheeks."

He shook his head angrily. "I don't want any help, and I'll rescue Miriael on my own."

He swung on his heel and marched off into the mist. Everyone stared after him, open-mouthed. Kiet was the first to react.

"Wait here!" she told the others. "I'll talk to him. He doesn't mean it. He *can't* mean it."

18

Ferren was a grey silhouette in the mist as Kiet ran after him. She caught him up just before he reached the final row of awnings. "What's wrong with you?" she demanded.

He shook off her hand as she clutched at his arm. She darted forward instead, to stand blocking his way.

He stopped and scowled. "It's me and her. Nothing to do with you."

"Oh?" She curled her lip. "Is this more of your vow to serve her? Is this you being true and loyal forever and ever?"

"You wouldn't understand."

"Phah! You like saying that! I think you *want* this to be a doomsday mission. I think you want to die for love so you can prove how much you've always loved her. Then she might be grateful and love you back—except she'll never get to hear about it. You'll be dead, and she'll be—whatever they're going to do to her."

His only response was to push past her and walk on. She ran round in front to block him and bring him to a halt again.

"You really think you can rescue her on your own? You think it'll be as easy as sneaking round in their Camp like you did before."

He was breathing heavily. "It won't be easy. It'll be almost impossible. But it's what I have to do."

"'What I have to do!' Listen to yourself! You want to play the doomed hero, don't you?"

"I was wrong about Miriael. I blamed her for going back up to Heaven and leaving me. I need to do the right thing now."

Kiet sniffed. *Miriael probably intended to go back up into Heaven anyway,* she thought. But she didn't utter the thought aloud.

"So now you have to make amends? You have to punish yourself and die for her?"

"I'll do everything I can to rescue her."

Kiet shook her head. "Not true."

Ferren looked puzzled.

"You're not doing everything you can to rescue her," Kiet pointed out. "If you were, you'd accept help when people offer it. She'll have a better chance of being rescued by a whole team of people. A better chance than you going in to get yourself killed."

"I don't want other people getting themselves killed."

"Or you don't want to share your heroic role? You're so perverse. When you've got friends who'll help you—"

"They're *your* friends."

"My friends can be yours."

"Nobody risks their life out of friendship."

"No? Only for love? Only for your stupid idea of love, that's all in your head anyway?" Kiet wished she could pick him up shake him... shake all the nonsensical ideas right out of him. "I'd rather have friends like my friends than have someone love me with your sort of love."

Ferren glared at her, and she glared right back.

"If you really cared for Miriael, you'd do everything you could to rescue her. Instead of playing the doomed hero. You're more in love with yourself. It's all selfishness."

Ferren stopped glaring. He was considering the new perspective, she could see.

"Friends care for each other and do things for each other," she went on. "If you were a friend to your angel..."

He sucked thoughtfully at his lips. "I *thought* we were friends as well," he said at last.

"You were."

"What?"

"I mean, the idea of being in love was all on your side. But she was a friend to you as you were a friend to her."

"You think so?"

"I was amazed. Everyone was amazed. No one would've believed a Celestial could be a friend to one of us."

"Oh."

"The most amazing thing ever. You don't realise how lucky you were. And still could be. But if you want to throw it all away for..."

Kiet didn't finish her sentence, and didn't need to. An entirely new expression had appeared on Ferren's face. She had converted him.

"All right," he said.

"All right? So you'll accept our help?"

"Yes. I suppose it makes sense."

"'Course it does." She plucked at his arm, and this time he didn't shake her off. "Let's go and tell the others before they give up on you."

As they made their way back through the rows of awnings, Kiet offered some further advice.

"And be positive. No more doom and gloom. No more doomsday mission. They need you to lead and inspire them. Show confidence."

The young Nesters were still waiting in the mist. Their eyes lit up when they saw that Ferren was coming back with Kiet.

"He's changed his mind," she told them.

"Yes, I'll lead anyone who chooses to come with me," he said in a loud, ringing voice. "An expedition into the Bankstown Camp! If you want to come—my thanks! I'll be very glad to have your help."

19

The sun was setting by the time they returned to the Nesters territory. They planned to start off at dawn, meeting on the flat, grassy field in front of the thicket. Kiet went off to her family nest to pack food and clothes for a few days. Then she collected Peeper on his zither from Bross's parents, who'd been taking care of him.

"Something to tell you, little one." She put down her backpack and sat leaning against a bush with the zither on her lap. Moon and stars were blanketed by the mist, and the night was very dark.

"I'm going to be gone for a few days. Ferren too. But I'll ask Bross's parents to look after you again, shall I?"

Peeper began to utter a doleful sound on the word "gone", and the sound rose higher and higher until she had to break off.

"Why 'gone'? Why-y-y? Why-e-e-e-e-e?"

"Shush! I'm going to a very dangerous place. Not safe for you."

"I'll be left all alo-o-o-o-o-ne!"

"No, you'll be with Bross's parents. You like them, don't you?"

"I want to be with you-o-o-o! Let me come too-o-o-o!"

"Shush! Shush!" Kiet rocked the zither gently back and forth, but the Morph was inconsolable.

"Let me-e-e-e! With you-o-o-o-o-o-o!"

"It's too dangerous, little one."

"No-o-o! Doesn't matter dangerous! With you-o-o-o!"

"How could I carry you all the way?"

"Tie me to your pack! Ple-e-e-ease!"

Kiet considered. It *was* possible, she could fasten the zither onto her backpack. But still…

"I'm not taking you into the Camp," she said firmly.

"As far as you can! Then I'll be happy-e-e! As far as you can!"

He was so mournful and pleading, she didn't have the heart to say no.

"Only the journey, then. Not inside the Camp."

"Thank you! Thank you-o-o!"

She headed back to the spare nest. Ferren had completed his packing and was already asleep. Very quietly, she lay down on her bedding. After all the day's events and decisions, she hardly expected to drop off straightaway. But she did—and slept through until morning.

She woke to the sound of Ferren's voice. He had his pack on his back, and was holding her pack out to her.

"Wait, there's something I have to do first," she said.

She found some cords and tied the zither onto her pack. Peeper let out a soft peep-peep of contentment. Ferren's eyes widened in surprise, but he made no comment.

Five minutes later, they came out to the field in front of the thicket. Curling wisps of vapour rose from the ground like steam, and the sun shone more strongly than it had shone for days.

"I think the mist's lifting," said Ferren.

"Just at the right time," Kiet agreed.

Five volunteers were present and waiting: Kiet's closest friends and family. There was thin, gangling Flens with his big nose, roly-poly Ethany and Gibby with her fair hair and dainty features. Tadge had included himself, and so too, unexpectedly, had Rhinn.

"I'm only coming to keep an eye on you all," she said. "To make sure you don't do anything reckless."

"We already are," laughed Flens.

Bross was the only one still to turn up. They stood around yawning and blinking and rubbing their eyes. When Bross appeared a few minutes later, Ferren pointed the direction and set off.

"We head north until we see an overbridge," he said. "Then we just follow it all the way to the Humen Camp. Every overbridge leads there."

20

Miriael had lost all sense of time. Lying on a trolley in a darkened room, day and night had ceased to exist. She knew she was inside the Bankstown Camp, but nothing told her if she was already in the surgeries or in some other building.

Hypers entered her room from time to time, but they didn't talk. They had transferred her from the flat top of the transport machine to a hospital trolley, and they had cut away her original bindings of tape. She was fastened to her new bed by tight, rubbery cuffs around her wrists and ankles. For food and drink, she had a bottle of sweet, fruity syrup suspended over her head, from which she drank through a tube.

She was startled when her room door was unlocked and an angel entered. The darkness in which she dwelt was instantly banished by the radiance of his aura. Unaccustomed to strong light, she had to close her eyes against the dazzle. But she didn't need to see to know who it was.

"Asmodai," she groaned.

The edge of his aura approached and touched the side of her trolley. She still didn't look at him even when she opened her eyes. The black silhouette of a Hyper stood outlined in the doorway.

"Not pleased to see me? And after I made a special request to call on you, too."

She could tell he was smiling by the sound of his voice. Smiling and beautiful, with that sincere and sorrowful look in his eyes... All a lie!

"Doctor Saniette seems to be taking his time," he went on. "I thought he'd have had his surgeons start the dissection by now. I'm paying a visit for a couple of days, I must ask him."

Miriael gritted her teeth. "You're a...a..."

"Words fail you? Something to do with traitor and treachery, perhaps? Ah, poor Miriael, you have only yourself to blame. You should've known better than to fall in love with an angel."

She sneaked a glance at him, and he was exactly as she'd been picturing, exactly as she remembered. Even now, the perfection of his features took her breath away. But the evil in that perfection...

"Yes, I played my role well, didn't I? I surprised myself by how convincing I was. I think I must have sensed it and borrowed it from you, from everything you wished me to be. But, of course, as a being of pure spirit, I can't possibly fall in love in that way. It's beneath my nature."

"I thought you were a Watcher," Miriael brought out.

Asmodai laughed. "One of those pathetic creatures? *Please!* That was a tale I had to spin when you nearly found me out. Quite humiliating in the moment, believe me. However, you were in love with me long before then."

"No." Miriael denied it, though she knew it was true.

"Yes, you were in love with me," he continued smoothly. "Even though you made my skin crawl with your impurity and your degraded body."

For the first time, she raised her eyes and stared straight at him. "I may be impure, but at least I'm not evil."

"No, you're corrupted. And I may be what you call evil, but at least I remain a being of pure spirit. Infinitely far above you, poor Miriael."

He doesn't care about whether he's evil, she thought. Nothing she could attack him with would have any effect. She looked away.

"If you came here to gloat, you can leave now," she said. "I've finished talking to you."

"Gloat? Oh no! How inane! You should think more highly of me. I came to thank you."

"*Thank* me?" In her astonishment, she forgot about not talking.

"Indeed, for a most fascinating experience. I may not have the kind of nature that could fall in love with you, but I've enjoyed letting you fall in love with me. An indirect pleasure, as it were. It's been quite delicious, watching the feeling grow and grow in you, until you were utterly at its mercy. So helpless and hopeless! And all for me! Very gratifying! So thank you for the experience."

He was mocking her; she knew; even worse, he was telling the truth. She felt indescribably reduced and belittled.

Just leave, she thought, and clenched her mind against his words. *Leave, leave, leave!*

And finally he left.

"Goodbye, then," he said with a laugh. "I hope it was equally fascinating for you, though I don't suppose it was. Goodbye, poor Miriael."

21

The next time Miriael's room door opened, four Hypers of a different kind trooped in. Clad from top to toe in suits of white rubber, they looked like medical attendants rather than her usual black-suited warders. Miriael guessed at once that the moment of her dissection had arrived.

Another difference was that they spoke to her. "We're taking you to the operating theatre," one said. "It's all connected up for transmission to Doctor Saniette."

"Doctor Saniette? Won't he be there?"

"Not in person. He'll be overseeing it."

"Lie still now," a second attendant told her.

Compared to ordinary Hypers, their voices were smoother and quieter—and somehow more sinister. They wheeled her on her trolley out from the room and along a succession of corridors. Miriael registered light-panels on the ceiling and bare, white-tiled walls. A sharp smell of disinfectant lingered everywhere.

After what seemed like endless turns to the left or right, the two attendants in front opened a double door, and the two behind propelled the trolley through. The double door closed with a soft, slow swish.

Miriael found herself in a room bathed in icy, blueish light. All around were glass-fronted machines that winked red and green and gave off a low, continuous hum. More white-suited attendants sat at the machines. In the middle of the room, a battery of stronger lights lit up an empty space of floor.

"Here she is," said one of Miriael's four attendants. They wheeled the trolley forward and stationed it under the battery of lights.

"Now step back." Another set of Hypers clustered around the trolley and peered down at her. They were not only clad in white rubber, but wore white medical coats. Gauze masks covered their mouthslits, stethoscopes hung down around their necks.

A moment later, there was a brief pinging sound. Then loudspeakers crackled into life.

"Is she in position?" a strange, amplified voice demanded.

"Yes, Doctor Saniette."

Swivelling her head, Miriael saw that one surgeon wore a metal collar that held a microphone on a stalk in front of his chin.

"Equipment all ready and prepared?"

"Yes, Doctor."

"Mark the first incision."

"First incision being marked."

The surgeon with the microphone nodded to a colleague, who stepped forward and drew what looked like a pencil from a pouch strapped over his chest. He hovered the point of the pencil just in front of Miriael's right ear.

"Two inches long, a quarter inch deep," ordered the voice of Doctor Saniette. "No more, no—"

The voice cut out, the battery of lights cut out. The hum of the machines faded to silence, and the tiny red and green lights on the machines stopped winking. There were gasps and exclamations all around the operating theatre.

"What the—?"

After the gasps and exclamations came the curses. Their voices were no longer smooth and quiet, but tense and edgy.

"Dratted power's gone down!"

"It *can't* happen now!"

"Must be sabotage!"

"Not *again!*"

"I'll go check outside."

Miriael lay very still. In the darkness, she could hear footsteps moving away from the trolley. Had she been saved?

The voices talked on.

"You'd think they'd have caught him by now."

"They still don't know how he gets into our machines."

"Maybe it's more than one. Maybe a whole gang of them."

"This is the first sabotage since Doctor Saniette took over."

"*He'll* work it out."

The talk rambled on as they waited for the power to return. They sounded angry and impatient.

Then the double door swished, and a voice called out. "It's not just us! I checked! Half the Camp's gone black! This is the worst ever!"

Some of the Hypers went out to check for themselves; the rest hung around, grumbling. Miriael prayed that the lights would stay off forever.

Ten minutes later, though, the battery of lights flickered and came back on.

"Idiot technicians took their time," muttered one surgeon.

"We're supposed to be a priority zone here," said another.

Again they gathered around Miriael's trolley, peering down. But then came a cry from an attendant by the machines.

"It's not coming back up."

The surgeons turned. "Go through the startup process."

"Reset the settings."

"Don't you have power?"

"Yes, power but no function," answered the attendant.

"Same here," growled another attendant.

"And here," added another.

"Keep trying," ordered the surgeon with the microphone. "Try everything."

From where she lay, Miriael could see that none of the lights on the machines were winking red or green. There was no hum either, only sounds of frustration from the attendants as they pressed buttons and toggled switches in vain.

"That was more than a blackout," said one. "I think it was a power surge."

"Must've been," another confirmed. "I've got a burned-out network here."

The surgeon with the microphone swore profusely. "And I'm the one has to tell Doctor Saniette!" he snarled.

He lowered his voice and spoke into the microphone. "Doctor, I have bad news."

There was not even a crackle from the loudspeakers. He tried raising his voice, tapping the microphone, fiddling with various knobs on the collar round his neck. Still no response.

"It's gone dead!" he raged. "The connection's down!"

"You won't fix it again in a hurry," said the attendant who'd first spoken up. "If at all."

The surgeon stamped across, seized the attendant by both ears and twisted until he produced a scream of pain. Then he stamped back to the trolley.

"Why are you all watching? The dissection's over for today. Don't just stand there." He kicked at a wheel of the trolley. "Transport this specimen back to her room."

22

"Well, well, this *is* unexpected."

It was Asmodai again, lighting up her room with his aura. Miriael, reprieved from immediate dissection, retorted with spirit.

"You must be disappointed."

"Ah, Miriael, it doesn't matter to me what happens to you. Survive as long as you can. Although I doubt it'll be for much longer. I've just come from a discussion with Doctor Saniette."

"Phuh!" Miriael put all her contempt into the sound. "Humen-lover!"

"Hardly that. My path and Doctor Saniette's run side by side for a while. How it'll turn out in the end, who knows?"

"I do."

"Oh?" His smile conveyed complete indifference to her opinion. "At the moment, the Doctor's quite consumed by this sabotage business. It's been going on a few years, did you know? But gradually advancing from minor inconveniences to serious damage. The idea of a mystery saboteur—or saboteurs—inside his own Camp seems very unsettling to him. He seeks absolute control over everything around him, I suspect. And absolute obedience." He laughed. "Perhaps he's not aware of *my* history."

He was referring to his past as a follower of Lucifer, Miriael understood, when he'd joined in the first great act of disobedience. But she made no comment.

"Yes, he sees me as a cog in his ultimate invasion plan. Just another cog—and I let him believe it. I've always thought that was the flaw in our original rebellion. Lucifer was too proud to hide his true thoughts—he had to stand forth and declare our intentions even when we'd won only a third of Heaven's angels to our side. Too soon, too soon! *Not* a mistake I shall be making again."

He moved close to Miriael's trolley, and she felt his radiance beating down on her. "You have to admit, I'm far more subtle. By your own experience, wouldn't you say so?"

She clenched her teeth and said nothing.

"Poor Miriael." He shook his head as if in pity. "Such a poor conversationalist you've become! I used to enjoy talking to you once. I suppose it's hard to focus on anything other than yourself when you're awaiting news of your impending extinction. Shall I tell you what I know about that?"

Still she said nothing. After a long pause, he drew back a little.

"Your choice," he said.

Clearly, he wasn't going to tell her without being asked.

"Yes," she said.

"Yes what?"

"Tell me. Please."

He smiled. "Well, I think Doctor Saniette plans to start the dissection in the next two or three days. I can't be more precise than that. But the interesting thing is that he plans to do it himself. Apparently, he requires voice contact, monitor data and minute-by-minute updates, and those connections can't be restored. So, since his physical dimensions prevent him from entering the operating theatres in person, he'll be having you brought to him."

"Where?"

"In his dome. You'll see. No doubt they'll start transferring all the necessary equipment soon. If they haven't already started."

Miriael had hardly hoped for a permanent reprieve, but her spirits sank to hear the definite details of her fate.

"Of course, actual extinction may take a while. I have no idea how long he'll keep you conscious under dissection. Perhaps days. It's a pity you'll never have the chance to pass on your impressions of him. He's a very odd sort of life-form. To tell the truth, I can't work out exactly *what* he is."

Miriael was thinking about being conscious for days under dissection. She had learned about pain in her new part-physical body. In fact, her part-physical body was so very new and tender that even small sensations could be unbearably acute…

She was hardly listening when Asmodai uttered his final farewell, hardly noticed when her room door closed behind him.

23

The rescue team had been walking parallel to an overbridge for three days. They had climbed in and out of countless gullies filled with thornbushes, they had detoured around remnants of old stone and brickwork strangely encased in blocks of clear glass. One time they passed a rocky bluff into which what looked like giant staircases had been carved.

Ferren tried to lead by example. He still thought of himself as fulfilling his vow to serve Miriael, but he no longer thought of himself as being in love with her. They shared a friendship, and that was extraordinary enough. The rest, as Kiet said, had been all in his head.

He might have spoken of it to Kiet, but whenever the group stopped for a break, she went off to the side and sat with her pack on her lap. All her attention was given to Peeper, crooning and whispering to the Morph on the zither. When Ferren wandered near enough to catch a few words, he gathered that she was explaining the truth about Asmodai and his flying wing.

On the third night of their journey, he became aware of a dull pulsation, infinitely faint and far away. It was more a vibration in the ground than a sound in the air. He thought at once of the throbbing of huge machinery in the Bankstown Camp, as he'd heard it once before. When he pressed his ear to the ground, he was certain. They were coming close, less than a day away now.

He announced the news to the others in the morning. "We'll be coming to the Camp from a different side to where I broke in last time. We have to take care no one sees us. Best if we walk further away from the overbridge."

They set off once more. Over the course of the morning, the throbbing vibration grew louder and louder. A vast mass of shadows appeared on the horizon, shifting shadows that baffled the eye. Ferren explained about the canopies of wire that scanned the sky and shielded the Humen from overhead attack. Later, they saw a second overbridge converging towards the Camp on their other side, and kept as far as possible away from both. Later again, the ground changed under their feet to a glutinous sort of clay.

By now, Ferren would have expected to see the lake like a moat surrounding the Camp, with the embankment behind it. But something blocked his view, something not present where he'd broken in before. He saw one taller, cylindrical structure and many lower, squarish shapes. The shapes covered the entire area between one overbridge and the other.

All his plans for getting into the Camp depended on the moat and embankment. But the shapes might help hide their approach if Hypers weren't working in the area...

The shapes turned out to be stacks of construction materials: great metal tubes and girders. Rising above head height, the stacks provided perfect cover. Hypers *were* working there, shouting orders and clanging metal, but they were all in a special zone fenced off around the taller structure.

Giving that zone a wide berth, the rescue team slipped along the aisles between the stacks. They paused at the end of every stack, and someone peered out ahead, checking for danger. But the general storage area was deserted.

They must have passed fifty stacks by the time they saw open space ahead. Ferren signalled for extra caution, and they crept forward in the shadow of the final girders, crouching low.

The scene that appeared before them was exactly as he'd hoped. The same moat of black water, the same sheer embankment on the other side—and the same concrete drainage pipes that tunnelled through the embankment and stuck out above the surface of the water.

"That's our way in," he whispered, and pointed to a pipe as far away as possible from the overbridges to their left and right. "We'll take the one in the middle."

"Not now, though?" Ethany pointed to the massive gates where the two overbridges entered the Camp. "There's guards up there. We'll be seen."

Ferren nodded agreement. "All right, we'll wait for nightfall. Let's find a place to hide till then."

24

They found a better place to hide than they could ever have hoped for. Not far from the lake was a trench in the earth, and a mountainous stack of tubes had been laid crosswise over the top of it. Entering from the trench, they advanced on hands and knees right under the centre of the stack. It was like an underground cave open at one end.

"This can be our base," said Ferren, as they settled comfortably in the gloom. "We need somewhere to leave our packs behind."

Flens nodded. "I wondered how we were going to carry them into the Camp."

They all shrugged off their packs. Kiet looked thoughtfully at the zither fastened to hers.

"And I need somewhere to leave Peeper," she said.

Peeper was listening and understood. "Leave me-e-e-e?"

"You knew it would happen, little one. Only the journey, we said."

"Oh-oh-oh." Peeper didn't disagree, but sounded sad. Kiet didn't appear very happy about it herself.

"Someone could stay with him," Ferren suggested.

"Don't look at me," Kiet shot back at once. "I'm coming in with you."

"I could stay with him," Rhinn offered.

"Would you?" Kiet turned to her sister. "Please!"

"But only if Tadge stays with me too."

"Not me." Kiet's twelve-year-old brother shook his head. "I'm a fighter and a rescuer."

"That's what I'm worried about," said Rhinn.

"No fighting in the Camp," Ferren put in. "We aim to avoid fighting."

Kiet took her cue. "We need someone brave to protect Peeper and our packs. If the Humen discovered our base, then you'd *have* to fight. You'd have to defend this place to the death." She appealed to Ferren. "It's a very important role, isn't it?"

"Very."

"To the death." Tadge considered. "I'll defend it and drive them back too."

So it was decided that Tadge and Rhinn would stay guarding the base, while Ferren, Kiet, Flens, Bross, Gibby and Ethany went in to rescue the angel.

"Now we should rest and eat," said Ferren. "Have a nap if you can."

All ate; some rested with their backs against the walls of the trench; others lay full length on the ground and slept. Kiet sang lullabies to Peeper in a low voice.

Ferren had no hope of sleep. He studied the faces of the five young Nesters who would be breaking into the Camp with him—and felt suddenly, overwhelmingly *responsible*. They weren't as naive as Tadge, but they still viewed this expedition as more of an adventure than a doomsday mission. They had put their lives in his hands, and he was the only one who understood the very real chance that they'd all be killed...

When night fell, there was no moon, and the area of construction materials was in complete darkness. Everyone roused up, and Ferren led the rescue team outside. Remembering something he'd done last time, he found a spot where the clay underfoot was particularly soft.

"Watch me," he said.

Then he knelt, scooped up clay and rubbed it over his face. Flens caught on at once.

"Makes us harder to see in the dark," he said, and scooped up clay for himself.

Soon they were all smearing on clay. Tadge, who had come out with Rhinn to see them off, smeared his face too. Then they walked down to the water's edge.

Ferren intended to break in exactly as he had broken in before, then look for Doctor Saniette's surgeries when they were inside. Since the surgeries were surely important, he expected to find them somewhere near the centre of the Camp.

Rhinn and Tadge said their farewells as the rescue team waded into the water.

"Goodbye," they called out. "Goodbye and good luck."

Yes, we'll need it, thought Ferren. *We'll really, really need it.*

PART FOUR

DOCTOR SANIETTE

1

Breaking into the Bankstown Camp went perfectly to plan. The Humen expected angelic forces to attack from the air and had made the Camp impregnable with wire canopies overhead. They'd never thought to protect themselves against a ground-level infiltration, least of all by Residuals.

The rescue team crossed the moat without difficulty, forming a line and holding hands for the deeper parts. No part was so deep that they had to swim. Searchlights on the embankment swept their beams this way and that, yet never dipped down as low as the black water of the moat.

They helped one another up into the mouth of the concrete pipe, then shuffled forward through the echoing interior. Ferren, at the front, whispered warnings whenever the slime underfoot grew slippery. At the far end of the tunnel was an open drainage channel, deep enough to hide them from sight, that led on further into the Camp. It was the same as on his previous visit—and exactly what he'd been hoping for.

"Keep your heads down!" he whispered, and heard his whisper passed back all along the line.

He took one quick look before lowering his own head. He saw jets of steam, billowing smoke, spots of red fire and dark, hulking shapes of machinery. Then he ducked down out of sight and advanced along the channel in a crouch.

The pulse of heavy machinery seemed to throb through the ground and into his bones. He heard other sounds too:

Ussh-gaah! Ussh-gaah! Ussh-gaah!

Ussh-gaah! Ussh-gaah! Ussh-gaah!

Those were the sounds of Plasmatics, he knew. Trapped inside some of the nearby machines, straps of muscle, nerve and cartilage laboured tirelessly. Muscle, nerve and cartilage stolen from Residual bodies… He tried not to think about it.

The channel turned sharply left, then sharply right, then came to a branching junction. Ferren chose the branch that seemed most likely to lead towards the centre of the Camp.

In several places, they passed under huge corrugated hoses that crossed over the channel on frames. In another place, they heard a clatter of many boots and a Hyper bellowing out orders… They ducked even lower then.

From time to time, Ferren checked back to see that the others were still close behind. Kiet nodded and grinned, and Flens, next in line, gave him a thumbs-up. They probably thought he knew where he was going…

They cut through an area of thunderous clangs and rattles, then an area where an acrid smell forced them to clamp hands over their mouths and noses. A little further again, they made a sharp turn to the left and passed under a metal footbridge. Thirty yards ahead, the channel came to a dead end.

Ferren grimaced. They had been lucky to come so far inside the Camp hidden from view, but now the easy part of their expedition was over.

He led the way on to the final wall, then stopped. The wall was solid concrete, pierced by many small vents and outlets.

"Bunch up," he told the rescue team. "We have to work out our next step."

They huddled closer at the end of the channel.

"Straight to the surgeries," Flens suggested. "How far now?"

Ferren didn't respond immediately, and Kiet guessed the answer. "You don't know where they are."

"Probably in the centre of the Camp. Probably a quieter, cleaner area than this."

"*Probably!*"

"I never said I knew where they were." Ferren scowled. "I was looking for my sister before, I wasn't thinking about surgeries."

Flens whistled under his breath. "But this place is huge. We could be searching for ages."

"I never said it would be quick."

Kiet let out a sigh, then snapped her fingers. "All right, we'd better make a start if—"

"*Unauthorised intruders! Unauthorised intruders!*" Suddenly, the harsh voice of a Hyper rang out.

Everyone whirled and gaped in the direction of the footbridge thirty yards back. There on the bridge stood two black, rubber-clad Hypers.

"Saboteurs!" yelled the second Hyper. "It's the saboteurs! *We got 'em!*"

"Run!" cried Ferren and Kiet in the same moment. "Run for it!"

The rescue team jumped up out of the channel and ran. The Hypers swung off the footbridge and gave chase. There was a thirty-yard gap between hunters and hunted.

2

Running, running, desperately running! With Ferren and Kiet in the lead, the rescue team raced across a cinder track and came to a massive, plastic-sheathed cable supported on stanchions. It was too high for leaping over, so they dived under it. Ferren heard a tick-ticking sound and felt a tingling sensation as his back brushed against it. Then he was through to the other side and up on his feet again.

They had come to an area where a network of steel rails crisscrossed the ground. Ahead was a forest of torpedo-shaped cylinders standing vertically in racks. To their left, a group of three Hypers were busy on some work that sent showers of yellow sparks cascading in the darkness. Behind them, the hue and cry was louder than ever.

"Catch the saboteurs! Bring 'em down! Kill 'em!"

Ferren ran straight for the forest of cylinders. From the corner of his eye, he saw the three working Hypers drop their tools and turn to join the pursuit.

There were gaps between the racks of cylinders, just wide enough for a body to pass through. Plunging into the first gap, Ferren felt a sudden blast of icy cold. The cylinders were coated with frost and wreathed in tendrils of white vapour like frozen steam.

"Follow me!" he called out over his shoulder, and began switching direction this way and that among the racks. Perhaps they could lose their pursuers in the maze…

Then a loudspeaker blared out. *"All personnel to Zone Five Industrial! Seal off the zone! Apprehend unauthorised intruders!"*

Other loudspeakers repeated the message far and wide. Ferren stopped switching direction and ran straight. Their only chance was to escape from Zone Five Industrial before the whole area was sealed off.

A few minutes of running straight, and he came out into an open space where various kinds of wheeled machines were parked: machines with scoops, machines with bulldozer blades, machines with heavy, wheeled containers attached. The ground was grease-stained tarmac dotted with iron gratings.

He darted across with the others at his heels. They had made it as far as the first machine when a floodlight switched on overhead. Total illumination! They were instantly exposed in the stark, white glare.

Ferren cursed, swerved and dropped down behind the first machine. The others took shelter beside him. What now? They couldn't stay here, and they couldn't go on. There were shouts in the darkness from all sides as loudspeakers continued to blare and Hypers converged on the zone.

"Ow! Help!" gasped Gibby suddenly.

Ferren hardly registered her cry. Two Hypers had just emerged from the forest of cylinders. He peered out and watched as they skidded to a halt, scanning the parking area. They seemed to be deciding which way to start searching. A moment later, more Hypers emerged and came forward to join them.

"Harder! Harder!" he heard Kiet urge, and looked round.

Gibby was on her back on the ground, Bross had hold of her under the armpits, while Kiet and Flens tugged at something on her foot. Ferren didn't understand at first, only that they were pulling in opposite directions. Then he realised: the thing was an iron grating, lifted right up out of the ground. Gibby's foot must have slipped through and become trapped; now they were trying to haul it off.

No sooner had he realised what they were trying to do than they succeeded. Gibby stifled a moan of pain, and the grating came away from her foot.

"Wait a minute," Ferren said, as Kiet and Flens prepared to lower the grating to the ground. He was staring at the black hole that the grating had covered. There was an echoing emptiness and a glint of water far below.

Kiet stared too. "We can hide there!" she breathed.

No need for further calculation. Ferren jumped down first, praying that the drop wasn't too far or the water too deep. In fact, the drop was no more than his own height, and the depth of water only a few inches. He moved to the side and prepared to catch the others as they jumped down too.

One by one they came: Ethany, Gibby, Flens and Kiet. Bross came last, and Ferren whispered up to him before he jumped.

"We need to close the grating after us!"

"Right." Bross positioned the grating at the edge of the hole before he jumped down. Then he reached up, hooked his fingers into the slots and dragged it across. It took all his strength, and nobody else could have done it. Finally the grating slid back into place with a clang.

Only just in time. Boots clattered on the ground above, harsh Hypers' voices called back and forth.

"Spread out!" "Not too far!' "Check everything!" "Keep a line!" "Look inside the machines!"

In the hollow space under the grating, every sound had a hundred echoes. The rescue team stood motionless, hardly daring to breathe. But when a shadow passed close by over their heads, Ferren realised the danger. They might be visible if any Hyper peered down through the grating. He nudged those nearest to him and started everyone moving deeper into the darkness.

The boots and voices came and went, sounding nearer, then further, then nearer again.

They'll probably keep searching Zone Five Industrial for hours, thought Ferren.

As though she'd read his mind, Kiet produced a solution. She brought her mouth up close to his ear to whisper. "Maybe we could get clear of the area walking underground."

Ferren liked the idea. "Let's explore," he whispered back.

He intended to test how far they could go, but as soon as he and Kiet set off, the rest of the team went with them.

3

There were walls underground, but there were doorways and openings for passing through them. It was a secret realm of room-like spaces, with rows of piers holding up a low roof. At the front of the rescue team, Ferren and Kiet walked with arms upraised, guarding against the metal pipes that ran across overhead. Underfoot, hidden sills in the water made a different hazard.

"Watch your head here!" they warned over their shoulders, and "Careful here, don't trip!"

By now, their eyes had adjusted to the merest hint of light. They kept well away from the gratings, where the light was stronger. They could no longer hear sounds from above, only the slosh and splash of their own feet through the water.

After they had found and passed through openings in three walls, the gratings came to an end. Now dim light descended not from slatted grilles but circular vents much higher up, as if at the top of chimneys.

"It's a new area," muttered Ferren. "We've left those wheeled machines behind."

"What about Zone Five, though?" said Kiet.

He shrugged. "Who knows how far it goes?"

"The lights are still bright out there." Kiet pointed to the illumination coming down from the vents. "No way we can climb out yet."

They were about to go on when Ethany piped up behind. "Did anyone hear that?"

"Hear what?"

"I don't know. A water noise. Not us."

Everyone stood still and listened to the ripples from their own movements dying away. There was no other sound.

"Let's go on," said Ethany after a while. "I must've imagined it."

It was easy for imagination to run riot in this eerie, subterranean world, where everything seemed to repeat itself interminably. The tiniest sound spread out into a thousand echoes; the piers in their rows marched endlessly off into the darkness. Ferren's sense of time and distance became confused. How many openings in walls had they passed through now? How many pipes had they ducked beneath?

Sometimes the water rose as high as their calves, at other times it fell away to a squelching slime under their feet. In one room, a rhythmical thump of heavy machinery shook the ground overhead. In another room, a strange warmth radiated down from above, as from ovens or furnaces. Different types of vents let in differing amounts of light; overall, though, the darkness seemed to be deepening.

"Stop!' said Ethany suddenly. "I *did* hear something."

"I heard it too," Gibby confirmed.

Again they froze motionless; again there was nothing to be heard in the silence.

"It was behind us," Ethany insisted.

"Like someone following," Gibby agreed.

Gibby and Ethany had been at the back of the group as they walked. Ferren and Kiet looked at one another, eyes gleaming out from their clay-smeared faces.

"Could it be a Hyper?" Kiet wondered aloud.

"Waiting for a chance to call down the rest of them?" Ferren suggested.

"Didn't sound like a Hyper," said Gibby. She and Ethany had moved up to stand shoulder to shoulder with Bross and Flens.

"Why not?"

"Too…too stealthy."

Ferren nodded. It *was* hard to think of any Hyper moving softly and staying quiet.

"We should look for a way back up above ground," Kiet proposed, then dropped her voice to a whisper. "We can jump on whoever it is if they follow us out."

"Yes, we must've gone beyond Zone Five by now," said Ferren, not dropping his voice. "We'll look for a way back up, then."

The vents in this area were small and square, too small for anyone to squeeze through. They set off once more, bunching close together. When they came to the next wall and the next opening, the room ahead was even less promising. Here there were no vents at all; piers and pipes were invisible in the pitch-black darkness.

Ferren bit his lip. "Let's keep going. We'll do better further on."

They stepped forward into the darkness. With hands outstretched, Ferren and Kiet had to find their way around piers as well as duck under pipes. Very slowly, past row after row of piers, they advanced. At the same time, everyone was listening for the slightest out-of-place sound—any sound other than the watery wash of their own progress.

At last, Ferren saw the glimmer of a doorway ahead. In the light beyond, he could pick out the dim shapes of distant piers...

But even as he watched, a door closed over the doorway, and the light disappeared. Then followed the click of a lock.

He gasped—and so did Kiet, who had seen it too.

"Back!" He whirled and flapped at the group behind him. "No way through! Go back! Quick!"

A dreadful premonition had seized him. His anxiety communicated to the others, and at once they turned and hurried back towards the doorway they'd just come through. The opening showed between the piers as a dim square of light.

"Faster!" he urged.

But it was impossible to rush without banging into obstacles. There were grunts and yelps of pain...then a loud clunk and a splash as Bross ran into an overhead pipe and sat down suddenly. Ferren moved to help, but Kiet was already helping.

In that same moment, someone sped past on his other side. Dark in the darkness, a fast-moving body—not one of the rescue team. He sensed more than saw it, and made a move to step across and block it. But he was far too slow. Whoever it was had already gone past, racing for the same dim square of light...

His premonition proved correct. Whoever it was stopped in the doorway and swung that door shut too. In the next moment came the click of another lock.

4

Trapped! Perhaps it was a Hyper after all, who'd followed them with a plan to lock them in.

With Kiet in the lead, the others surged forward to the door that had just closed. She was the first to inspect the lock.

"Can't move it," she announced after a moment. "It's been jammed."

"The other one will be too, then," said Flens.

"Maybe there's some other hole in the walls," suggested Gibby.

"We should search all around," said Bross. "Right?"

"Right," Ferren agreed, since they seemed to be waiting on his approval. But he didn't join the search himself. He listened to the sounds of sloshing and splashing as they began to feel their way around the walls.

Then a smaller sloshing approached him in the dark.

"Ferren?" It was Kiet.

"Here."

She came close enough to whisper. "That lock that was jammed. It was done from the *inside.*"

She didn't need to spell out what she was thinking. If the lock had been jammed from the inside, then whoever it was must be still in the room with them. Ferren scanned all around, but the same pitch-black dark met his eyes in every direction.

Yet there was *something.* He sensed it rather than saw it—not at ground level, but as if hovering overhead. Very cautiously, without a ripple of water, he moved towards it. He raised a hand and touched a metal pipe…then his other hand touched a second pipe, intersecting with the first.

Sliding his hands along both pipes, he came to an end of cloth hanging down. He felt it between his fingers—

There was a sudden swoosh of movement as the cloth jerked away and a body swung down from above. Before he knew what was happening, a sinewy hand clamped over his face from behind. Something very cold and thin made contact with his Adam's apple.

"Don't move," murmured a strange, menacing voice in his ear.

"What is it?" Kiet called out in alarm. "Are you all right?"

The hand dropped away. "Tell them," the voice ordered.

"I think someone's holding a knife to my throat," Ferren brought out.

"Everyone stay where they are," the voice commanded. It didn't belong to a Hyper; it was a woman's voice, yet oddly hoarse and rusty-sounding.

Then a dazzling beam of light flashed full in Ferren's eyes, and he couldn't see a thing. The woman had switched on some kind of torch to illuminate the knife at his throat. In the next moment, she switched it off again.

"What are you doing in my territory?" The question was directed to Ferren along with the rest of the team. "Are you on the side of the Humen?"

It was impossible to guess what reply would please her, and everyone answered differently. "Yes." "No." "Sort of." "We weren't..."

"Straight answer!" she growled. "Don't think you can—*Stop!*"

Ferren was almost swept off his feet as the woman swung suddenly around. The torch snapped on again, pinning Kiet in its beam. She had been trying to work her way round behind their attacker's back.

"Little fool!" snarled the woman. "*You* answer me straight or he dies. What are you doing here?"

Kiet goggled at the knife held to Ferren's throat. "Don't hurt him," she begged.

The knife moved threateningly, and Ferren felt the blade's edge sharp against his skin.

"We came to the Camp to rescue an angel." Kiet babbled so fast she hardly seemed to know what she was saying. "Then we got spotted and chased before we'd even started. Chased down here! It's the truth! Please!"

"Rescue an angel! So you're on Heaven's side!"

"Yes. No. I don't know." Kiet flustered.

Ferren struggled to speak without moving his throat. "Better them than the Humen."

The woman snorted; but perhaps she meant it as a laugh. "Now I've heard everything. Tribespeople going against the Humen!"

Her voice no longer sounded quite so odd, as though she was recovering the habit of speech. Ferren wished he could turn round and look at her.

"You're one of us yourself," he challenged. "You're from a Residual tribe too."

She uttered a scornful; spitting sound. "Phah! I'm not anyone anymore. No tribe, no family. I left all of that behind long ago. A destroyer and a saboteur, I am. I do my work alone. *Killing* work."

"Please don't kill us," pleaded Ethany.

"She won't," said Ferren. "She's not our enemy."

"Is that so?" The woman swung her torch full in Ferren's face again. "I'm an enemy to anyone who's a risk to me. And you're a risk of blabbing about me to the Humen. All of you. I don't think I can let you live."

"It's six against one," said Kiet. "You can start killing, but you'll never finish. We'll charge you and finish you first."

"Not when I do this.' The torch switched off, and everything went instantly black again. "I don't need to see you to know where you are. I can finish you one by one."

Ferren was listening intently, not to her words but her voice, which sounded less and less odd all the time. In fact, it was starting to sound familiar.

"You could, but you won't," he said.

"Starting with you." The woman sounded savage yet puzzled.

Ferren only laughed, a laugh of absolute relief. Impossible joy welled up inside him.

"You need to fear me, boy."

"No." Ferren managed to speak through his laughter. "You're Shanna of the People."

Shocked silence followed. The woman sucked in air, then released it in a strangled, inarticulate sound. Ferren reached up and moved the hand that held the knife slowly away from his neck. At last he could turn to face his attacker, though he still couldn't see her.

"Who. Are. You?" she brought out, one word at a time.

"Me?" Again Ferren had to fight against the laughter that threatened to overwhelm him. "I'm Ferren of the People. Your little brother."

5

The torch switched back on.

"You can't be."

"Yes."

"No!"

"*Yes.*"

Ferren stood motionless as his sister played the light over his clay-smeared face. Not dazzling him but inspecting him.

"Don't move," she said in a whisper.

She sheathed her knife in her belt, knelt suddenly and scooped up a handful of water. She applied the water to his face and rubbed away the clay with gentle, wondering gestures. Ferren couldn't stop grinning; *her* mouth hung open in utter disbelief.

"It must be," she said at last. "It *is*. But you've changed."

"I'm two and a half years older." He laughed. "Now my turn."

He did as Shanna had done, scooping up water and washing her face. The dirt and grime on her skin was deeply ingrained, more of a permanent coating than a temporary camouflage. But he rubbed and rubbed, while the rest of the rescue team watched in respectful silence. Shanna held the torch so that he could see her emerging features.

What emerged was a face aged by hard experience rather than by years alone. There were furrows across her forehead, lines around her mouth and nose, and a scar that ran down all the way down her left cheek. With her hair pulled back in a tight knot, she looked like the most grim and formidable of warriors.

But she was still Shanna, and the expression in her eyes was the same as it had always been: deep and probing, wise and thoughtful. He stopped washing and wrapped his arms around her. So many times she'd hugged him when he was little! Now she was stiff—but only for a moment. Then she wrapped arms around him too.

The respectful silence gave way to curiosity, and he heard the others questioning one another.

"Are they brother and sister, then?"

"What's she doing down here?"

"She must be the one he came searching for before."

"How could she survive in the Humen Camp?"

Then Kiet, who knew more of the background, explained. "Her name's Shanna, and the Selectors took their parents for military service when he was very young. It was his sister who brought him up like a mother. Then the Selectors took her too. She must've escaped in the Camp."

"Yes, I escaped." Shanna disengaged herself from Ferren's arms, stepped back and shone the torch on Kiet and the others. "I'll tell you the whole story. But not here in the dark." She swung back to Ferren. "We'll go to one of my safe-holes. Right?"

Ferren merely grinned. He was too happy to care about where they went, or even about hearing Shanna's story. It was enough to have found her again. He'd always kept a last, irrational shred of hope, but most of his hope had died after he'd seen what happened to Residuals in the baths. Yet suddenly, incredibly—here she was!

In a dream, he followed with the rest as his sister led the way. He didn't see how she opened the lock in the door, and hardly registered the rooms they passed through. She had switched off her torch again, and led them in single file through row after row of dimly lit piers.

Finally they came to a hole in a wall that wasn't a doorway. A small number of bricks had been pulled out, sufficient for a body to squeeze through. On the other side was a cave with a raised, dry floor and walls of packed earth. Light filtered down through a chimney overhead.

"Cosy as a nest!" Gibby exclaimed.

They settled themselves cross-legged on the floor. Shanna turned to her brother and began her story.

6

"You remember that day the Selectors took me away? As soon as we were out of sight of the Home Ground, they put chains on me and led me along as their prisoner."

"I remember." Ferren nodded. "And I know what happens in military service."

"We all do," put in Kiet. "He told us."

"The pit and the baths?"

"Yes."

"I don't have to explain, then. I was with half a dozen men and women from other tribes, and they drove us with sharp pointed sticks and pushed us into a bath. We were packed in side by side so tight we couldn't move. Then they began clambering over us and putting wads of stuff in our mouths. Soft, fluffy stuff it was, but with some kind of chemical in it. I held my breath so as not to inhale the fumes. I must've been the only one that fought against it. And I still ended up sluggish and sleepy because I had to breath a bit through my nose.

"Next thing, they started clipping wires onto us. I had clips attached to my fingers, ears and toes. But as soon as they'd finished clipping, I got the wad of stuff halfway out of my mouth, so I didn't have to breathe through it. Then I managed to pull the clips off my fingers. Lucky, I suppose—they must all have been looking the other way in the moment. And they still didn't notice when they covered us up with a black plastic sheet. Then there was a hum of equipment and a sort of humming in my toes and ears, where the other clips were still attached.

"It was the strangest feeling, I can't describe it. In my head, I mean. It was like being drained and drawn out, as if I couldn't quite catch my breath. But not actual breath, it wasn't physical. For a moment, I couldn't remember who I was or what I was doing there or anything. But I must've remembered I'd been trying to get the clips off me, and I managed to reach up and yank away the ones on my ears. That made the difference. With four clips gone, their equipment couldn't work on me. Suddenly I could think again.

"I lay there under the black plastic, listening to the sounds of Hypers outside. But after a while, there were no more sounds, only the hum of the equipment. The Hypers had left. So I crawled out and found a place to hide in a corner of the pit behind the equipment. That was as far as I could go. Then I passed out.

"I woke up, though, when an alarm started beeping and the Hypers came back. You know what happens next, do you?"

"Yes," said Ferren through gritted teeth. Like everyone else, he'd been caught up in the story, which was all the more vivid because of his own memories.

"The jelly sucked out of the bath?"

"Yes. And the butchery afterwards."

"Good. So I don't need to tell you. I saw all of that, and I vowed revenge. Nothing else mattered. I don't know, maybe something changed in me, maybe I wasn't quite the same person. But I *had* to have revenge."

"You never thought to escape the Camp?" asked Ferren. "You never tried to return home?"

Shanna looked at him and shook her head sadly. "Sorry, little brother. No, I stayed secretly in the Camp and tried to do as much damage as I could. I learned to become a saboteur. Small things at first, like puncturing hoses, turning on taps, turning off valves. But I built up gradually to bigger and better kinds of damage. Especially when I learned to communicate with Plasmatics."

"Communicate with… What, by shouting numbers at them?"

"No, that's what Hypers do. Mathematical orders. I can't do that. I signal to them by touching them and tapping on them."

Ferren remembered the muscles and nerves and internal organs he'd seen, and shuddered at the thought of touching them. Shanna smiled at his reaction.

"I always hoped I'd be able to talk to them, like the people they once were. But it's impossible. They can't answer back, they can only obey orders. I like to think that, when they obey my orders, at least they're revenging themselves on the Humen." She grinned with satisfaction.

"My last sabotage fused a whole lot of electrical equipment and blacked out half-a-dozen zones. I'll do something even better next time."

"You can't!" Ferren protested. "We're here to rescue Miriael, then we're getting out of this Camp for good. You have to come with us."

"Oh." Shanna sucked at her lip and looked thoughtful. "You want me to come back to being normal? That's not so easy, little brother."

"I won't lose you again. I *won't!*"

"Hmm. I don't want to lose you again either." Shanna gave herself a shake and changed the subject. "So the angel you're rescuing is called Miriael?"

"Yes. We think she's being held in the surgeries."

Kiet chimed in. "But we don't know where the surgeries are. Do you?"

"Of course. Do you want me to take you there?"

"Please."

"Now?"

"Yes."

"All right. You're going to need help, I can see."

7

Shanna had a small stock of weapons in her safe-hole, which she distributed before they set out. Ferren, Kiet, Gibby and Ethany each received a knife, and Flens a weighted cosh.

"That's all, sorry," she told Bross. "I can't give you what I need myself."

"I'll fight with my hands if we have to fight," Bross replied.

Leaving the safe-hole, they made their way through more water-filled rooms, then came to a tunnel that ended in a vertical shaft. Half-a-dozen rungs at the side of the shaft led to a solid manhole cover at the top. Shanna climbed out first, and the rescue team followed.

They were in a different kind of area here, with khaki buildings like immense sheds of corrugated iron. The only windows were high in the walls, and the walls were marked with numbers and letters in red paint.

They glided along in the shadows. There was nobody about outside; inside, the sheds were bright with light and alive with noise and activity.

"This is the secret weapons area," Shanna whispered to Ferren, in a moment when they waited for the others to catch up. "The new Doctor brought new military devices, and they're making more and more of them."

"What?"

"Don't know, the sheds are too well secured. I only overheard Hypers talking about secret weapons."

A hundred yards further on, they left the buildings behind and came to an area of flat concrete dotted with small caps like white enamel mushrooms. Puddles of scummy, yellow liquid lay everywhere on the concrete, giving off a foul-smelling vapour.

"It won't hurt," said Shanna, and strode forward into the vapour.

They soon learned where the puddles came from. There was a gurgle underground, and the mushroom caps disgorged an overflow of yellow liquid. Half a minute later, with a greedy, slurping sound, the mushroom caps sucked the liquid back in again. Vomiting and swallowing, vomiting and swallowing ...

The rescue team dodged the overflows as well as they could. Shanna didn't even bother.

"Hear that?" she said, pointing. "That's the Main Belt."

Ferren didn't understand, but he could hear the noise: a grinding, clanking sort of rumble. As they advanced across the concrete area, the noise swelled to a loud, continuous thunder.

The source emerged finally through the vapour. The Main Belt was a conveyor belt running over the ground. As they watched, they saw crates, drums, canisters and cargoes of every kind pass slowly by, as if borne on some great river.

"This way," Shanna whispered to Ferren and signalled to the rest.

She led them closer on a curving route. Here the vapour grew thinner and the concrete was dry. Ahead was a low platform alongside the conveyor belt.

"Flat on your bellies and crawl," she instructed. "There can be Hypers on the Main Belt."

They crawled the last part of the way and arrived at the back of the platform. Now they could see the rollers revolving under the belt and the moving surface of rubber above.

"We have to cross that?" Ferren whispered.

"When it's safe, yes." Shanna raised her head above the level of the platform, cautiously higher and higher. Then she ducked down again in a hurry.

"Not safe," she hissed. "Stay hidden. Hypers."

Ferren squeezed in with the others behind the platform—but not before he caught a glimpse of the Hypers. There were four of them approaching on top of the belt, and they were clad not in black but white rubber.

Unusual...but he had seen such Hypers once before, he remembered. *Then* they had been assisting the old Bankstown Doctors to inject doses of jelly into the foreheads of ordinary soldiers. Medical attendants...

He kept his head down as they went past. But as soon as Shanna risked a tiny peek, he did too. The Hypers were travelling along the belt with a wheeled trolley, two in front and two behind. Of the two in front, one carried a rolled-up cloth under his arm, the other carried a large, long bag. There was something on top of the trolley itself, but covered over with a white sheet...

Then Ferren gasped. Hanging down, escaping from under the sheet, was a mass of bright golden hair. Utterly distinctive, utterly unmistakable!

"It's her—" Shanna's hand clamped over his mouth before he could utter another word.

But he fought to stay watching. The Hypers hadn't heard him anyway. As the trolley travelled further along the belt, Kiet and the others took a peek too.

"It *is!*" murmured Kiet. "It's the angel!"

"No one else has hair like that," Flens confirmed.

Shanna released Ferren's mouth. "We're going the wrong way, then," she said. "They might've come *from* the surgeries, but they're not going there now."

Ferren jumped to his feet. The Hyper and trolley were rapidly disappearing into the distance. "We have to follow!"

"Right. We can do that." Shanna also jumped to her feet. "I know where the Main Belt goes. We can detour and catch it up again at the next fork."

It wasn't far, and they ran fast. Ferren hardly noticed or cared where they were running. They were taking risks now, but luck was with them.

A few minutes later, they emerged from a labyrinth of tanks and pipes, and saw the fork ahead. The primary conveyor belt veered to the right, carrying away the crates and drums and other cargoes, while a separate, secondary belt started up on the left. They arrived just in time to see the four white-suited Hypers manoeuvre the trolley off the Main Belt and wheel it onto the secondary belt.

Shanna groaned.

"Where are they taking her now?" Ferren asked.

"To the new Doctor. That belt leads straight to his dome."

"Doctor Saniette?"

"If that's what he's called. The giant monster."

Kiet spoke up before Ferren could respond. "That's where we rescue her, then."

8

"Far enough! We'll take over from here. What else have you brought?"

"Surgical instruments, all sterilised. As Doctor Saniette required."

Miriael, under her sheet on the trolley top, heard a harsh female voice followed by the smoother, quieter tone of an attendant from the surgeries.

"Good. Let's have a look at her, then."

The sheet was plucked off, and Miriael found herself gazing up into the face of a strange type of Hyper. Whereas ordinary Hypers typically adopted a brutally male appearance, the features of this Hyper were oddly feminised. Long, artificial eyelashes veiled her eyeslits, red cupid's bow lips had been painted round her mouthslit. Only her mask of black rubbery skin followed the usual pattern.

She seemed to find Miriael equally odd. "Not a normal angel, this one," she commented.

"A unique case," said one of the attendants. "Surviving in our atmosphere without an aura. And she eats and drinks like a Residual."

The red cupid's bow formed the shape of a sneer. "I wouldn't mind dissecting her myself."

Then the face went away, and four attendants gathered around. Miriael saw that she was in some sort of chamber with curtains at either end and stainless steel tables along the sides.

A moment later, the strange Hyper returned, wheeling one of the tables. For the first time, Miriael noticed the copper circuitry snaking across her shoulders and a bulge like a plastic blister on her back. Her movements were unnaturally springy, and she was clearly much taller than the attendants. A new type of augmented Hyper in Doctor Saniette's army? Miriael remembered the figures she'd seen in the dust cloud alongside the overbridge, bounding along in great, six-foot strides…

"Lay the instruments out here." The augmented Hyper tapped a tray on top of the table. "Ready for him to use. We'll winch the tray up to him first."

One attendant opened up a bag, another unfurled a rolled-up cloth. Inside the cloth were dozens of shiny instruments tucked into dozens of soft, padded pockets.

"Show them all to her as you lay them out." A malevolent smile reshaped the cupid's bow. "Let her see what to expect."

So Miriael was shown the instruments to be used for her dissection: scalpels, forceps, scissors and retractors. From the bag came clamps and clips, gauzes and dressings, suction bulbs, syringes and kidney dishes. She tried to close her mind to what she was seeing.

"How does the Doctor use ordinary-size instruments?" one attendant asked. "With his huge hands…"

"His hands aren't his hands, not the way you think of hands." The augmented Hyper raked the questioner with a look of contempt. "He has the very finest touch. You have no idea the things he can do."

Nothing more was said until every item of equipment was neatly arranged on the tray. Then the augmented Hyper raised her voice and called out.

"Right, take them in. Equipment goes up first, then the angel."

Several ordinary black Hypers stepped forward into view. No doubt they'd been standing there all along. They took hold of Miriael's trolley and wheeled her towards the curtains at the far end of the chamber.

As the curtains parted, a wide interior space opened up ahead. She glimpsed enormous white pillars descending to the ground…and, in the same moment, felt an oppressive pressure building inside her head. It was the same experience she'd had when the giant Doctor had passed above her on the overbridge…

9

Doctor Saniette's dome loomed larger and larger as the rescue team approached. It was a hundred feet high, and as wide as it was high. Transparent panels at the top shed brightness across the night sky. Lower down, glowing panels of a different kind revealed the shadow of a colossal figure within.

"Brr!" muttered Shanna. "I hate that place. Gives me the creeps."

She led them towards the back of the dome until their advance was blocked by a wire fence.

"Don't touch, it's electrical," she warned. "It'll knock you flat."

"Then how—" Ferren began, but found himself addressing empty air. His sister was heading for a gate in the fence, and a red plastic box at the side of the gate.

Naturally, the gate was locked. Shanna produced a screwdriver from a pouch on her belt and attacked the screws of the box. Ferren guessed at once that there were Plasmatics inside.

Soon the cover of the box came away. Peering over his sister's shoulder, he saw a mass of veined tissue and glistening, string-thin tendons. The tissue was alive and quietly palpitating, the tendons attached to hooked levers at the sides of the box.

Shanna studied the Plasmatics for a moment, then reached in and touched with her fingertips at certain points. She seemed to be murmuring under her breath. Her fingertips made tiny up-and-down movements as if playing on some infinitely delicate musical instrument.

It took several minutes. Then, finally, the gate unlocked and swung slowly open. Shanna breathed a sigh of relief.

"I can't always communicate with them," she confessed.

They passed through the gate, weapons at the ready. On the other side, the dome rose forty yards away. The space in between was a parking area for bucket-trains, such as Ferren had seen on his previous visit to the Camp. There were three of them, each with a snub-nosed hauling engine at the front, coupled to half-a-dozen buckets on wheels.

They made their way between the bucket-trains, moving with stealth, checking in all directions. The only light was the faint, dull glow from the dome, and there was nobody around.

Suddenly, Shanna detoured to the hauling engine at the head of one particular machine. Ferren and the other followed, mystified. They were even more mystified when she crouched and knelt on the tiny footplate behind the engine.

"Thought so!" she exclaimed with satisfaction. "I recognised the markings."

"What markings?" Ferren saw nothing distinctive about this engine compared to the others.

She pointed to the steel plate that covered the back of the engine. "See where I loosened the screws? I remember the Plasmatics in this engine. I communicated very well with these."

Ferren was amazed. "You remember individual Plasmatics?"

"They're all different when you get to know them," she said, and gave him a lopsided grin.

Of course, he thought, *these are the only beings she's known for two and a half years.*

She rose from the footplate, stepped away from the engine and became brisk and efficient again. "Right, you all want to get on with the rescue. Let's go and work out how to do it."

She led the team forward to the dome. To Ferren's surprise, it wasn't built with solid material, although rigid ribs supported the structure. Between the ribs were panels of plastic fabric, no thicker than canvas.

"We can cut our way in," he said.

In fact, Shanna was already cutting. She made a foot-long incision with her knife, stuck her head through and spied out the scene inside. A minute later, she withdrew her head again.

"We've come to a good spot," she told them in a whisper. "Everybody quiet now."

With swift strokes, she extended the incision upwards and downwards. Then she stepped through, and the rescue team followed.

10

Inside the dome, the air was warm and stuffy with a faintly sweet smell. When they entered, they faced a wall of head-high cabinets displaying row upon row of dials and switches. Around them and above them was a framework of scaffolding, all metal tubes and horizontal boards. Wires and cables ran over the ground and went up the side of the scaffolding.

The cabinets blocked their vision across the interior, while the scaffolding obscured their vision looking up. They had a sense of dazzling, bright lights shining down from high above, and the sense of some towering white shape on which they shone.

"That's him." Shanna pointed to the white shape. "I think he's facing the other way."

"Have you been here before?" Ferren asked in a whisper.

Shanna grimaced. "In here? You must be joking. But I saw the dome going up round the new Doctor when they built it."

"Oh, right. So you don't know where they'd have put Miriael?"

"No, but she'd have come in through the main entrance. Opposite side to us. Let's look around."

She led the way past the cabinets until they came to a gap. There was something at the other end of the gap, something curved and gleaming. They couldn't tell what it was until they came right up to it: a massive steel cylinder, ten feet in diameter.

"No, not here," Shanna warned, as Ferren prepared to squeeze between cylinder and cabinet. "Let's find another gap."

But as Shanna signalled for everyone to go back, suddenly they pushed forward.

"Hyper!" hissed Flens. "Stay hidden!"

Tightly crammed into the narrow space, they all froze and held their breath.

A moment later, Ferren saw the Hyper stride past. He came and went in the blink of an eye, not even glancing in their direction. They continued to wait.

Then Flens peeked out around the corner of the cabinet.

"He's stopped," he reported, shaking his head. "Looks like he's on guard duty."

Everyone craned to look. The black-suited figure had taken up position just a few paces away. He stood with legs firmly planted, his long-barrelled weapon resting butt-down on the ground beside him. He wasn't looking in their direction and hadn't noticed the cut they'd made in the wall of the dome. But he would surely notice if they came out now.

"We could be stuck here for ages," Ferren whispered in his sister's ear.

Shanna clicked her tongue. "All right, then. I think we can jump him before he can reach for his weapon."

"Then what? Cut his throat?"

"Hypers don't have windpipes or arteries. But I know a way to deal with him, if we're quick." She turned to Bross. "You're the strongest. Hold him down, and we'll get him on his back."

She peeked out around the cabinet and held up her hand so they could all see her three extended fingers. "On the count of three."

She folded over a first finger. "One." Then a second finger. "Two." Then a third. "*Three!*"

They swept out of the gap, and the Hyper hardly had time to swivel his head. Shanna charged into him and knocked him over. Kiet pulled his weapon away, Ferren and the others grabbed arms and legs.

"Onto his back!" ordered Shanna.

The Hyper let out a vicious hiss, but he was too surprised to call out.

As they rolled him flat on his back, Bross pressed down on his shoulders. Shanna covered his mouthslit with one hand; with the other, she reached for his forehead. Her fingers worked at something—at the plug where all Hypers had their doses injected.

Ferren gasped as he understood. Shanna was unscrewing the plug in his forehead!

The Hyper didn't have the chance to get over his surprise. Shanna finished unscrewing, the plug came away in her hand and a jet of escaping vapour shot forth like steam. A million colours, a million images, dispersing into the air...

"Don't look," warned Shanna.

She took her hand away from his mouthslit, but no sounds emerged. The glare from his eyeslits turned blank and dull.

"Now onto his front," Shanna ordered.

The jet of escaping vapour was already less intense. When they rolled him over, the hole in his forehead pressed against the ground, so that the colours and images leaked out more slowly.

Ferren felt the arm he was gripping grow gradually limp.

"Is he dead?" he asked Shanna.

"No. More like...depressurised. They can revive him with another dose. But he'll be quiet for us now."

"What do we do with him?" asked Kiet.

Shanna cocked an ear. The interior of the dome murmured with quiet activity, as before. They had disposed of the Hyper with a minimum of noise and had drawn no attention.

"He can stay here," she said.

The left the inert body and continued on around the back of the cabinets. They didn't have to go far before they found another gap, and this time there was no cylinder in the way at the other end. They crept forward and peered out. Although Hypers milled about at ground level, they were preoccupied with their tasks, and the rescue team was at no risk of being spotted.

Every eye was drawn upwards. The interior of the dome was a breathtaking sight, with the tiers of scaffolding that rose against the walls all around. Long cables dangled down to the ground from out of the brightness above. And Doctor Saniette...

At first, Ferren hardly realised he was seeing Doctor Saniette. The giant loomed so large it was impossible to take him in as a whole. Ferren squinted up at his legs and white medical coat in disbelief. He could take in only a vague impression of a vast bulk higher up, while the great head and face were completely hidden from view.

Dropping his gaze, Ferren discovered a new wonder. Doctor Saniette's legs terminated not in feet but in something more like hooves…and the hooves were actually massive steel cylinders. The very same as the steel cylinder which had stood in their way earlier… It wasn't only in size that Doctor Saniette was different.

"Winch her up!"

A shout of command came from the middle of a group of Hypers, followed by a creak and rattle of machinery. Then one of the cables that hung down from the roof of the dome went suddenly taut. As it moved upwards, four attached chains also went taut, lifting a flat, rectangular frame from the ground.

Ferren gaped. The frame rising above the heads of the surrounding Hypers was the frame of a stretcher. And someone lay on it…someone with bright, golden hair…

"It's her!"

Shanna pulled him back into the shadows of the cabinets and hissed a warning to everyone. "Stay hidden!"

Ferren protested, but in a lowered voice now. "We have to save her! She's being winched up to the Doctor!"

"We have to have a plan first."

"No time!"

"You can't fight that many Hypers. Plan first."

"Yes, plan first." Kiet agreed with Shanna. "I've got an idea."

"So have I," whispered Flens.

Shanna made them all draw back a little further. "So let's hear your ideas," she said. "Let's see if they fit with mine."

11

The pressure continued to intensify in Miriael's head. As she went up higher and higher, she thought that her skull would burst.

Approaching the level of the Doctor's shoulders, she saw a thirty-foot gantry spanning the dome, all the way from the scaffolding on one side to the scaffolding on the other. A gang of Hypers awaited her on the gantry. When her stretcher arrived, they caught it by the chains, pulled it in and locked the frame in place.

Miriael blinked in the brightness. The tray of surgical instruments was already in place, winched up before her. The Hypers retreated to the scaffolding at the sides.

Then Doctor Saniette's head leaned forward over her. At the centre of his face was a single gigantic, bulging eye. Like a fly's eye, its gelatinous surface was divided into a hundred separate facets—and each facet gave back a reflection of herself and her stretcher. Miriael's mind swam...

She couldn't tell what his skin was made of. He had no proper mouth, only a black oval pad from which a dozen wires emerged. The wires ran round out of sight behind the back of his neck. When he spoke, his voice echoed and re-echoed as if reproduced through a great many speakers.

"Well, angel, here you are. I've been searching for you, you know."

The tone was carefully modulated, as if held under control. Miriael lay still and strove to resist the pressure in her head.

"Now you'll play your part and make your contribution," he went on. "A unique specimen. I can't help thinking you survived especially for my benefit. The benefit of my great goal. No?"

He seemed to expect a reply, but Miriael wouldn't give him one.

"I've devoted all my energies to the quest for knowledge, you see. Complete and absolute knowledge. A trillion trillion trillion pieces of information I've absorbed. But there has always been one relative shortfall: the Heavenly realm and the nature of angels. With your aid, I shall now make good on those deficits."

"You can't learn from me." She tried to sound dismissive. "I'm not a normal angel."

"Not now, indeed. But your memories contain all the elements of normal angel experience. Your life in Heaven, your training, your instincts and impulses. It's not what you are, it's what you *have been* that interests me. Every particle of your body and mind carries the imprint of your past, which I shall extract and absorb, one tiny sliver at a time. Then I shall fully understand, as you could never do yourself. I shall understand *everything*."

Was there a note of gloating in the calm, quiet tone?

"You're insane," said Miriael.

"On the contrary, I am the very essence of rationality. What I know and do and understand is all for the sake of making the world a better place. Perfectly safe and secure. A perfect place."

"Perfect for *you*."

"No, for everyone. Everyone other than me, because *I* have to bear the weight of it. I alone, the ultimate being of my kind. Do you imagine it's a pleasure to have my level of mental capacity and my degree of consciousness?"

His voice was changing and breaking up as he spoke. Miriael had the impression of someone attempting to pronounce a great many sentences all at the same time.

"It is agony, let me tell you, *agony*. To remain endlessly, endlessly on guard, to calculate innumerable risks, to encompass an infinity of possibilities—too much for one mind! But *I* do it! I can and I must! Eternal vigilance! The price of omniscience!'

"You can't be omniscient," Miriael objected. "Omniscience belongs to—"

"To *me!*' The mouthpad quivered, the whole face shook. It was as though invisible forces were pulling Doctor Saniette in a dozen different directions. "Because I can! Ultimate being! My gift and my curse!"

He was like a volcano about to explode. But instead he quietened, the fluctuations of his voice steadied, and he went back to his carefully modulated tone.

"Objective, impartial and rational," he observed. "I remain under control."

There was a swishing sound as he raised one arm and adjusted a battery of lights mounted on the gantry. Miriael closed her eyes as the glare fell full upon her—but not before she glimpsed the peculiar stump-like end of his arm. In place of a normal hand and fingers, he had a leathery pad like an animal's paw, from which sprouted an enormous number of bristling filaments.

She strained against the bonds that fastened her to the stretcher. They were soft rather than hard, yet strangely unyielding.

Doctor Saniette must have noticed her struggles. "Those bonds will only tighten the more you pull at them. I advise against it." His great head rotated towards the tray of surgical instruments. "And now I must choose the means for making the first incision. I think you'll admire the artistry of my surgery. Experiencing it from the other side, as it were. A more inward form of appreciation."

12

Kiet was counting. "Twenty and one…twenty and two…twenty and three…" She murmured under her breath and left a long pause after each number. She wanted to give Ferren as much time as possible.

She had taken up position in the gap between the cabinets. When she looked back over her shoulder, she could see Ethany, Gibby and Bross busy on the wall of the dome. They were hacking out a large, square panel of the plastic fabric. She had given Bross her knife, since he hadn't received one from Shanna earlier.

Shanna herself had already left, reluctantly. Their means of escape had been her idea, and only she could carry it out. Still, she was unhappy to miss out on a more active role—and doubly unhappy that the most dangerous role fell to her brother.

At present, Ferren was out of sight, ascending the scaffolding behind the Doctor's back. When he reached the right level, he would come round to the front, where the angel's stretcher had been fixed onto some kind of bridge across the dome. Kiet was counting to a hundred as a way to time his arrival.

The only role almost as dangerous as Ferren's was the role of decoy and diversion, which Flens had taken on. Kiet couldn't see him either, but she knew he was behind the cabinets on the other side of the dome, working out where to run and how to escape. Daredevil Flens! She hoped he wouldn't take unnecessary risks.

"Seventy and five...seventy and six...seventy and seven..."

Not long now. Their only chance of success was perfect synchronisation. Glancing over her shoulder again, she saw that Ethany, Gibby and Bross had almost completed their task. She caught Gibby's eye and mouthed, *Hurry, hurry, hurry!*

"Eighty and two...eighty and three...eighty and four..."

Flens had just appeared in a gap between cabinets on the other side. He gave her a thumbs up: *Ready to go!* She shook her head and signalled back: *Not yet!* He retreated out of sight, but she knew he was watching.

"Eighty and nine...ninety...ninety and one..."

She looked up into the roof of the dome, shielding her eyes. The bridge was a mere silhouette, the tiers of scaffolding dissolved into the light. She couldn't actually see Ferren, but that didn't mean he wasn't there.

"Ninety and eight...ninety and nine...one hundred."

The moment had come. Kiet could only hope that Ferren was in place and ready to take advantage of the diversion. She raised a hand and gave Flens a big thumbs up.

Flens came rushing out across the floor of the dome like a madman. "Yaroo! Yaroo!" He flailed his arms and yelled at the top of his voice. "I'm your saboteur! Come and get me! Yaroo!"

Far enough, thought Kiet. *They've all seen you.*

Still he kept coming, until he was twenty paces away from the nearest Hypers. Then he spun on his heel and raced back the way he'd come.

The Hypers on the floor of the dome stared as if stunned. Then a commanding voice set them in motion. "Catch him! Catch the saboteur!"

In the next moment, Flens disappeared from view behind the cabinets. The Hypers all ran towards the spot where they'd last seen him. But even before they reached it, a muffled shout rang out from somewhere else entirely.

"Yaroo! Yaroo! Catch me if you can!"

Kiet dropped back to join Ethany, Gibby and Bross. They held up a great sheet of plastic fabric, ready to play their part.

13

erren had climbed the scaffolding behind the Doctor's back, hidden from Hypers on the ground. Sometimes he had scaled ladders from tier to tier, at other times he had shinned up the vertical tubes themselves.

Viewed from behind, the white medical coat was like a great, snow-covered hillside. Ferren had heard a strange-sounding voice on the way up, no doubt the Doctor speaking to Miriael. But by the time he reached the topmost tier, the voice was silent.

He crept out from behind the Doctor's shoulders and started to circle around on the scaffolding. He saw a bridge-like gantry that spanned the dome, he saw a battery of lights and medical equipment and Miriael tied down on her stretcher. It could have been so simple to run across and cut her bonds—but it wasn't.

His heart sank as he took in the gangs of Hypers waiting at either end of the gantry. He would have to fight through three of them on one side or four on the other. Impossible!

He shook his head and looked upwards. The only other route to the stretcher was by way of the cable that had raised it aloft. A single cable descended from a pulley to a ring attached by chains to the corners of the stretcher. If he could slide down the cable...

But how to reach the pulley? It was mounted overhead on a supporting rib that converged with others to arch across the top of the dome. Would the rib bear his weight?

He didn't stop to think, just jumped from scaffolding to rib and began climbing up. The rib had perforations and a flange that made it easy to grip. Soon he passed beyond panels of plastic fabric to the transparent panels that crowned the uppermost part of the dome. The further he climbed, the more he found himself tilting over backwards.

But the tilt wasn't the worst; what he hated was the feeling of exposure. He was surely in plain sight to the Hypers on the scaffolding, if one of them happened to glance up… He had to struggle against the urge to twist his head and look round. He couldn't do anything about it anyway.

He concentrated on his climbing, and at last he reached his goal. Still no one had spotted him or called out. He lowered himself into position on the pulley, wrapping arms and legs around it. Below he could see Doctor Saniette's skull with a mat of something like hair under a hairnet. The huge face was invisible, bent over Miriael on her stretcher. She appeared to have her eyes closed.

He had reached his position only just in time. A moment later, wild yelling and shouting rose from the bottom of the dome. "Yaroo! Yaroo!" Flens was launching the diversion.

The Doctor swung his great head away from Miriael and looked down. The Hypers on the scaffolding were looking down too. Far below, the Hypers at ground level were now scurrying round, giving chase to the intruder.

Ferren clambered over the pulley, gripped the cable in both hands and slid down. His palms were hot and burning with the speed of his descent. He came to the ring—and Miriael opened her eyes. Wide blue eyes staring up at him in amazement …

Still Doctor Saniette hadn't noticed, nor had the Hypers on the scaffolding. In fact, Doctor Saniette seemed to be stamping his hooves as though trying to trample some noxious insect. Ferren heard a drumming sound from the ground and sensed a vast shaking and vibration. But he stayed focused on his task.

Miriael was bound by straps around her wrists and ankles. Not metal, at least… He swung down onto the frame of her stretcher and reached for the knife that Shanna had given him, tucked into the top of his loincloth. No time to greet Miriael, no time to even look at her. He began sawing at the first strap with his blade. Back and forth, back and forth…

"Whoa! Look! Residual!" One of the Hypers on the scaffolding had spotted him.

The first strap parted. Ferren switched across to the second.

"What's he doing here?"

"Must be a bunch of 'em snuck in!"

The shouts came from both ends of the gantry now. But Doctor Saniette was still looking down at the ground, still stamping his hooves up and down.

"Put them down…put them down…mustn't be…put them down," he rumbled in his strange, echoey voice.

Faster and faster Ferren sawed with his knife. The second strap parted, and he started on the third.

"Doctor!" "Doctor!" "Doctor Saniette!" The Hypers on the scaffolding waved and yelled and tried to redirect the Doctor's attention. Then they stepped onto the gantry and came forward themselves.

The third strap parted. Only one to go! Ferren spoke to Miriael out of the corner of his mouth. "Get ready to jump."

"What?" Miriael didn't understand, but she rose on one knee on the stretcher. The last strap held her pinned by her left ankle.

The Hypers advanced from both ends of the gantry—but cautiously. The whole structure shook, thanks to the vibrations of Doctor Saniette's stamping.

Ferren cut through the last strap and looked down. Most of the Hypers at ground level had gone off in pursuit of Flens. There in the exact spot planned stood Kiet, Ethany, Gibby and Bross with their sheet of plastic. They held it stretched out taut between them like a trampoline.

"Jump!" Ferren told Miriael, and pointed. On two knees now, she goggled at the square sheet forty or fifty feet below

"So small!" she gasped. "What if I—"

Ferren gave her a push and sent her toppling over the edge of the stretcher.

He couldn't stay watching to see how she landed; in that same instant, Doctor Saniette's rumble changed to a wordless roar. Ferren looked round and saw an immense, multi-faceted eye hovering over him. *Now* the Doctor was paying attention.

Ferren had no time to take aim, he could only hope. The gantry had stopped shaking, and Hypers from both sides were rushing towards him.

He stepped off the frame of the stretcher and dropped.

14

"Here she comes!"

Looking up into the brightness, Kiet saw the angel plummeting towards them. She braced and pulled back hard, along with Ethany, Gibby and Bross.

At first she thought the angel was going to miss her landing. Then Miriael half-extended a wing and came down right in the middle of the sheet. She rebounded from the plastic, high in the air. Kiet watched as she spread both wings and glided to the ground two yards away.

"Hold steady!" cried Bross.

Ferren was falling even before the angel had touched down. He was more compact than Miriael and fell faster. When he hit the sheet, it turned out he was also far heavier. Taken by surprise, Kiet barely kept her grip and almost lost her balance. The others stumbled too.

Ferren didn't bounce. His weight brought the sheet to the ground, where he lay sprawling and winded. But at least they had broken his fall.

Kiet darted forward. "You all right?"

He nodded mutely and held up a hand. Kiet caught hold of the hand and hauled him to his feet. There was no time to lose. Hypers had seen the rescue and were calling out across the floor of the dome.

"Catch 'em!"

"Kill 'em!"

"Keep that angel alive! Surround them! Kill them, not her!"

The last cry came from a strange female-looking Hyper, whose shoulders were covered in copper circuitry. She had sprung up on top of a cabinet and was directing operations from the other side of the dome.

A thunderous drumming drowned out all cries. Doctor Saniette was stamping his great hooves again, and rotating as he stamped. There was a screech of metal as his lumbering limbs collided with the scaffolding, then a prolonged grating, scraping, creaking sound. A large section of scaffolding leaned away from the wall and toppled slowly to the ground.

Still towing Ferren, Kiet followed the others back to the same gap where she'd kept watch before. Behind them, shouts of pursuit turned into shouts of alarm. As they plunged between the cabinets, the scaffolding struck the floor with a tremendous, clanging crash.

They ran on, straight out through the gaping square hole that Gibby, Ethany and Bross had cut in the panel.

The night outside was suddenly quiet compared to the noise and chaos going on in the dome. Bross pointed and led the way across the parking area. Shanna stood beside the snub-nosed engine at the front of the bucket-train, signalling to them.

Kiet turned to Ferren. "She's set it up, your sister. Got your breath back yet?"

"Yes, all right now," said Ferren, and let go of her hand.

Everyone headed for the wheeled buckets, which were only big enough for one person in each. Ethany and Gibby helped Miriael into a bucket, then dived into separate buckets themselves. Bross took the first bucket behind Shanna, who had squeezed into the narrow space on the footplate at the back of the engine. Kiet climbed into the very last bucket, while Ferren climbed into the last but one. Still there was one member of the rescue team missing.

"Flens!" cried Kiet.

Even as she spoke his name, Flens appeared. He ran across the parking area from a different direction, grinning from ear to ear.

"Here I am!"

They pointed him to his bucket, and he jumped in.

"Let's go!" Bross called to Shanna.

The Plasmatics in the engine were primed and ready. There was a sudden lurch, a squeak of wheels, and the bucket-train moved forward. Kiet looked back at Doctor Saniette's dome.

No one had come out after them—and no one was likely to now. The dome was no longer a hemisphere, but a formless shape of lumps and bulges. Many of its supporting ribs must have collapsed, so that the fabric sagged or hung in folds. As Kiet watched, the whole structure appeared to shift and rotate…

The bucket-train trundled out through the gate of the parking area and kept going.

15

Ferren crouched low and arranged his feet between chunks of coal or rock in the bottom of his bucket. The bucket-train moved slowly away from the centre of the Camp, towards the nearest exit bridge.

Although he couldn't help wishing Shanna would go faster, Ferren understood the plan. He'd seen for himself on his previous visit how wheeled trains moved about in the Camp with no one driving them. The Plasmatics in the engines followed mathematical instructions; usually, the Hypers who gave the instructions walked alongside, but not always. No one would ever imagine that Plasmatics might be under instructions of a different kind. Hidden inside the buckets, the rescue team could travel a long way without arousing suspicion.

They hadn't gone far when sirens sounded all across the Camp. Then loudspeakers added their blare: *"Warning! Major incident! Doctor Saniette! Attention Doctor Saniette!"*

A bustle of activity sprang up everywhere. Lights came on, orders were shouted, Hypers began running in the direction of the dome. Ferren ducked his head well out of sight. The bucket-train made no sudden deviations but trundled on at the same steady pace.

The sound and feel of the wheels under his bucket told Ferren they were passing along a paved roadway. On either side, he could hear the boots of Hypers and harsh voices calling out.

"What's happening?"

"What do we do?"

"Has everyone gone mad?"

"*He* has!"

Two minutes later, the bucket-train left the roadway again. Now they were crossing softer ground that crunched under their wheels. This was a darker, quieter area, with no Hypers around. After a while, Ferren risked a small peek above the rim of his bucket.

What he saw were pyramids of ash and cinders, some high and some low. Here and there were glowing, red embers exposed among the cinders.

A whistle of amazement from Kiet redirected his attention. She too was peeking out.

"Where is it?" she cried.

At first he didn't understand why she was scanning the part of the Camp they'd left behind. Then he worked out what should have been still visible above the pyramids—but wasn't.

"The dome! It's gone!"

Staring out backwards from the bucket-train, they weren't watching the pyramids at the sides and didn't see a pair Hypers emerge from the shadow of a particular pile of cinders. They jumped when one of the two spoke up.

"Hey! What was that?"

Ferren and Kiet ducked instantly out of sight—too late. They hadn't been seen, but they had been heard.

"Someone's voice."

"Two voices."

"Must've come from that train."

"See anyone with it?"

"Nah. Where's it heading, anyway?"

"Under whose orders?"

"Needs investigating."

Hypers' boots scrunched over the ground as they swung to follow the bucket-train. Then one of the two barked a mathematical formula.

"34c times 9.8 plus 6 squared!"

They were ordering the train to a halt, and for a moment the engine at the front reduced speed. But only for a moment—then it accelerated again.

"What the—?"

Shanna did that! Ferren exulted. *She overrode their command!*

Secrecy was impossible; now Shanna was trying to outpace pursuit. The train accelerated—but the two Hypers accelerated after it.

"34c times 9.8 plus 6 squared!" Once more the order rang out, in jerky gasps of breath.

This time, the engine barely slowed. When it sped up again, they were travelling faster than ever. Ferren braced against the sides of his bucket as everything rattled around him.

Clangg!

The sound came from Kiet's bucket at the back of the train. Then a Hyper yelled out in triumph.

"I see 'em! I see 'em all! Intruders! Saboteurs!"

A black, rubber-clad head had come into view, rising high above the back of Kiet's bucket. One of the Hypers had latched on and was about to climb in. Kiet jumped up to confront him.

Ferren jumped up too. The Hyper carried a weapon that he recognised by its cone-shaped nozzle—a flamethrower! Kiet grabbed hold of it, and the Hyper twisted it this way and that, trying to break her hold.

Ferren strained forward, but couldn't reach around Kiet to attack her attacker. He dived down to the bottom of his bucket and came up with a chunk of rock in either hand.

He was intending to throw… But the Hyper had forced Kiet backwards and downwards, and was leaning over her in her bucket. *Now* the black, rubber-clad head was within reach!

Ferren swung with one chunk of rock and smashed it against one side of the Hyper's head. The Hyper looked up, a puzzled glare in his eyeslits. Ferren swung with his second chunk of rock and delivered an even better blow to the other side.

The Hyper roared with rage, lost his balance and fell backwards. He had lost his grip on the flamethrower too, which Kiet still held on to.

"Yaroo!" shouted Kiet, as Flens had done.

There were more cheers behind Ferren from Gibby and Ethany, who had been watching the fight. But the moment of victory was short-lived.

The second Hyper was still jogging along without attempting to catch up. He didn't need to. He had a small black box with a silver spike in his hand, and he was speaking into it.

"Intruder alert. Zone Thirteen, Section Six, heading north. Watch for rogue train. Intruder alert."

16

For the moment, nothing changed. The noises of the Camp continued as before, the area through which they were passing remained quiet. The Hyper with the black box fell further and further behind, and eventually dropped out of sight. When the bucket-train emerged from the pyramids onto a road, Shanna slowed to their previous speed. The road seemed to be a main thoroughfare, but at present empty and deserted.

They could now see what had happened to Doctor Saniette's dome. A muffled bellow in the distance drew their attention—and there was the dome like a slowly moving mountain! Doctor Saniette had not only collapsed it but detached it from the ground. Enveloped in its folds, he now blundered blindly this way and that, carrying the whole thing with him. By the sound of his frustrated bellowing, he was trying to shake it off. Luckily, his lumbering path was nowhere near the route they were travelling.

They were still watching when a flare shot high in the air overhead. Floating down from the top of its arc, it painted the scene around them in garish, green light. Then loudspeakers crackled and blared into life.

"Intruder alert! Rogue train! Close gates on bridges! Guard all exits!"

The blare was deafening, and a thousand other noises soon joined in all across the Camp. By the light of the flare, Ferren could see that the road they were on wasn't empty after all; two hundred yards ahead was a gang of a dozen marching Hypers.

Shanna must have communicated with the Plasmatics, because the bucket-train leaped forward once again. Faster and faster it accelerated. By the time it reached the Hypers, it was hurtling along at a speed Ferren would never have believed possible.

Taken by surprise, the Hypers scattered and dived out of the way. They yelled and shouted and shook their fists.

Still the bucket-train accelerated. Obscure shapes of machinery and industrial plant flashed past left and right. Ferren held on to the side of his bucket, crouching low and looking out. He could see where the overhead shields of wire came to an end not far ahead—which surely indicated the end of the Camp too. Not far to go!

They were even closer than he thought. They swung onto a wider road that led straight up to an opening in the embankment, straight up to a bridge and an overbridge beyond. But the gate on the bridge was closed and defended by armed guards.

"Heads down!" yelled Shanna from her place behind the engine.

She was clearly hoping to smash through the gate. She kept the bucket-train moving at top speed. The armed guards knelt and raised their weapons to their shoulders.

In the next moment, a volley of projectiles raked the front and sides of the bucket-train. But the Hypers were firing too fast to aim accurately, and the metal walls of the buckets were as solid as any armour. Projectiles ricocheted harmlessly away.

We still have a chance, thought Ferren—

—and then suddenly they didn't. Tall, lithe figures in black came racing in to reinforce the guards. Like cats they moved, covering the ground in great springs and bounds, all carrying flamethrowers. Ferren saw them and groaned.

Shanna must have seen them too. She swung the bucket-train off the road and accelerated away from the danger.

"Queen-Hypers!" she yelled back. "I'll try for another bridge!"

But the Queen-Hypers, as she called them, hadn't come as reinforcements for this bridge alone. When the bucket-train veered away, they gave chase.

Even at top speed, Shanna couldn't outdistance them. In no time at all, they came up level with the last bucket in the train. Kiet shrank down out of sight as the first flamethrower spat fire.

There was a tremendous sizzling roar, and the air filled with red and yellow flames. Ferren watched, transfixed with horror, until the Queen-Hypers came up level with his own bucket. He dropped down and took cover just before a new burst of fire shot across. He could see the flames over his head and smell the flamethrower smell of burning fuel. But the flames couldn't touch him as long as he stayed curled up at the bottom of his bucket.

Would the Queen-Hypers climb up on the train and shoot fire down from above? Instead, he heard the flames beating on the metal walls of the bucket. Did they think they could burn a hole through his armour?

Then he realised how the interior of the bucket was warming up. In a matter of minutes, it was stifling hot. When he touched the walls now, the metal burned his fingertips. So that was their plan! He could hardly breath for the heat.

They're going to roast us alive, he thought. *We'll be roasted like meat in an oven.*

The bucket-train rattled on as fast as ever, so the flamethrowers couldn't yet have reached Shanna and her Plasmatics at the front. But he saw what seemed like a dull red glow in the side of his bucket, and everything appeared to him through a wavering haze of heat. Or perhaps the wavering was in his mind, and he was about to faint... He smelled a smell of singeing hair and knew it was his own.

Then, all at once, the roaring stopped, the flames no longer beat on the walls of his bucket. Had the Queen-Hypers called off the attack? Had their flamethrowers run out of fuel, or what? In the relative quiet, a deep-down vibration sounded in his ears.

Still the train sped on, never faltering. He raised his head cautiously above the rim of his bucket.

The Queen-Hypers had fallen back, loping along thirty paces to the rear of Kiet's bucket. As he watched, the top of Kiet's head appeared, then her whole head and shoulders. She still held the flamethrower that she'd snatched from the Hyper.

He gulped fresh air into his lungs and swivelled to look forward. They were travelling parallel to the embankment, and there was an opening in it just a hundred yards ahead. An opening meant an exit bridge and a gate... He looked and saw the road that led up to the exit.

"There's our escape!" he cried, and turned back to Kiet. "We can do it!"

But Kiet was looking in a different direction—and suddenly Ferren understood the deep-down vibration he'd heard before.

Thrungg! Thrungg! Thrungg! Thrungg!

Doctor Saniette was no longer in the distance. He had shaken off the enveloping dome, and could now see and move freely again. His giant hooves pounded the ground, his column-like legs covered a dozen yards with every stride, he smashed and trampled everything in his path.

Thrungg! Thrungg! Thrungg! Thrungg!

His single, huge eye was fixed upon the bucket-train as he approached.

17

"I—will—will—keep—control! Con—trol! Con—trol!"

The Doctor's voice was an echoing boom, strangely disjointed. He stomped down on stainless steel tanks and crashed through tall glass vessels, spattering liquid. His once-white medical coat was covered in smears. In his wake, he trailed cords and cables from the dome he had left behind.

Ferren watched helplessly. The Doctor wasn't advancing directly towards them, but towards the exit where they would have made their escape. He intended to cut them off before they could reach the bridge.

"Hang on!" Shanna shouted back to Ferren and the rest.

She was trying to coax more speed out of the Plasmatics in the engine. But although the Doctor appeared slow and clumsy, his huge strides made him faster than he looked. He arrived before them at the road leading up to the bridge and planted his great hooves across it.

Shanna kept going as though to head right past him and on to another exit. She drove the train across the road—then suddenly threw a ninety-degree turn. She was aiming to detour around him before he could react. The buckets bucked and rattled, skidded as they swung wildly after the engine.

"I will—I will—I will—I will—" Doctor Saniette saw what they were doing and shuffled his left hoof further across.

Shanna let out a wail of despair. The Doctor bent at the knees and lowered a hand to scoop them up. Ferren saw the hand coming towards them—a hand without fingers, only a black, leathery pad that bristled with filaments.

Then Shanna swerved the other way, so abruptly that he was flung off his feet. The bucket tilted on its wheels, teetered for a moment and nearly went over. Then it came back upright again.

Ferren found himself at the bottom of his bucket, looking up at Doctor Saniette like a tower soaring above him. Cylindrical steel hooves, dirtied white legs, white coat with smears... From high overhead came an inarticulate bellow.

Ferren hardly realised what was happening until it happened. Shanna's last swerve had redirected the bucket-train right between the Doctor's legs! The snub-nosed engine passed through, then Bross's bucket, then Miriael's...

"I—con—I will—control—keep—trol!'

Doctor Saniette's voice was like a hundred voices all speaking at once. But perhaps he didn't understand or couldn't see where the bucket-train had got to. He seemed to be straightening at the knees, yet he didn't move to close the gap between his hooves.

Bucket after bucket went through. Ferren flinched instinctively as he came in under the white medical coat like a hanging curtain. He twisted his neck to watch the Doctor's vast bulk passing over his head. As he emerged on the other side, he jumped to his feet and whooped in triumph.

Kiet, coming through right behind him, whooped too. She also flourished her flamethrower and, by accident or design, her fingers squeezed the trigger. A great gout of flame leaped forth from the cone-shaped nozzle. It played over the Doctor's trousered legs and the underside of his coat—and the material caught fire.

Whoooosh! The coat went up in a sheet of flame.

The bucket-train went careening on towards the bridge. Ferren heard Shanna shout something from the front, but the words didn't register. He was too busy gaping at the sight behind him.

As the towering, white figure came increasingly into view, there were tongues of flame licking and spreading all over his clothing. As if searching for the source of the fire, Doctor Saniette swung his arms and beat about this way and that. But his clumsy efforts did nothing to put out the flames.

Kranngg!

A tremendous crash pitched Ferren against the back wall of his bucket. When he looked round, Shanna had charged the engine into a gate that spanned the roadway at the start of the bridge.

The engine lost speed, but it was still moving forward. The gate was a high barrier of steel mesh—tough steel, but not impenetrable. Already the engine's nose had made a hole in the strands and continued to push through.

So close to freedom! Beyond the gate was the bridge across the moat, then the overbridge across dry land.

Sparks flew and metal screeched on metal. A notice board fell from the gate and crashed to the roadway. Several armed Hypers who stood nearby remained strangely inactive. One by one, the rescue team ducked their heads when their bucket arrived at the gate and scraped through.

The friction took its toll. By the time Ferren's bucket reached the gate, the engine had lost all momentum. He could hear the wheels slipping and spinning as the train laboured along. But still inching forward…

And then, at last, they were through. Suddenly, the train discovered new energy and surged forward again. They'd escaped!

There were several Hypers on this side of the gate too, but also strangely inactive. Ferren realised they were all gawping at something behind him…at Doctor Saniette…

He swung around, and an incredible sight met his eyes.

18

Doctor Saniette was still burning. He had turned in the direction of the escaping intruders, but seemed to have lost control of his own actions. His arms hung down, his legs were splayed, his whole body shook and heaved.

Except it wasn't exactly a body.

The fire had peeled away his coat and clothing, which floated down in charred scraps of material. Underneath were hundreds of ordinary-size Doctors, all fastened in side-by-side and one on top of the other. Strapped around a hinged skeleton, they made up the shape of torso, head and shoulders. Each wore a white medical coat, each had wires coming out of the back of his skull. Individually, they were just like the original Bankstown Doctors—except that their wires came together in thicker and thicker bundles, running all the way up from the limbs to the head.

They might have been tiny single cells in a gigantic organism. At present, though, the organism was unravelling, and the cells were falling apart.

Ferren stared wide-eyed. Although the bucket-train sped on across the bridge, Shanna was probably the only one not watching the disintegration of the giant Doctor.

The flames that had burned away his coat and clothing had now spread to the coats of the individual Doctors. All over the great body, tiny mouths opened up in tiny O's of agony. Their screams made no sound, but they were screaming.

No longer did the overall shape bear any resemblance to a human being. Individual Doctors hung part-way out from the skeleton frame, as if struggling to free themselves. Some had broken out of their harnesses of straps, yet the wires in their skulls held them back. They waved tiny, helpless hands and continued to scream.

Ominous ripples ran through the colossal legs and torso. Doctor Saniette was unable to support his own weight. His head wobbled on his shoulders, he swayed and staggered. His right leg took one vague step towards the bridge, and his left leg dragged after it. But he wasn't walking, only floundering.

He's going to fall, thought Ferren. *He's going to fall on us.*

They had left the embankment behind and were almost across the moat. But Doctor Saniette was eighty feet tall, at least as high as the moat was wide. If he fell full-length...

He lurched forward another step, then a half-step. Then his hooves and legs came to a dead stop. But his head and shoulders were still moving forward. He was tipping over at the top.

"Faster, faster!" yelled Ferren, as the bucket-train left the bridge and started along the overbridge.

Further and further the Doctor tilted. He couldn't have regained balance if he'd tried, and he wasn't trying. He didn't even put out his arms to break his fall. In slow motion, like a mighty tower, he toppled over straight towards the bucket-train.

Ferren stood frozen in his bucket. He looked up at a hundred Doctors descending upon him, a hundred tiny, shrieking mouths rushing down on top of him.

Kerwhummpff!

The giant body hit the bridge with a tremendous crashing, crunching sound. Debris flew up in all directions, along with a great spray of water from the moat. The monstrous head smashed down on the roadway just twenty feet short of the bucket-train.

But although they hadn't been crushed, they didn't escape untouched. As the overbridge collapsed under Doctor Saniette's head and body, the section along which they were travelling broke off and pivoted upwards on a pair of still-standing pylons. Suddenly the roadway leaped underneath them and sent them flying.

19

Time stood still. For one long, eternal moment, the train seemed to hover in mid-air. Even when they started to descend, it was as though they were floating. But the impact when they landed jarred every bone in Ferren's body.

They landed on bare ground alongside the overbridge. Incredibly, the buckets had sailed upright through the air and came down still upright on their wheels.

Ferren picked himself up from where he'd been thrown at the bottom of his bucket. Half-stunned, he clambered over the side and jumped out. All along the train, the others were also climbing out. Everyone seemed dazed and bemused.

It took a minute to adjust. Then Flens let forth a great shout, "We did it!"

Gibby skipped about, and Bross waved a fist in the air. "We did, we did, we did it!"

Ferren looked at the ruin and wreckage they'd left behind. The vast bulk of Doctor Saniette stretched from one side of the moat to the other; the bridge and part of the overbridge lay flattened beneath him. No one could chase after them without climbing over his great body. At present, there was no sign that anyone even thought of chasing after them.

Smoke still drifted above the fallen giant, but the splash and spray from the moat had extinguished the fires. Many of the small, ordinary Doctors who made up his body hung limp in their harnesses; others wriggled and squirmed as they sought to escape. Broken struts of the hinged skeleton to which they were attached stuck out here and there.

Ferren heard a whistle of amazement. "Whew! Look at that!"

It was Shanna, surveying the scene and shaking her head.

"We came to rescue an angel, and ended up destroying the Doctor," said Ferren.

"And all his tiny Doctors inside him." Shanna laughed. "I never dreamed of a sabotage like this."

"You've achieved the ultimate revenge."

"I suppose I have."

"Nothing more to do. You can join us now."

"Seems like I already have, little brother." Shanna laughed again and wrapped an arm over his shoulder.

"You'll be able to come round all the tribes with us. We're organising a Residual Alliance..."

But he was talking to himself. Shanna had caught sight of Miriael walking towards them—and her mouth hung open, her eyes were wide with wonder. It was the first time she'd had a proper view of the angel, Ferren realised—and she'd always been fascinated by the idea of angels.

"This is Miriael," he told her. "She's on our side and helping with the Residual Alliance."

Shanna just stared and stared. She appeared to have difficulty breathing.

"And this is my sister, Shanna," Ferren told Miriael. "She's been hiding all this time in the Humen Camp."

"I never thought..." Shanna found her voice, but hardly seemed to know what she was saying. "A real, live angel. I never thought it could happen to me. Meeting a real, live angel."

"Yes, we just rescued her," said Ferren.

Miriael smiled. "I'm not a very good example of an angel. Real angels have auras and don't eat mortal food. I think I'm a sort of hybrid."

"You still look…" Shanna couldn't find the words to say how she looked.

Miriael switched her attention to Ferren, and a troubled expression displaced her smile.

"Where's Kiet?" she asked. "You know, your friend from the Nesters. She was with us before, but I can't see her now."

20

Bross…Gibby…Ethany…Flens… Ferren looked round, but there was no Kiet.

He raised his voice. "Where's Kiet? What's happened to her?"

The others had been gazing at the ruin of Doctor Saniette. They were equally surprised to discover that Kiet wasn't with them.

"She must be still in her bucket," said Ethany.

Everyone made a beeline for Kiet's bucket at the end of the train—but the bucket wasn't there. At the back of Ferren's bucket, the coupling hook that should have linked to Kiet's bucket hung down unattached. They stared in amazement.

"Where's it gone?" muttered Ferren.

"Snapped right off," said Flens.

"When did it happen?" Shanna wondered.

"Maybe when the overbridge jumped up under us," Ethany suggested.

"It could be in the moat," said Bross.

They all turned to take another look at the moat. But they hadn't seen a partially submerged bucket before, and they didn't see one now.

"Maybe it fell in a very deep spot," said Gibby without much hope.

"Or sank down in the mud," added Ethany.

"Maybe it broke off earlier," said Miriael.

Everyone looked to Ferren, since he'd been riding in the bucket ahead of Kiet's. He racked his brains. *Of course* he should have seen what happened to her... She'd been there when she'd fired the flamethrower, but was she still there when they charged into the gate? Was she still there when they'd come through onto the bridge? He must have been looking in the right direction because he'd been looking at the Doctor—yet somehow it was only the Doctor he'd seen. It was stupid and impossible, but he couldn't remember.

"I don't know," he mumbled miserably. "Didn't anyone else see?"

There was a general shaking of heads. They'd all been looking upwards at the Doctor, not down at the buckets.

Ferren stuck out his chin. "The Humen might've got hold of her," he said. "We have to go and search."

He set off towards the moat, but Shanna hauled him back. "No! Wait! There are Hypers!"

Half-a-dozen black figures had now appeared along the top of the embankment. They were pointing at the fallen body of Doctor Saniette and the flattened bridge beneath him.

"They're not interested in us," said Ferren. "Anyway, she has to be rescued. Who's coming?"

But nobody was enthusiastic.

"We can't walk up where they can see us," Gibby objected.

"It'd be suicide," Bross agreed.

Ferren snorted. "It was suicide going in before."

"But at least we knew what we were doing," said Flens.

"Yes, going up through a drainage pipe," Ferren retorted. "We can do that again."

"But this time they're *watching!*" cried Ethany, with an edge in her voice. "They'll be *waiting* for us."

Ferren refused to listen. "I won't leave her there. They could be killing her or torturing her."

"We don't know if she's in their hands," Miriael pointed out. "It's all guesswork."

Ferren rounded on her. "We rescued you! *Kiet* helped rescue you!"

It was like an accusation, and Miriael looked suddenly guilty. "I didn't deserve… You shouldn't have…" She dropped her eyes. "All right, I'll come."

"*No!*" snapped Shanna. "It doesn't make sense! Not now! We have to choose our moment."

She still kept a grip on Ferren's arm, and he couldn't shake her off.

"Look!" cried Flens. "Look there!"

Everyone followed the line of his pointing arm. Two Queen-Hypers had just slid down the embankment into the moat. Chest-high in the water, they waded towards the broken hulk of Doctor Saniette. Small, pale Doctors wriggled in their straps at their approach, like maggots in a carcass.

"It's not safe here," said Ethany. "We have to get back to our base."

"*Then* we can work out how to search for Kiet." Bross turned to Ferren. "We'll all help as long as…"

But Ferren wasn't listening. Images of Kiet captured and tortured filled his mind, until he couldn't think straight. With a sudden, violent jerk, he broke away from Shanna and strode back towards the moat. Voices called out behind him.

"Stop!"

"Don't let him…!"

"He's gone mad!"

Shanna caught up with him at the water's edge and brought him to a halt. The others rushed round and blocked his way.

"Nobody else has to come," he growled. "I'll go on my own, and you can't stop me."

"Yes, we can," said Shanna. "Bross?"

There was a momentary exchange of glances. Then Ferren heard his sister say, "Just do it."

The blow came out of nowhere. There was an explosive impact on the point of his jaw, his head jolted back—then nothing. Ferren went out like a light.

21

Miriael didn't understand where they were going. Shanna and Bross supported Ferren's weight between them, his arms draped over their shoulders. The others led the way, scanning around as they walked. They went past a second bridge over the moat and approached a third.

"Here's the area," said Flens. "We weren't far from where we went in, after all."

The area was a storage zone for construction materials. They made their way to a trench that burrowed under a great stack of girders.

"This is our base," Ethany explained to Miriael. "Rhinn and Tadge will be waiting for us."

Even as she spoke, a fierce command rang out in the dark.

"Halt! Who goes there?"

Gibby laughed. "Hello Tadge! We're back!"

"At last!" another voice called out. "We were sick with worry."

"That's Rhinn," Ethany told Miriael, and dropped her voice to a whisper. "Tadge and Rhinn are Kiet's family."

One by one, the rescue team and Miriael dropped down into the trench, which was like a cave under the girders. Tadge and Rhinn appeared as dim shapes in the darkness, but Miriael was clearly recognisable to them.

"You brought back the angel!" Rhinn clapped her hands. "You did it *and* came back safe and sound. So it wasn't a doomsday mission!"

"What's wrong with *him?*" asked Tadge, meaning Ferren.

"It's a long story," said Shanna.

"Who's *she?*" Tadge demanded, meaning Shanna.

"Tell us what happened," said Rhinn.

There was a long moment of silence. Tadge and Rhinn hadn't yet noticed their sister's absence, and nobody wanted to break the news.

"Not all safe and sound, not yet," Flens began. "We don't know where—"

"Your sister's missing," Gibby blurted out all at once.

"What?" cried Tadge and Rhinn in the same breath. "*What?*"

A lamentation started up in the depths of the cave, high-pitched and wailing. Miriael recognised the unmistakable sound of a Morph.

"We'll tell you about it," Flens said to Tadge and Rhinn. "But we haven't given up on her, so you mustn't either."

Bross helped Shanna lean Ferren back against a wall of the trench. Then he went over to join the others explaining about Kiet to Tadge and Rhinn. Miriael saw Shanna taking her brother's pulse and came across to question her.

"He'll be all right, won't he?"

"He'll be fine, don't worry. His breathing's good, and his pulse is perfect." Shanna lowered Ferren's hand gently to the ground. "Crazy, crazy little brother."

"He must really care for Kiet," said Miriael. "I never guessed."

Shanna nodded. "And she cares for him. You should've seen her when I was threatening to slit his throat underground."

"Threatening to slit…?"

"Before I knew it was him. She was ready to take me on. Savage as a wildcat. If I *had* hurt him, I don't know what she'd have done."

"Mmm." Miriael thought about Ferren's fixation on *her*. "That would be good, if the two of them…" She didn't finish her sentence, and Shanna didn't ask.

Meanwhile, Tadge and Rhinn had been learning about their sister's mysterious disappearance. Tadge's voice rose up from the middle of the huddle.

"We'll go there! We'll find her!"

Shanna heard him and twisted round. "Not inside the Humen Camp, you can't. You don't know anything about the place."

"No, not inside, then." Rhinn spoke up before Tadge. "But we'll search all around outside."

Ferren groaned, as though something said had percolated through to him. But he didn't wake up, and his eyes stayed shut.

In spite of all attempts to discourage them, Tadge and Rhinn went off to search. Miriael and Shanna sat leaning against the trench wall next to Ferren. Miriael had a question on her mind, and after a while she brought it up.

"You lived inside the Humen Camp how long?"

"Two and a half years."

"So you must have seen and learned a lot. What do you think will happen with Doctor Saniette gone?"

Shanna shrugged. "The Camp seemed to speed up when he arrived. Him and his Queen-Hypers and secret weapons. The whole place started buzzing with efficiency. He gave them a new sense of purpose…a goal to work for…" She reflected a moment. "But it was all his influence. He controlled and organised everything. I don't think they'll ever invade Heaven without him driving them on."

For Miriael, the answer to her question immediately aroused more questions, but she didn't get to ask them. At that moment Ferren stirred and opened his eyes.

"Ah, he's back with us!" Shanna quietened her brother with a hand on his shoulder. "Lie still now. Give yourself time. Don't wake up all at once."

"You…you…knocked me out," he muttered thickly.

"Bross did."

"You told him…punch me."

Miriael began to back away. "I'll leave you two alone," she murmured.

She felt embarrassed to speak with Ferren right now. She had no doubt he'd led the mission to rescue her—and she'd only needed rescuing because of her folly over Asmodai! She hadn't deserved him to risk his life for her…nor Kiet's life either…

She looked around for something to do. The others were talking together in low voices, and she didn't know how to join in. Then she heard the sad sound of the Morph, much softer now, but no less grieving.

Grieving for Kiet? she wondered. She decided to go and sing him a soothing song. Perhaps she could make him feel better…

Twenty minutes later, she was still singing. Dawn had broken, and the first faint light shone down into the trench beyond the girders.

Suddenly there was a scuffling, and a pair of legs appeared in the light. In the next moment, a body jumped down into the trench and came scurrying forward. A head poked in under the girders—Tadge's head.

"Guess what we found!" he crowed.

22

They had found Kiet. Rhinn helped her down into the trench, Tadge went back to support her under the arm and lead her into the cave. She was sagging with exhaustion, laughing and crying at the same time.

Everyone clustered round, then drew back to give her air.

"You looked on the wrong side of the bridge!" Tadge told them. "Your buckets all came down on this side—hers was on the other!"

"We never thought—"

"But *we* did!" Tadge was bursting with triumph.

Kiet spoke up for herself. "When Doctor Saniette fell on the bridge... My bucket..." Kiet had to keep pausing to draw breath. "The roadway split apart right in front of my bucket. You went up and I went down."

"We went flying through the air," said Gibby.

"And I just stopped and dropped. I came down in the moat. My bucket landed upside down in the water."

"We saw it!" Tadge put in. "With wreckage and metal and slabs of stuff all around. And Doctor Saniette really close—"

"Shush, Tadge," said Rhinn. "Let her tell it."

"I was trapped," Kiet went on with a shudder. "The bucket wouldn't turn over. I had a pocket of air inside, but I couldn't get out."

"Whew!" Ethany shuddered in sympathy.

"So then I pushed and rocked the bucket back and forth. Back and forth and back and forth, and it still wouldn't turn over. I'd used up all my air, I was almost suffocating. Then, at last, it tipped and went over."

The strength was gradually returning to Kiet's voice. Like everyone else, she was caught up in the momentum of her story.

"Then I crawled out, and there was Doctor Saniette. His head straight in front of me. And all those tiny, wriggling Doctors waving their hands and opening their mouths. I think they must've been trying to call to me, but no sound came out. Then three of those specially tall Hypers…you know the ones, with humps on their backs and lipstick…"

"Queen-Hypers," said Shanna.

"Yes, them. They waded along by the side of the body to the head, and they started cutting some of the tiny Doctors free. I hid behind my bucket, but I couldn't move or they'd have seen me. I was stuck there ages and ages."

"We hadn't come looking for her yet," Tadge explained—and was immediately shushed again by Rhinn.

"Then a whole lot of ordinary Hypers turned up with stretchers. They loaded the Doctors who'd been cut free onto the stretchers and went off with them. I decided… I had to get far enough away before I came up onto dry land. But I thought of a trick to stay invisible in the water. On my back."

"On your back?" There were several murmurs of surprise, including Miriael's.

"It was only shallow water, you see. I pulled myself backwards on my elbows, and only my nose above the surface. Holding my breath half the time. I went a long, long way parallel to the edge of the moat, but I didn't try to crawl out. Not until those special Hypers couldn't see me in the dark."

"Then we came and found her," said Tadge.

This time Rhinn didn't shush him but continued the story herself. "We went under the overbridge where it hadn't collapsed, and we were searching on the other side. Then we came nearer to the moat, and I spotted this waterlogged figure crawling—"

"*I* spotted her first," said Tadge.

"No, you were looking the other way."

"Was not."

"You *were*."

"*Not!*"

The others laughed: a laugh of sheer relief. The world was back to normal.

"Who cares, she's here and she's safe," said Flens.

The story had reached its conclusion. Miriael, listening at the back, had been holding up the zither so that the Morph could hear every word. Now she came forward.

"Here's somebody else that wants to see you," she said, and offered the zither for Kiet to take. "He was afraid you'd never come back. You wouldn't believe how unhappy he was."

"Peeper!" Kiet's tired face lit up. "I'm here, little one."

She shifted across to the nearest wall, leaned back and placed the zither on her lap. The Morph made a contented chirruping sound as she began to croon to him.

She's learned to communicate better than I ever did, thought Miriael, noting that Kiet didn't need the rhymes and tune of actual singing.

Gradually, the others moved away, not wanting to intrude. There was an intimacy to the communication between Kiet and her Morph that put everyone else at a distance.

Still, Miriael continued to keep an eye on her. She wasn't entirely surprised when, a little later, Kiet rose with the zither in her hands and went across to sit next to Ferren by the opposite wall.

23

As the sun rose higher, Shanna went out to reconnoitre Humen activity. She reported that Hypers were milling around Doctor Saniette's body like a swarm of ants, but there were no Hypers in the construction zone looking for *them*. She recommended resting up through the day in their base, then heading off after sunset. Dog-tired after the night just gone, the others agreed at once.

Miriael was settling down to sleep when Shanna approached.

"What do you think?" Shanna pointed to Ferren and Kiet, side by side with their heads together.

"Looks like they've both recovered."

Shanna clicked her tongue. "I didn't mean that. I meant the two of them as a pair."

"Yes, why not?" Miriael had her own reasons for liking the idea.

"I doubt he's even thought about it. He hardly knows his own feelings, my little brother."

"What about her?"

"Probably not as slow as him." Shanna shrugged. "She's amazingly attractive, don't you think? With that dark red hair and deep brown eyes."

"Is she? I don't think much about beauty."

"No, you wouldn't need to," Shanna said, then dropped her gaze. "It's different with Kiet's sort of beauty. You don't see it at first, until you really look at her. Whereas *you*...."

Miriael heard the adulation in her voice and quickly changed the subject. "I've been thinking about what you said before, that the Humen will never invade Heaven without Doctor Saniette driving them on. What did you mean?"

Shanna looked up. "What I said."

"But was it just something Doctor Saniette hoped to do one day? Or a definite plan?"

"A definite plan. I overheard two Queen-Hypers talking about it. Doctor Saniette came to this Camp with a plan to invade Heaven, and he was in a hurry to carry it out. Very soon, from the way they were talking."

"But how? Boost-beams could never lift up enough soldiers for an attack. Did he have some other way?"

"Don't know, they didn't say. All I know is, he was producing all kinds of secret weapons, and that's what it was for. An invasion of Heaven."

Miriael didn't like the sound of that. She pursed her lips and sank into her own thoughts.

After a while, Shanna broke the silence. "But it can't happen now, right? It was Doctor Saniette's plan, and he's finished. Who's left to carry it out?"

Miriael shook her head. "*He's* finished, but some of the individual Doctors he was made from survived. You heard what Kiet said about Queen-Hypers cutting them free."

"What, you think they'll put them back together and create a new giant Doctor?"

"No-o. I don't think they could do that."

"Then what?"

"I'm just saying. Doctor Saniette was preparing to invade Heaven just three or four months after the defeat of the original Bankstown

Doctors. A whole Humen army was obliterated then. That's how fast they can rebuild."

"But without another Doctor Saniette…"

"Yes, they'll be disorganised for a long while."

"Years and years and years."

"I hope so." Miriael put on a smile. "No need to worry yet."

AND THE STORY REACHES ITS FINALE...

For a long while, the Humen have been working towards a great invasion of Heaven. All they needed was the right leader—and now that leader has arrived!

Meanwhile, the representatives of the tribes assemble at Ferren's old Home Ground to launch the Residual Alliance. What they don't know is that someone is watching their every move...

This is the climax for which readers of the Ferren books have been waiting. There's a love triangle to resolve between Ferren, Kiet and Zonda, and another twist to the relation between Miriael and Asmodai. But, above all, there's the incredible clash of armies as the action moves right up into Heaven itself.

Ferren, Miriael, Kiet and their friends will have to choose a side. They could be saboteurs, they could be warriors—and they could decide the outcome of the most important battle ever fought!

Read a sample chapter at www.ferren.com.au!

FERREN AND THE INVADERS OF HEAVEN is coming soon from IFWG Publishing!

Appendix 1

Chronology of the Millenary War

1961	USSR sends first human into space
1969	US lands first human on the moon
2028	The Venables-Hirsch experiment
2031	Inauguration of Project Olympus
2033	The Trespass upon Heaven
	The Devastation at Mount Horeb
2034	Start of the Age of the Undead
2038	The Depopulation of New York
2075	Many Fallen Angels allowed back into Heaven
2079	Decision on excluding human souls from Heaven
	Supreme Trinity withdraws to Seventh Altitude
	War Council of great archangels takes control
2088	The First United Earth Congress
2089–94	The False Truce
2094	The Great Collapse
2094–2112	Period of the Long Famine
2223	First appearance of Plasmatics
2228	First appearance of Hypers
2262–91	Construction of the Endless Wall
2305	The Declaration of Material Being
2436–40	The Weather Wars
2440–2543	The Hundred Years' Blizzard in North America
2742	Humen colonies set up in the Burning Continents
2755	Extinction of the colonies
2904	Foundation of the South American Empire
2912	First appearance of force-fields and boost-beams
2927–45	The Wars of Doctor Mengis and Doctor Genelle
2943–45	The Campaign of the Five Zones
3003–3022	Rise of the ten original Bankstown Doctors
3023	Bankstown Doctors destroyed at Battle of Picton

APPENDIX 2
ANGELOLOGY: TRADITIONAL LORE ON ANGELS IN THIS BOOK

Traditionally, Heaven is composed of seven distinct Heavens; in this book, Heaven has seven distinct Altitudes. Angels are divided into nine Orders, from Seraphim on the highest level, through Cherubim, Ofanim, Dominions, Virtues, Powers and Principalities, down to the lowest levels of Archangels and Angels. But, since 'angels' also applies to beings of all Orders and 'archangels' to the highest captains of Heaven, I've renamed the lowest Orders as Junior Angels and Archangels.

Anaitis: an important female angel also known as Anahita.

archon: any angel of high rank can be called an archon.

Asmodai: an angel of the Order of Principalities.

Barachiel: ruler of the planet Jupiter and of the zodiacal sign of Scorpio, Barachiel is a Seraph who has dominion over lightning.

Bethor: one of seven high angels who share in ruling the 196 provinces of Heaven. In the previous book, he visited the earthbound Miriael and urged her to improve her spiritual condition.

Cedrion: an important angel who rules in the south. Like Bethor, he tried and failed to stop Miriael from eating mortal food.

Fallen Angels, the: led by Lucifer (q.v.), the original Fallen Angels rebelled against the will of God and were cast down into Hell. A second smaller group of Fallen Angels were the Grigori (q.v.). Early Church fathers such as St Jerome believed that the Fallen Angels would eventually repent and be allowed to return to Heaven, which is what has happened in the backstory to this book.

Grigori, the (or Watchers): according to the Apocrypha and a reference in Genesis, the Grigori were angels sent down by God to watch over the early development of humankind. However, they fell in love and lust with mortal women, leading to the birth of a race of giants called Nephelim. They also taught skills to humankind and encouraged them to develop more quickly than the divine plan permitted. God punished them as a lesser class of Fallen Angels.

Jehoel: the principal angel over fire, and the angel who holds the Leviathan in check. (Leviathan is the great monster of the deep, often in the form of a sea-dragon.)

Lucifer: the name 'Lucifer' is so well established as Satan's angelic name that I've continued to use it, although it comes from a misreading of the Hebrew Bible. Majority scholarly opinion is that Satan's angelic name was probably Samael. As for the name 'Satan', the word actually means 'adversary', so a more literal translation would be 'the Satan', which is what I've used in The Ferren Trilogy.

Mendrion: a ruling angel of the Seventh Hour of Night.

Miriael: in traditional angelology, Miriael is a minor angel who is also a warrior. In *Ferren and the Angel,* she fell to Earth, lost her aura and chose to side with the Residuals.

Uriel: an Angel of the Presence, who is one of the four greatest archangels along with Michael, Gabriel and Raphael. Regent of the Sun, he controls the south and is included among the Angels of Destruction. When serving as an agent of divine punishment, he carries the fiery Sword of God, re-christened as the Sword of Judgement in The Ferren Trilogy. In the previous book, he threatened to use the Sword on Miriael, but was unable to find her guilty of any sin.

Zophiel: an angel also known as God's spy, Zophiel is a standard bearer in battle.

Caveat: there are endless variations in Christian sources (especially the *Apocrypha*), Jewish sources (especially the *Kabbalah*) and Islamic sources (especially Sufi texts). There's good evidence for the facts I've given as traditional, but other versions also exist.

About the Author

Richard was born in Yorkshire, England, then migrated to Australia at the age of twenty-one. He was always trying to write, but could never finish the stories he began. Instead he drifted around as a singer, songwriter and poet, then became a university tutor and finally a university lecturer. But after twenty-five years of writer's block, he finally finished the cult novel, *The Vicar of Morbing Vyle*.

When he contracted his next book to a major publisher, he immediately resigned his lectureship to follow his original dream. Since then, he's produced seventeen books of fantasy, SF and horror/supernatural, ranging from Children's to Young Adult to Adult. Best known internationally for *Worldshaker* and its sequels, he's won many awards in France and Australia.

He lives with partner Aileen near Wollongong, south of Sydney, between golden beaches and green escarpment. Walking Yogi the Labrador while listening to music is his favourite relaxation—when he's not writing like a mad workaholic, catching up all on those wasted twenty-five years…

His Ferren Trilogy website is at www.ferren.com.au and his author website is at www.richardharland.au. You can email him at author@ferren.com.au.

For all aspiring writers, he's put up a comprehensive 145-page guide to writing fantasy fiction at www.writingtips.com.au.

OTHER BOOKS BY RICHARD HARLAND

For YA Readers

The Ferren Trilogy:
>*Ferren and the Angel* (Book 1)

Worldshaker
Liberator
Song of the Slums

For Younger Readers

the Wolf Kingdom quartet:
>*Escape!*
>*Under Siege*
>*Race to the Ruins*
>*The Heavy Crown*

Sassycat
Walter Wants to Be a Werewolf

For Adult Readers

The Vicar of Morbing Vyle
The Black Crusade
the Eddon and Vail series:
>*The Dark Edge*
>*Taken By Force*
>*Hidden From View*